REAPER MAN

A Discworld Novel

By the same author:

THE CARPET PEOPLE

THE DARK SIDE OF THE SUN

STRATA

TRUCKERS

DIGGERS

WINGS

THE UNADULTERATED CAT
(with Gray Jolliffe)

GOOD OMENS
(with Neil Gaiman)

The Discworld series:

THE COLOUR OF MAGIC

THE LIGHT FANTASTIC

EQUAL RITES

MORT

SOURCERY

WYRD SISTERS

PYRAMIDS

GUARDS! GUARDS!

ERIC
(with Josh Kirby)

MOVING PICTURES

REAPER MAN

BY

TERRY PRATCHETT

A ROC BOOK

ROC
Published by the Penguin Group
Penguin Books USA Inc., 375 Hudson Street,
New York, New York 10014, U.S.A.
Penguin Books Ltd, 27 Wrights Lane,
London W8 5TZ, England
Penguin Books Australia Ltd, Ringwood,
Victoria, Australia
Penguin Books Canada Ltd, 10 Alcorn Avenue,
Toronto, Ontario, Canada M4V 3B2
Penguin Books (N.Z.) Ltd, 182–190 Wairau Road,
Auckland 10, New Zealand

Penguin Books Ltd, Registered Offices:
Harmondsworth, Middlesex, England

First published in the United States of America by Roc, an imprint
of New American Library, a division of Penguin Books USA Inc.

First published in Great Britain by Victor Gollancz Ltd.

Roc is a trademark of New American Library, a division of
Penguin Books USA Inc.

Printed in Canada

ISBN 0-575-04979-0

REAPER MAN

The Morris dance is common to all inhabited worlds in the multiverse.

It is danced under blue skies to celebrate the quickening of the soil and under bare stars because it's springtime and with any luck the carbon dioxide will unfreeze again. The imperative is felt by deep-sea beings who have never seen the sun and urban humans whose only connection with the cycles of nature is that their Volvo once ran over a sheep.

It is danced innocently by raggedy-bearded young mathematicians to an inexpert accordion rendering of "Mrs Widgery's Lodger" and ruthlessly by such as the Ninja Morris Men of New Ankh, who can do strange and terrible things with a simple handkerchief and a bell.

And it is never danced properly.

Except on the Discworld, which is flat and supported on the backs of four elephants which travel through space on the shell of Great A'Tuin, the world turtle.

And even there, only in one place have they got it right. It's a small village high in the Ramtop Mountains, where the big and simple secret is handed down across the generations.

There, the men dance on the first day of spring, backwards and forwards, bells tied under their knees, white shirts flapping. People come and watch. There's an ox roast afterwards, and it's generally considered a nice day out for all the family.

But that isn't the secret.

The secret is the *other* dance.

And that won't happen for a while yet.

There is a ticking, such as might be made by a clock. And, indeed, in the sky there is a clock, and the ticking of freshly minted seconds flows out from it.

At least, it looks like a clock. But it is in fact exactly the opposite of a clock, and the biggest hand goes around just once.

There is a plain under a dim sky. It is covered with gentle rolling curves that might remind you of something else if you saw it from a long way away, and if you did see it from a long way away you'd be very glad that you were, in fact, a long way away.

Three grey figures floated just above it. Exactly what they were can't be described in normal language. Some people might call them cherubs, although there was nothing rosy-cheeked about them. They might be numbered among those who see to it that gravity operates and that time stays separate from space. Call them auditors. Auditors of reality.

They were in conversation without speaking. They didn't need to speak. They just changed reality so that they had spoken.

One said, It has never happened before. Can it be done?

One said, It will have to be done. There is a *personality*. Personalities come to an end. Only forces endure.

It said this with a certain satisfaction.

One said, Besides . . . there have been irregularities. Where you get personality, you get irregularities. Well-known fact.

One said, He has worked inefficiently?

One said, No. We can't get him there.

One said, That is the point. The word is *him*. Becoming a personality *is* inefficient. We don't want it to spread. Supposing gravity developed a personality? Supposing it decided to *like* people?

One said, Got a crush on them, sort of thing?

One said, in a voice that would have been even chillier if it was not already at absolute zero, No.

One said, Sorry. Just my little joke.

One said, Besides, sometimes he wonders about his job. Such speculation is dangerous.

One said, No argument there.

One said, Then we are agreed?

One, who seemed to have been thinking about something, said, Just one moment. Did you not just use the singular pronoun, "my"? Not developing a personality, are you?

One said, guiltily, Who? Us?

One said, Where there is personality, there is discord.

One said, Yes. Yes. Very true.

One said, All right. But watch it in future.

One said, Then we are agreed?

8

They looked up at the face of Azrael, outlined against the sky. In fact, it *was* the sky.

Azrael nodded, slowly.

One said, Very well. Where is this place?

One said, It is the Discworld. It rides through space on the back of a giant turtle.

One said, Oh, one of *that* sort. I hate them.

One said, You're doing it again. You said "I".

One said, No! No! I didn't! I never said "I"! . . . oh, bugger . . .

It burst into flame and burned in the same way that a small cloud of vapour burns, quickly and with no residual mess. Almost immediately, another one appeared. It was identical in appearance to its vanished sibling.

One said, Let that be a lesson. To become a personality is to end. And now . . . let us go.

Azrael watched them skim away.

It is hard to fathom the thoughts of a creature so big that, in real space, his length would be measured only in terms of the speed of light. But he turned his enormous bulk and, with eyes that stars could be lost in, sought among the myriad worlds for a flat one.

On the back of a turtle. The Discworld – world and mirror of worlds.

It sounded interesting. And, in his prison of a billion years, Azrael was bored.

And this is the room where the future pours into the past via the pinch of the now.

Timers line the walls. Not hour-glasses, although they have the same shape. Not egg-timers, such as you might buy as a souvenir attached to a small board with the name of the holiday resort of your choice jauntily inscribed on it by someone with the same sense of style as a jelly doughnut.

It's not even sand in there. It's seconds, endlessly turning the *maybe* into the *was*.

And every lifetimer has a name on it.

And the room is full of the soft hissing of people living.

Picture the scene . . .

And now add the sharp clicking of bone on stone, getting closer.

9

A dark shape crosses the field of vision and moves up the endless shelves of sibilant glassware. Click, click. Here's a glass with the top bulb nearly empty. Bone fingers rise and reach out. Select. And another. Select. And more. Many, many more. Select, select.

It's all in a day's work. Or it would be, if days existed here.

Click, click, as the dark shape moves patiently along the rows.

And stops.

And hesitates.

Because here's a small gold timer, not much bigger than a watch.

It wasn't there yesterday, or wouldn't have been if yesterdays existed here.

Bony fingers close around it and hold it up to the light.

It's got a name on it, in small capital letters.

The name is *DEATH*.

Death put down the timer, and then picked it up again. The sands of time were already pouring through. He turned it over experimentally, just in case. The sand went on pouring, only now it was going upwards. He hadn't really expected anything else.

It meant that, even if tomorrows could exist here, there weren't going to be any. Not any more.

There was a movement in the air behind him.

Death turned slowly, and addressed the figure that wavered indistinctly in the gloom.

WHY?

It told him.

BUT THAT IS . . . NOT RIGHT.

It told him that No, it was right.

Not a muscle moved on Death's face, because he hadn't got any.

I SHALL APPEAL.

It told him, *he* should know that there was no appeal. Never any appeal. Never any appeal.

Death thought about this, and then he said:

I HAVE ALWAYS DONE MY DUTY AS I SAW FIT.

The figure floated closer. It looked vaguely like a grey-robed and hooded monk.

It told him, We know. That is why we're letting you keep the horse.

*

10

The sun was near the horizon.

The shortest-lived creatures on the Disc were mayflies, which barely make it through twenty-four hours. Two of the oldest zigzagged aimlessly over the waters of a trout stream, discussing history with some younger members of the evening hatching.

"You don't get the kind of sun now that you used to get," said one of them.

"You're right there. We had proper sun in the good old hours. It were all yellow. None of this red stuff."

"It were higher, too."

"It was. You're right."

"And nymphs and larvae showed you a bit of respect."

"They did. They did," said the other mayfly vehemently.

"I reckon, if mayflies these hours behaved a bit better, we'd still be having proper sun."

The younger mayflies listened politely.

"I remember," said one of the oldest mayflies, "when all this was fields, as far as you could see."

The younger mayflies looked around.

"It's still fields," one of them ventured, after a polite interval.

"I remember when it was *better* fields," said the old mayfly sharply.

"Yeah," said his colleague. "And there was a cow."

"That's right! You're right! I remember that cow! Stood right over there for, oh, forty, fifty minutes. It was brown, as I recall."

"You don't get cows like that these hours."

"You don't get cows at all."

"What's a cow?" said one of the hatchlings.

"See?" said the oldest mayfly triumphantly. "That's modern Ephemeroptera for you." It paused. "What were we doing before we were talking about the sun?"

"Zigzagging aimlessly over the water," said one of the young flies. This was a fair bet in any case.

"No, before that."

"Er . . . you were telling us about the Great Trout."

"Ah. yes. Right. The Trout. Well, you see, if you've been a good mayfly, zigzagging up and down properly – "

" – taking heed of your elders and betters – "

11

" – yes, and taking heed of your elders and betters, then eventually the Great Trout – "

Clop

Clop

"Yes?" said one of the younger mayflies.

There was no reply.

"The Great Trout what?" said another mayfly, nervously.

They looked down at a series of expanding concentric rings on the water.

"The holy sign!" said a mayfly. "I remember being told about that! A Great Circle in the water! Thus shall be the sign of the Great Trout!"

The oldest of the young mayflies watched the water thoughtfully. It was beginning to realise that, as the most senior fly present, it now had the privilege of hovering closest to the surface.

"They say," said the mayfly at the top of the zigzagging crowd, "that when the Great Trout comes for you, you go to a land flowing with . . . flowing with . . ." Mayflies don't eat. It was at a loss. "Flowing with water," it finished lamely.

"I wonder," said the oldest mayfly.

"It must be really good there," said the youngest.

"Oh? Why?"

"'Cos no one ever wants to come back."

Whereas the oldest things on the Discworld were the famous Counting Pines, which grow right on the permanent snowline of the high Ramtop Mountains.

The Counting Pine is one of the few known examples of borrowed evolution.

Most species do their own evolving, making it up as they go along, which is the way Nature intended. And this is all very natural and organic and in tune with mysterious cycles of the cosmos, which believes that there's nothing like millions of years of really frustrating trial and error to give a species moral fibre and, in some cases, backbone.

This is probably fine from the species' point of view, but from the perspective of the actual individuals involved it can be a real pig, or

12

at least a small pink root-eating reptile that might one day evolve into a real pig.

So the Counting Pines avoided all this by letting other vegetables do their evolving for them. A pine seed, coming to rest anywhere on the Disc, immediately picks up the most effective local genetic code via morphic resonance and grows into whatever best suits the soil and climate, usually doing much better at it than the native trees themselves, which it usually usurps.

What makes the Counting Pines particularly noteworthy, however, is the way they count.

Being dimly aware that human beings had learned to tell the age of a tree by counting the rings, the original Counting Pines decided that this was *why humans cut trees down.*

Overnight every Counting Pine readjusted its genetic code to produce, at about eye-level on its trunk, in pale letters, its precise age. Within a year they were felled almost into extinction by the ornamental house number plate industry, and only a very few survive in hard-to-reach areas.

The six Counting Pines in this clump were listening to the oldest, whose gnarled trunk declared it to be thirty-one thousand, seven hundred and thirty-four years old. The conversation took seventeen years, but has been speeded up.

"I remember when all this wasn't fields."

The pines stared out over a thousand miles of landscape. The sky flickered like a bad special effect from a time travel movie. Snow appeared, stayed for an instant, and melted.

"What was it, then?" said the nearest pine.

"Ice. If you can call it ice. We had *proper* glaciers in those days. Not like the ice you get now, here one season and gone the next. It hung around for ages."

"What happened to it, then?"

"It went."

"Went where?"

"Where things go. Everything's always rushing off."

"Wow. That was a sharp one."

"What was?"

"That winter just then."

"Call that a winter? When I was a sapling we had winters – "

Then the tree vanished.

After a shocked pause for a couple of years, one of the clump said: "He just went! Just like that! One day he was here, next he was gone!"

If the other trees had been humans, they would have shuffled their feet.

"It happens, lad," said one of them, carefully. "He's been taken to a Better Place,* you can be sure of that. He was a *good* tree."

The young tree, which was a mere five thousand, one hundred and eleven years old, said: "What sort of Better Place?"

"We're not sure," said one of the clump. It trembled uneasily in a week-long gale. "But we think it involves . . . sawdust."

Since the trees were unable even to sense any event that took place in less than a day, they never heard the sound of axes.

Windle Poons, oldest wizard in the entire faculty of Unseen University –

– home of magic, wizardry and big dinners –

– was also going to die.

He knew it, in a frail and shaky sort of way.

Of course, he mused, as he wheeled his wheelchair over the flagstones towards his ground-floor study, in a *general* sort of way everyone knew they were going to die, even the common people. No one knew where you were before you were born, but when you *were* born, it wasn't long before you found you'd arrived with your return ticket already punched.

But wizards *really* knew. Not if death involved violence or murder, of course, but if the cause of death was simply a case of running out of life then . . . well, you knew. You generally got the premonition in time to return your library books and make sure your best suit was clean and borrow quite large sums of money from your friends.

He was one hundred and thirty. It occurred to him that for most of his life he'd been an old man. Didn't seem fair, really.

And no one had said anything. He'd mentioned it in the Un-

---

* In this case, three better places. The front gates of Nos 31, 7, and 34 Elm Street, Ankh-Morpork.

common Room last week, and no one had taken the hint. And at lunch today they'd hardly spoken to him. Even his old so-called friends seemed to be avoiding him, and he wasn't even *trying* to borrow money.

It was like not having your birthday remembered, only worse.

He was going to die all alone, and no one cared.

He bumped the door open with the wheel of the chair and fumbled on the table by the door for the tinder box.

That was another thing. Hardly anyone used tinder boxes these days. They bought the big smelly yellow matches the alchemists made. Windle disapproved. Fire was important. You shouldn't be able to switch it on just like that, it didn't show any respect. That was people these days, always rushing around and . . . fires. Yes, it had been a lot warmer in the old days, too. The kind of fires they had these days didn't warm you up unless you were nearly on top of them. It was something in the wood . . . it was the wrong sort of wood. Everything was wrong these days. More *thin*. More fuzzy. No real life in anything. And the days were shorter. Mmm. Something had gone wrong with the days. They were shorter days. Mmm. Every day took an age to go by, which was odd, because days *plural* went past like a stampede. There weren't many things people wanted a 130-year-old wizard to do, and Windle had got into the habit of arriving at the dining-table up to two hours before each meal, simply to pass the time.

Endless days, going by fast. Didn't make sense. Mmm. Mind you, you didn't get the sense now that you used to get in the old days.

And they let the University be run by mere boys now. In the old days it had been run by *proper* wizards, great big men built like barges, the kind of wizards you could look up to. Then suddenly they'd all gone off somewhere and Windle was being patronised by these boys who still had some of their own teeth. Like that Ridcully lad. Windle remembered him clearly. Thin lad, sticking-out ears, never wiped his nose properly, cried for his mother in the dorm on the first night. Always up to mischief. Someone had tried to tell Windle that Ridcully was Archchancellor now. Mmm. They must think he was daft.

Where was that damn tinder box? Fingers . . . you used to get proper fingers in the old days . . .

Someone pulled the covers off a lantern. Someone else pushed a drink into his groping hand.

"Surprise!"

In the hall of the house of Death is a clock with a pendulum like a blade but with no hands, because in the house of Death there is no time but the present. (There was, of course, a present *before* the present now, but that was also the present. It was just an older one.)

The pendulum is a blade that would have made Edgar Allan Poe give it all up and start again as a stand-up comedian on the scampi-in-a-casket circuit. It swings with a faint whum-whum noise, gently slicing thin rashers of interval from the bacon of eternity.

Death stalked past the clock and into the sombre gloom of his study. Albert, his servant, was waiting for him with the towel and dusters.

"Good morning, master."

Death sat down silently in his big chair. Albert draped the towel over the angular shoulders.

"Another nice day," he said, conversationally.

Death said nothing.

Albert flapped the polishing cloth and pulled back Death's cowl.

ALBERT.

"Sir?"

Death pulled out the tiny golden timer.

DO YOU SEE THIS?

"Yes, sir. Very nice. Never seen one like that before. Whose is it?"

MINE.

Albert's eyes swivelled sideways. On one corner of Death's desk was a large timer in a black frame. It contained no sand.

"I thought that one was yours, sir?" he said.

IT WAS. NOW THIS IS. A RETIREMENT PRESENT. FROM AZRAEL HIMSELF.

Albert peered at the thing in Death's hand.

"But . . . the sand, sir. It's *pouring*."

QUITE SO.

"But that means . . . I mean . . . ?"

IT MEANS THAT ONE DAY THE SAND WILL ALL BE POURED, ALBERT.

"I know that, sir, but . . . you . . . I thought Time was something that

16

happened to other people, sir. Doesn't it? Not to *you*, sir." By the end of the sentence Albert's voice was beseeching.

Death pulled off the towel and stood up.

COME WITH ME.

"But you're *Death*, master," said Albert, running crab-legged after the tall figure as it led the way out into the hall and down the passage to the stable. "This isn't some sort of joke, is it?" he added hopefully.

I AM NOT KNOWN FOR MY SENSE OF FUN.

"Well, of course not, no offence meant. But listen, you can't die, because you're Death, you'd have to happen to yourself, it'd be like that snake that eats its own tail — "

NEVERTHELESS, I AM GOING TO DIE. THERE IS NO APPEAL.

"But what will happen to *me*?" Albert said. Terror glittered on his words like flakes of metal on the edge of a knife.

THERE WILL BE A NEW DEATH.

Albert drew himself up.

"I really don't think I could serve a new master," he said.

THEN GO BACK INTO THE WORLD. I WILL GIVE YOU MONEY. YOU HAVE BEEN A GOOD SERVANT, ALBERT.

"But if I go back — "

YES, said Death. YOU WILL DIE.

In the warm, horsey gloom of the stable, Death's pale horse looked up from its oats and gave a little whinny of greeting. The horse's name was Binky. He was a real horse. Death had tried fiery steeds and skeletal horses in the past, and found them impractical, especially the fiery ones, which tended to set light to their own bedding and stand in the middle of it looking embarrassed.

Death took the saddle down from its hook and glanced at Albert, who was suffering a crisis of conscience.

Thousands of years before, Albert had opted to serve Death rather than die. He wasn't exactly immortal. Real time was forbidden in Death's realm. There was only the ever-changing *now*, but it went on for a very long time. He had less than two months of real time left; he hoarded his days like bars of gold.

"I, er . . . ." he began. "That is — "

YOU FEAR TO DIE?

"It's not that I don't want . . . I mean, I've always . . . it's just that life is a habit that's hard to break . . ."

17

Death watched him curiously, as one might watch a beetle that had landed on its back and couldn't turn over.

Finally Albert lapsed into silence.

I UNDERSTAND, said Death, unhooking Binky's bridle.

"But you don't seem worried! You're really going to *die?*"

YES. IT WILL BE A GREAT ADVENTURE.

"It will? You're not afraid?"

I DO NOT KNOW HOW TO BE AFRAID.

"I could show you, if you like," Albert ventured.

NO. I SHOULD LIKE TO LEARN BY MYSELF. I SHALL HAVE EXPERIENCES. AT LAST.

"Master . . . if you go, will there be – ?"

A NEW DEATH WILL ARISE FROM THE MINDS OF THE LIVING, ALBERT.

"Oh." Albert looked relieved. "You don't happen to know what he'll be like, do you?"

NO.

"Perhaps I'd better, you know, clean the place up a bit, get an inventory prepared, that sort of thing?"

GOOD IDEA, said Death, as kindly as possible. WHEN I SEE THE NEW DEATH, I SHALL HEARTILY RECOMMEND YOU.

"Oh. You'll see him, then?"

OH, *YES*. AND I MUST LEAVE NOW.

"What, so soon?"

CERTAINLY. MUSTN'T WASTE TIME! Death adjusted the saddle, and then turned and held the tiny hour-glass proudly in front of Albert's hooked nose.

SEE! I HAVE TIME. AT LAST, I HAVE *TIME*!

Albert backed away nervously.

"And now that you have it, what are you going to do with it?" he said.

Death mounted his horse.

I AM GOING TO *SPEND* IT.

The party was in full swing. The banner with the legend "Goodebye Windle 130 Gloriouse Years" was drooping a bit in the heat. Things were getting to the point where there was nothing to drink but the punch and nothing to eat but the strange yellow dip with the highly suspicious tortillas and *nobody minded*. The wizards chatted with

18

the forced jolliness of people who see one another all day and are now seeing one another all evening.

In the middle of it all Windle Poons sat with a huge glass of rum and a funny hat on his head. He was almost in tears.

"A genuine Going-Away party!" he kept muttering. "Haven't had one of them since old 'Scratcher' Hocksole Went Away," the capital letters fell into place easily, "back in, mm, the Year of the Intimidating, mm, Porpoise. Thought everyone had forgotten about 'em."

"The Librarian looked up the details for us," said the Bursar, indicating a large orangutan who was trying to blow into a party squeaker. "He also made the banana dip. I hope someone eats it soon."

He leaned down.

"Can I help you to some more potato salad?" he said, in the loud deliberate voice used for talking to imbeciles and old people.

Windle cupped a trembling hand to his ear.

"What? What?"

"More! salad! Windle?"

"No, thank you."

"Another sausage, then?"

"What?"

"Sausage!"

"They give me terrible gas all night," said Windle. He considered this for a moment, and then took five.

"Er," shouted the Bursar, "do you happen to know what time – ?"

"Eh?"

"What! Time?"

"Half past nine," said Windle, promptly if indistinctly.

"Well, that's nice," said the Bursar. "It gives you the rest of the evening, er, free."

Windle rummaged in the dreadful recesses of his wheelchair, a graveyard for old cushions, dog-eared books and ancient, half-sucked sweets. He flourished a small green-covered book and pushed it into the Bursar's hands.

The Bursar turned it over. Scrawled on the cover were the words: Windle Poons Hys Dyary. A piece of bacon rind marked today's date.

19

Under Things to Do, a crabbed hand had written: Die.

The Bursar couldn't stop himself from turning the page.

Yes. Under tomorrow's date, Things to Do: Get Born.

His gaze slid sideways to a small table at the side of the room. Despite the fact that the room was quite crowded, there was an area of clear floor around the table, as if it had some kind of personal space that no one was about to invade.

There had been special instructions in the Going Away ceremony concerning the table. It had to have a black cloth, with a few magic sigils embroidered on it. It had a plate, containing a selection of the better canapés. It had a glass of wine. After considerable discussion among the wizards, a funny paper hat had been added as well.

They all had an expectant look.

The Bursar took out his watch and flicked open the lid.

It was one of the new-fangled pocket watches, with hands. They pointed to a quarter past nine. He shook it. A small hatch opened under the 12 and a very small demon poked its head out and said, "Knock it off, guv'nor, I'm pedalling as fast as I can."

He closed the watch again and looked around desperately. No one else seemed anxious to come too near Windle Poons. The Bursar felt it was up to him to make polite conversation. He surveyed possible topics. They all presented problems.

Windle Poons helped him out.

"I'm thinking of coming back as a woman," he said conversationally.

The Bursar opened and shut his mouth a few times.

"I'm looking forward to it," Poons went on. "I think it might, mm, be jolly good fun."

The Bursar riffled desperately through his limited repertoire of small talk relating to women. He leaned down to Windle's gnarled ear.

"Isn't there rather a lot of," he struck out aimlessly, "washing things? And making beds and cookery and all that sort of thing?"

"Not in the kind of, mm, life *I* have in mind," said Windle firmly.

The Bursar shut his mouth. The Archchancellor banged on a table with a spoon.

"Brothers – " he began, when there was something approaching silence. This prompted a loud and ragged chorus of cheering.

" – As you all know we are here tonight to mark the, ah, *retirement*" – nervous laughter – "of our old friend and colleague Windle Poons. You know, seeing old Windle sitting here tonight puts me in mind, as luck would have it, of the story of the cow with three wooden legs. It appears that there was this cow, and – "

The Bursar let his mind wander. He knew the story. The Archchancellor always mucked up the punch line, and in any case he had other things on his mind.

He kept looking back at the little table.

The Bursar was a kindly if nervous soul, and quite enjoyed his job. Apart from anything else, no other wizard wanted it. Lots of wizards wanted to be Archchancellor, for example, or the head of one of the eight orders of magic, but practically no wizards wanted to spend lots of time in an office shuffling bits of paper and doing sums. All the paperwork of the University tended to accumulate in the Bursar's office, which meant that he went to bed tired at nights but at least slept soundly and didn't have to check very hard for unexpected scorpions in his night-shirt.

Killing off a wizard of a higher grade was a recognised way of getting advancement in the orders. However, the only person likely to want to kill the Bursar was someone else who derived a quiet pleasure from columns of numbers, all neatly arranged, and people like that don't often go in for murder.*

He recalled his childhood, long ago, in the Ramtop Mountains. He and his sister used to leave a glass of wine and a cake out every Hogswatchnight for the Hogfather. Things had been different, then. He'd been a lot younger and hadn't known much and had probably been a lot happier.

For example, he hadn't known that he might one day be a wizard and join other wizards in leaving a glass of wine and a cake and a rather suspect chicken vol-au-vent and a paper party hat for . . .

. . . someone else.

There'd been Hogswatch parties, too, when he was a little boy. They'd always follow a certain pattern. Just when all the children were nearly sick with excitement, one of the grown-ups would say, archly, "I think we're going to have a special visitor!" and,

---

* At least, until the day they suddenly pick up a paper-knife and carve their way out through Cost Accounting and into forensic history.

amazingly on cue, there'd be a suspicious ringing of hog bells outside the window and in would come . . .

. . . in would come . . .

The Bursar shook his head. Someone's grandad in false whiskers, of course. Some jolly old boy with a sack of toys, stamping the snow off his boots. Someone who *gave* you something.

Whereas *tonight* . . .

Of course, old Windle probably felt different about it. After one hundred and thirty years, death probably had a certain attraction. You probably became quite interested in finding out what happened next.

The Archchancellor's convoluted anecdote wound jerkily to its close. The assembled wizards laughed dutifully, and then tried to work out the joke.

The Bursar looked surreptitiously at his watch. It was now twenty minutes past nine.

Windle Poons made a speech. It was long and rambling and disjointed and went on about the good old days and he seemed to think that most of the people around him were people who had been, in fact, dead for about fifty years, but that didn't matter because you got into the habit of not listening to old Windle.

The Bursar couldn't tear his eyes away from his watch. From inside came the squeak of the treadle as the demon patiently pedalled his way towards infinity.

Twenty-five minutes past the hour.

The Bursar wondered how it was supposed to happen. Did you hear – *I think we're going to have a very special visitor* – hoofbeats outside?

Did the door actually open or did He come through it? Silly question. He was renowned for His ability to get into sealed places – *especially* into sealed places, if you thought about it logically. Seal yourself in anywhere and it was only a matter of time.

The Bursar hoped He'd use the door properly. His nerves were twanging as it was.

The conversational level was dropping. Quite a few other wizards, the Bursar noticed, were glancing at the door.

Windle was at the centre of a very tactfully widening circle. No one was actually avoiding him, it was just that an apparent random Brownian motion was gently moving everyone away.

Wizards can see Death. And when a wizard dies, Death arrives in person to usher him into the Beyond. The Bursar wondered why this was considered a plus –

"Don't know what you're all looking at," said Windle, cheerfully.

The Bursar opened his watch.

The hatch under the 12 snapped up.

"Can you knock it off with all this shaking around?" squeaked the demon. "I keeps on losing count."

"Sorry," the Bursar hissed. It was nine twenty-nine.

The Archchancellor stepped forward.

"'Bye, then, Windle," he said, shaking the old man's parchment-like hand. "The old place won't seem the same without you."

"Don't know how we'll manage," said the Bursar, thankfully.

"Good luck in the next life," said the Dean. "Drop in if you're ever passing and happen to, you know, remember who you've been."

"Don't be a stranger, you hear?" said the Archchancellor.

Windle Poons nodded amiably. He hadn't heard what they were saying. He nodded on general principles.

The wizards, as one man, faced the door.

The hatch under the 12 snapped up again.

"Bing bing bong bing," said the demon. "Bingely-bingely bong bing bing."

"What?" said the Bursar, jolted.

"Half past nine," said the demon.

The wizards turned to Windle Poons. They looked faintly accusing.

"What're you all looking at?" he said.

The seconds hand on the watch squeaked onwards.

"How are you feeling?" said the Dean loudly.

"Never felt better," said Windle. "Is there any more of that, mm, rum left?"

The assembled wizards watched him pour a generous measure into his beaker.

"You want to go easy on that stuff," said the Dean nervously.

"Good health!" said Windle Poons.

The Archchancellor drummed his fingers on the table.

"Mr Poons," he said, "are you quite *sure*?"

Windle had gone off at a tangent. "Any more of these toturerillas? Not that I call it proper food," he said, "dippin' bits of hard bikky in sludge, what's so special about that? What I could do with right now is one of Mr Dibbler's famous meat pies – "

And then he died.

The Archchancellor glanced at his fellow wizards, and then tiptoed across to the wheelchair and lifted a blue-veined wrist to check the pulse. He shook his head.

"That's the way I want to go," said the Dean.

"What, muttering about meat pies?" said the Bursar.

"No. Late."

"Hold on. Hold on," said the Archchancellor. "This isn't right, you know. According to tradition, Death *himself* turns up for the death of a wiz – "

"Perhaps He was busy," said the Bursar hurriedly.

"That's right," said the Dean. "Bit of a serious flu epidemic over Quirm way, I'm told."

"Quite a storm last night, too. Lots of shipwrecks, I daresay," said the Lecturer in Recent Runes.

"And of course it's springtime, when you get a great many avalanches in the mountains."

"And plagues."

The Archchancellor stroked his beard thoughtfully.

"Hmm," he said.

Alone of all the creatures in the world, trolls believe that all living things go through Time backwards. If the past is visible and the future is hidden, they say, then it means you must be facing the wrong way. Everything alive is going through life back to front. And this is a very interesting idea, considering it was invented by a race who spend most of their time hitting one another on the head with rocks.

Whichever way around it is, Time is something that living creatures possess.

Death galloped down through towering black clouds.

And now he had Time, too.

The time of his life.

*

24

Windle Poons peered into the darkness.

"Hallo?" he said. "Hallo. Anyone there? What ho?"

There was a distant, forlorn soughing, as of wind at the end of a tunnel.

"Come out, come out, wherever you are," said Windle, his voice trembling with mad cheerfulness. "Don't worry. I'm quite looking forward to it, to tell the truth."

He clapped his spiritual hands and rubbed them together with forced enthusiasm.

"Get a move on. Some of us have got new lives to go to," he said.

The darkness remained inert. There was no shape, no sound. It was void, without form. The spirit of Windle Poons moved on the face of the darkness.

It shook its head. "Blow this for a lark," it muttered. "This isn't right at all."

It hung around for a while and then, because there didn't seem anything else for it, headed for the only home it had ever known.

It was a home he'd occupied for one hundred and thirty years. It wasn't expecting him back and put up a lot of resistance. You either had to be very determined or very powerful to overcome that sort of thing, but Windle Poons had been a wizard for more than a century. Besides, it was like breaking into your own house, the old familiar property that you'd lived in for years. You knew where the metaphorical window was that didn't shut properly.

In short, Windle Poons went back to Windle Poons.

Wizards don't believe in gods in the same way that most people don't find it necessary to believe in, say, tables. They know they're there, they know they're there for a purpose, they'd probably agree that they have a place in a well-organised universe, but they wouldn't see the point of *believing*, of going around saying, "O great table, without whom we are as naught". Anyway, either the gods are there whether you believe or not, or exist only as a function of the belief, so either way you might as well ignore the whole business and, as it were, eat off your knees.

Nevertheless, there is a small chapel off the University's Great Hall, because while the wizards stand right behind the philosophy as outlined above, you don't become a successful wizard by getting up gods' noses even if those noses only exist in an ethereal or metaphorical sense. Because while wizards don't believe in gods they know for a fact that *gods* believe in gods.

And in this chapel lay the body of Windle Poons. The University had instituted twenty-four hours' lying-in-state ever since the embarrassing affair thirty years previously with the late Prissal "Merry Prankster" Teatar.

The body of Windle Poons opened its eyes. Two coins jingled onto the stone floor.

The hands, crossed over the chest, unclenched.

Windle raised his head. Some idiot had stuck a lily on his stomach.

His eyes swivelled sideways. There was a candle on either side of his head.

He raised his head some more.

There were two more candles down there, too.

Thank goodness for old Teatar, he thought. Otherwise I'd already be looking at the underside of a rather cheap pine lid.

Funny thing, he thought. I'm thinking. Clearly.

Wow.

Windle lay back, feeling his spirit refilling his body like gleaming molten metal running through a mould. White-hot thoughts seared across the darkness of his brain, fired sluggish neurones into action.

It was never like this when I was alive.

But I'm not dead.

Not alive and not dead.

Sort of non-alive.

Or un-dead.

Oh *dear* . . .

He swung himself upright. Muscles that hadn't worked properly for seventy or eighty years jerked into overdrive. For the first time in his entire life, he corrected himself, better make that "period of existence", Windle Poons' body was entirely under Windle Poons' control. And Windle Poons' spirit wasn't about to take any lip from a bunch of muscles.

Now the body stood up. The knee joints resisted for a while, but they were no more able to withstand the onslaught of will-power

26

than a sick mosquito can withstand a blowtorch.

The door to the chapel was locked. However, Windle found that the merest pressure was enough to pull the lock out of the woodwork and leave fingerprints in the metal of the doorhandle.

"Oh, goodness," he said.

He piloted himself out into the corridor. The distant clatter of cutlery and the buzz of voices suggested that one of the University's four daily meals was in progress.

He wondered whether you were allowed to eat when you were dead. Probably not, he thought.

And could he eat, anyway? It wasn't that he wasn't hungry. It was just that . . . well, he knew how to think, and walking and moving were just a matter of twitching some fairly obvious nerves, but how exactly did your stomach work?

It began to dawn on Windle that the human body is not run by the brain, despite the brain's opinion on the matter. In fact it's run by dozens of complex automatic systems, all whirring and clicking away with the kind of precision that isn't noticed until it breaks down.

He surveyed himself from the control room of his skull. He looked at the silent chemical factory of his liver with the same sinking feeling as a canoe builder might survey the controls of a computerised supertanker. The mysteries of his kidneys awaited Windle's mastery of renal control. What, when you got right down to it, *was* a spleen? And how did you make it go?

His heart sank.

Or, rather, it didn't.

"Oh, *gods*," muttered Windle, and leaned against the wall. How did it work, now? He prodded a few likely-looking nerves. Was it *systolic . . . diastolic . . . systolic . . . diastolic . . .*? And then there were the lungs, too . . .

Like a conjuror keeping eighteen plates spinning at the same time – like a man trying to programme a video recorder from an instruction manual translated from Japanese into Dutch by a Korean rice-husker – like, in fact, a man finding out what total self-control really means, Windle Poons lurched onwards.

*

27

The wizards of Unseen University set great store by big, solid meals. A man couldn't be expected to get down to some serious wizarding, they held, without soup, fish, game, several huge plates of meat, a pie or two, something big and wobbly with cream on it, little savoury things on toast, fruit, nuts and a brick-thick mint with the coffee. It gave him a lining to his stomach. It was also important that the meals were served at regular times. It was what gave the day shape, they said.

Except for the Bursar, of course. He didn't eat much, but lived on his nerves. He was certain he was anorectic, because every time he looked in a mirror he saw a fat man. It was the Archchancellor, standing behind him and shouting at him.

And it was the Bursar's unfortunate fate to be sitting opposite the doors when Windle Poons smashed them in because it was easier than fiddling with the handles.

He bit through his wooden spoon.

The wizards revolved on their benches to stare.

Windle Poons swayed for a moment, assembling control of vocal chords, lips and tongue, and then said: "I think I may be able to metabolise alcohol."

The Archchancellor was the first one to recover.

"Windle!" he said. "We thought you were dead!"

He had to admit that it wasn't a very good line. You didn't put people on a slab with candles and lilies all round them because you think they've got a bit of a headache and want a nice lie down for half an hour.

Windle took a few steps forward. The nearest wizards fell over themselves in an effort to get away.

"I am dead, you bloody young fool," he muttered. "Think I go around looking like this all the time? Good grief." He glared at the assembled wizardry. "Anyone here know what a spleen is supposed to do?"

He reached the table, and managed to sit down.

"Probably something to do with the digestion," he said. "Funny thing, you can go through your whole life with the bloody thing ticking away or whatever it does, gurgling or whatever, and you never know what the hell it's actually for. It's like when you're lying in bed of a night and you hear your stomach or something

28

go *pripple-ipple-goinnng*. It's just a gurgle to *you*, but who knows what marvellously complex chemical exchange processes are really going – "

"You're an *undead*?" said the Bursar, managing to get the words out at last.

"I didn't *ask* to be," said the late Windle Poons irritably, looking at the food and wondering how the blazes one went about turning it into Windle Poons. "I only came back because there was nowhere else to go. Think I want to be here?"

"But surely," said the Archchancellor, "didn't . . . you know the fella, the one with the skull and the scythe – "

"Never saw him," said Windle, shortly, inspecting the nearest dishes. "Really takes it out of you, this un-dyin'."

The wizards made frantic signals to one another over his head. He looked up and glared at them.

"And don't think I can't see all them frantic signals," he said. And he was amazed to realise that this was true. Eyes that had viewed the past sixty years through a pale, fuzzy veil had been bullied into operating like the finest optical machinery.

In fact two main bodies of thought were occupying the minds of the wizards of Unseen University.

What was being thought by most of the wizards was: this is terrible, is it really old Windle in there, he was such a sweet old buffer, how can we get rid of it? *How can we get rid of it?*

What was being thought by Windle Poons, in the humming, flashing cockpit of his brain, was: well, it's true. There is life after death. And it's the same one. Just my luck.

"Well," he said, "what're you going to do about it?"

It was five minutes later. Half a dozen of the most senior wizards scurried along the draughty corridor in the wake of the Archchancellor, whose robes billowed out behind him.

The conversation went like this:

"It's *got* to be Windle! It even talks like him!"

"It's not old Windle. Old Windle was a lot older!"

"Older? Older than *dead*?"

"He's said he wants his old bedroom back, and I don't see

29

why I should have to move out – "

"Did you see his eyes? Like gimlets!"

"Eh? What? What d'you mean? You mean like that dwarf who runs the delicatessen on Cable Street?"

"I mean like they bore into you!"

" – it's got a lovely view of the gardens and I've had all my stuff moved in and it's not fair – "

"Has this ever happened before?"

"Well, there was old Teatar – "

"Yes, but he never actually died, he just used to put green paint on his face and push the lid off the coffin and shout 'Surprise, surprise – '"

"We've never had a *zombie* here."

"He's a zombie?"

"I think so – "

"Does that mean he'll be playing kettle drums and doing that bimbo dancing all night, then?"

"Is that what they do?"

"Old Windle? Doesn't sound like his cup of tea. He never liked dancing much when he was alive – "

"Anyway, you can't trust those voodoo gods. Never trust a god who grins all the time and wears a top hat, that's my motto."

" – I'm damned if I'm going to give up my bedroom to a zombie after waiting *years* for it –"

"Is it? That's a funny motto."

Windle Poons strolled around the inside of his own head again.

Strange thing, this. Now he was dead, or not living any more, or whatever he was, his mind felt clearer than it had ever done.

And control seemed to be getting easier, too. He hardly had to bother about the whole respiratory thing, the spleen seemed to be working after a fashion, the senses were operating at full speed. The digestive system was still a bit of a mystery, though.

He looked at himself in a silver plate.

He still looked dead. Pale face, red under the eyes. A dead body. Operating but still, basically, dead. Was that fair? Was that justice? Was that a proper reward for being a firm believer in reincarnation for almost 130 years? You come back as a *corpse*?

No wonder the undead were traditionally considered to be very angry.

Something wonderful, if you took the long view, was about to happen.

If you took the short or medium view, something horrible was about to happen.

It's like the difference between seeing a beautiful new star in the winter sky and actually being *close* to the supernova. It's the difference between the beauty of morning dew on a cobweb and actually being a fly.

It was something that wouldn't normally have happened for thousands of years.

It was about to happen now.

It was about to happen at the back of a disused cupboard in a tumbledown cellar in the Shades, the oldest and most disreputable part of Ankh-Morpork.

Plop.

It was a sound as soft as the first drop of rain on a century of dust.

"Maybe we could get a black cat to walk across his coffin."

"He hasn't got a coffin!" wailed the Bursar, whose grip on sanity was always slightly tentative.

"Okay, so we buy him a nice new coffin and then we get a black cat to walk across it?"

"No, that's stupid. We've got to make him pass water."

"What?"

"Pass water. Undeads can't do it."

The wizards, who had crowded into the Archchancellor's study, gave this statement their full, fascinated attention.

"You sure?" said the Dean.

"Well-known fact," said the Lecturer in Recent Runes flatly.

"He used to pass water all the time when he was alive," said the Dean doubtfully.

"Not when he's dead, though."

"Yeah? Makes sense."

"*Running* water," said the Lecturer in Recent Runes suddenly. "It's *running* water. Sorry. They can't cross over it."

"Well, *I* can't cross running water, either," said the Dean.

"Undead! Undead!" The Bursar was becoming a little unglued.

"Oh, stop teasing him," said the Lecturer, patting the trembling man on the back.

"Well, I can't," said the Dean. "I sink."

"Undead can't cross running water even on a *bridge.*"

"And is he the only one, eh? Are we going to have a plague of them, eh?" said the Lecturer.

The Archchancellor drummed his fingers on his desk.

"Dead people walking around is unhygienic," he said.

This silenced them. No one had ever looked at it that way, but Mustrum Ridcully was just the sort of man who would.

Mustrum Ridcully was, depending on your point of view, either the worst or the best Archchancellor that Unseen University had had for a hundred years.

There was too much of him, for one thing. It wasn't that he was particularly big, it was just that he had the kind of huge personality that fits any available space. He'd get roaring drunk at supper and that was fine and acceptable wizardly behaviour. But then he'd go back to his room and play darts all night and leave at five in the morning to go duck hunting. He shouted at people. He tried to *jolly them along.* And he hardly ever wore proper robes. He'd persuaded Mrs Whitlow, the University's dreaded housekeeper, to make him a sort of baggy trouser suit in garish blue and red; twice a day the wizards stood in bemusement and watched him jog purposefully around the University buildings, his pointy wizarding hat tied firmly on his head with string. He'd shout cheerfully up at them, because fundamental to the make-up of people like Mustrum Ridcully is an iron belief that everyone else would like it, too, if only they tried it.

"Maybe he'll die," they told one another hopefully, as they watched him try to break the crust on the river Ankh for an early morning dip. "All this healthy exercise can't be good for him."

Stories trickled back into the University. The Archchancellor had gone two rounds bare-fisted with Detritus, the huge odd-job troll at the Mended Drum. The Archchancellor had arm-wrestled with the Librarian for a bet and, although of course he hadn't won, still had his arm afterwards. The Archchancellor wanted the University to form its own football team for the big city game on Hogswatchday.

Intellectually, Ridcully maintained his position for two reasons. One was that he never, ever, changed his mind about anything. The other was that it took him several minutes to understand any new idea put to him, and this is a very valuable trait in a leader, because anything anyone is still trying to explain to you after two minutes is probably important and anything they give up after a mere minute or so is almost certainly something they shouldn't have been bothering you with in the first place.

There seemed to be more Mustrum Ridcully than one body could reasonably contain.

Plop. Plop.

In the dark cupboard in the cellar, a whole shelf was already full.

There was exactly as much Windle Poons as one body could contain, and he steered it carefully along the corridors.

I never expected this, he thought. I don't *deserve* this. There's been a mistake somewhere.

He felt a cool breeze on his face and realised he'd tottered out into the open air. Ahead of him were the University's gates, locked shut.

Suddenly Windle Poons felt acutely claustrophobic. He'd waited years to die, and now he had, and here he was stuck in this – this *mausoleum* with a lot of daft old men, where he'd have to spend the rest of his life being dead. Well, the first thing to do was get out and make a proper end to himself –

"'Evening, Mr Poons."

He turned around very slowly and saw the small figure of Modo, the University's dwarf gardener, who was sitting in the twilight smoking his pipe.

"Oh. Hallo, Modo."

"I 'eard you was took dead, Mr Poons."

"Er. Yes. I was."

"See you got over it, then."

Poons nodded, and looked dismally around the walls. The University gates were always locked at sunset every evening, obliging students and staff to climb over the walls. He doubted very much that he'd be able to manage that.

He clenched and unclenched his hands. Oh, well . . .

"Is there any other gateway around here, Modo?" he said.

"No, Mr Poons."

"Well, where shall we have one?"

"Sorry, Mr Poons?"

There was the sound of tortured masonry, followed by a vaguely Poons-shaped hole in the wall. Windle's hand reached back in and picked up his hat.

Modo relit his pipe. You see a lot of interesting things in this job, he thought.

In an alley, temporarily out of sight of passers-by, someone called Reg Shoe, who was dead, looked both ways, took a brush and a paint tin out of his pocket, and painted on the wall the words:

DEAD YES! GONE NO!

. . . and ran away, or at least lurched off at high speed.

The Archchancellor opened a window onto the night.

"Listen," he said.

The wizards listened.

A dog barked. Somewhere a thief whistled, and was answered from a neighbouring rooftop. In the distance a couple were having the kind of quarrel that causes most of the surrounding streets to open their windows and listen in and make notes. But these were only major themes against the continuous hum and buzz of the city. Ankh-Morpork purred through the night, *en route* for the dawn, like a huge living creature although, of course, this was only a metaphor.

"Well?" said the Senior Wrangler. "I can't hear anything special."

"That's what I mean. Dozens of people die in Ankh-Morpork every day. If they'd all started coming back like poor old Windle, don't you think we'd know about it? The place'd be in uproar. More uproar than usual, I mean."

"There's always a *few* undead around," said the Dean, doubtfully. "Vampires and zombies and banshees and so on."

"Yes, but they're more *naturally* undead," said the Archchancellor. "They know how to carry it off. They're born to it."

"You can't be born to be undead," the Senior Wrangler* pointed out.

"I mean it's traditional," the Archchancellor snapped. "There were some very respectable vampires where I grew up. They'd been in their family for centuries."

"Yes, but they drink blood," said the Senior Wrangler. "That doesn't sound very respectable to me."

"I read where they don't actually need the actual blood," said the Dean, anxious to assist. "They just need something that's in blood. Hemogoblins, I think it's called."

The other wizards looked at him.

The Dean shrugged. "Search me," he said. "Hemogoblins. That's what it said. It's all to do with people having iron in their blood."

"I'm damn sure I've got no iron goblins in *my* blood," said the Senior Wrangler.

"At least they're better than zombies," said the Dean. "A much better class of people. Vampires don't go shuffling around the whole time."

"People can be turned into zombies, you know," said the Lecturer in Recent Runes, in conversational tones. "You don't even need magic. Just the liver of a certain rare fish and the extract of a particular kind of root. One spoonful, and when you wake up, you're a zombie."

"What type of fish?" said the Senior Wrangler.

"How should I know?"

"How should anyone know, then?" said the Senior Wrangler nastily. "Did someone wake up one morning and say, hey, here's an

* The post of Senior Wrangler was an unusual one, as was the name itself. In some centres of learning, the Senior Wrangler is a leading philosopher; in others, he's merely someone who looks after horses. The Senior Wrangler at Unseen University was a philosopher who looked *like* a horse, thus neatly encapsulating all definitions.

idea, I'll just turn someone into a zombie, all I'll need is some rare fish liver and a piece of root, it's just a matter of finding the right one? You can see the queue outside the hut, can't you? No. 94, Red Stripefish liver and Maniac root . . . didn't work. No. 95, Spikefish liver and Dum-dum root . . . didn't work. No. 96 – "

"What are you talking about?" the Archchancellor demanded.

"I was simply pointing out the intrinsic unlikelihood of – "

"Shut up," said the Archchancellor, matter-of-factly. "Seems to me . . . seems to me . . . look, death must be going on, right? Death has to happen. That's what bein' alive is all about. You're alive, and then you're dead. It can't just stop happening."

"But he didn't turn up for Windle," the Dean pointed out.

"It goes on all the time," said Ridcully, ignoring him. "All sorts of things die all the time. Even vegetables."

"But I don't think Death ever came for a potato," said the Dean doubtfully.

"Death comes for everything," said the Archchancellor, firmly.

The wizards nodded sagely.

After a while the Senior Wrangler said, "Do you know, I read the other day that every atom in your body is changed every seven years? New ones keep getting attached and old ones keep on dropping off. It goes on all the time. Marvellous, really."

The Senior Wrangler could do to a conversation what it takes quite thick treacle to do to the pedals of a precision watch.

"Yes? What happens to the old ones?" said Ridcully, interested despite himself.

"Dunno. They just float around in the air, I suppose, until they get attached to someone else."

The Archchancellor looked affronted.

"What, even wizards?"

"Oh, yes. Everyone. It's part of the miracle of existence."

"Is it? Sounds like bad hygiene to me," said the Archchancellor. "I suppose there's no way of stopping it?"

"I shouldn't think so," said the Senior Wrangler, doubtfully. "I don't think you're supposed to stop miracles of existence."

"But that means everythin' is made up of everythin' else," said Ridcully.

"Yes. Isn't it *amazing*?"

"It's disgusting, is what it is," said Ridcully, shortly. "Anyway, the point I'm making . . . the point I'm *making* . . ." He paused, trying to remember. "You can't just abolish death, that's the point. Death can't die. That's like asking a scorpion to sting itself."

"As a matter of fact," said the Senior Wrangler, always ready with a handy fact, "you *can* get a scorpion to – "

"Shut up," said the Archchancellor.

"But we can't have an undead wizard wandering around," said the Dean. "There's no telling what he might take it into his head to do. We've got to . . . put a stop to him. For his own good."

"That's right," said Ridcully. "For his own good. Shouldn't be too hard. There must be dozens of ways to deal with an undead."

"Garlic," said the Senior Wrangler flatly. "Undead don't like garlic."

"Don't blame them. Can't stand the stuff," said the Dean.

"Undead! Undead!" said the Bursar, pointing an accusing finger. They ignored him.

"Yes, and then there's sacred items," said the Senior Wrangler. "Your basic undead crumbles into dust as soon as look at 'em. And they don't like daylight. And if the worst comes to the worst, you bury them at a crossroads. That's surefire, that is. And you stick a stake in them to make sure they don't get up again."

"With garlic on it," said the Bursar.

"Well, yes. I suppose you could put garlic on it," the Senior Wrangler conceded, reluctantly.

"I don't think you should put garlic on a good steak," said the Dean. "Just a little oil and seasoning."

"Red pepper is nice," said the Lecturer in Recent Runes, happily.

"Shut up," said the Archchancellor.

Plop.

The cupboard door's hinges finally gave way, spilling its contents into the room.

Sergeant Colon of the Ankh-Morpork City Guard was on duty. He was guarding the Brass Bridge, the main link between Ankh and Morpork. From theft.

When it came to crime prevention, Sergeant Colon found it safest to think big.

There was a school of thought that believed the best way to get recognised as a keen guardian of the law in Ankh-Morpork would be to patrol the streets and alleys, bribe informants, follow suspects and so on.

Sergeant Colon played truant from this particular school. *Not*, he would hasten to say, because trying to keeping down crime in Ankh-Morpork was like trying to keep down salt in the sea and the only recognition any keen guardian of the law was likely to get was the sort that goes, "Hey, that body in the gutter, isn't that old Sergeant Colon?" *but* because the modern, go-ahead, intelligent law officer ought to be always one jump ahead of the contemporary criminal. One day someone was bound to try to steal the Brass Bridge, and then they'd find Sergeant Colon right there waiting for them.

In the meantime, it offered a quiet place out of the wind where he could have a relaxing smoke and probably not see anything that would upset him.

He leaned with his elbows on the parapet, wondering vaguely about Life.

A figure stumbled out of the mist. Sergeant Colon recognised the familiar pointy hat of a wizard.

"Good evening, officer," its wearer croaked.

"Morning, y'honour."

"Would you be kind enough to help me up onto the parapet, officer?"

Sergeant Colon hesitated. But the chap *was* a wizard. A man could get into serious trouble not helping wizards.

"Trying out some new magic, y'honour?" he said, brightly, helping the skinny but surprisingly heavy body up onto the crumbling stonework.

"No."

Windle Poons stepped off the bridge. There was a squelch.*

---

* It is true that the undead cannot cross running water. However, the naturally turbid river Ankh, already heavy with the mud of the plains, does not, after having passed through the city (pop. 1,000,000) necessarily qualify under the term "running" or, for that matter, "water".

Sergeant Colon looked down as the waters of the Ankh closed again, slowly.

Those wizards. Always up to something.

He watched for a while. After several minutes there was a disturbance in the scum and debris near the base of one of the pillars of the bridge, where a flight of greasy stairs led down to the water.

A pointy hat appeared.

Sergeant Colon heard the wizard slowly climb the stairs, swearing under his breath.

Windle Poons reached the top of the bridge again. He was soaked.

"You want to go and get changed," Sergeant Colon volunteered. "You could catch your death, standing around like that."

"Hah!"

"Get your feet in front of a roaring fire, that's what I'd do."

"Hah!"

Sergeant Colon looked at Windle Poons in his own private puddle.

"You been trying some special kind of underwater magic, y'honour?" he ventured.

"Not exactly, officer."

"I've always wondered about what it's like under water," said Sergeant Colon, encouragingly. "The myst'ries of the deep, strange and wonderful creatures . . . my mum told me a tale once, about this little boy what turned into a mermaid, well, not a mer*maid*, and he had all these adventures under the s– "

His voice drained away under Windle Poons' dreadful stare.

"It's boring," said Windle. He turned and started to lurch away into the mist. "Very, very boring. Very boring indeed."

Sergeant Colon was left alone. He lit a fresh cigarette with a trembling hand, and started to walk hurriedly towards the Watch headquarters.

"That face," he told himself. "And those eyes . . . just like whatsisname . . . who's that bloody dwarf who runs the delicatessen on Cable Street . . ."

"Sergeant!"

Colon froze. Then he looked down. A face was staring up at him from ground level. When he'd got a grip on himself, he made out the sharp features of his old friend Cut-Me-Own-Throat Dibbler, the Discworld's walking, talking argument in favour of the theory that mankind had descended from a species of rodent. C. M. O. T. Dibbler liked to describe himself as a merchant adventurer; everyone else liked to describe him as an itinerant pedlar whose money-making schemes were always let down by some small but vital flaw, such as trying to sell things he didn't own or which didn't work or, sometimes, didn't even exist. Fairy gold is well known to evaporate by morning, but it was a reinforced concrete slab by comparison to some of Throat's merchandise.

He was standing at the bottom of some steps that led down to one of Ankh-Morpork's countless cellars.

"Hallo, Throat."

"Would you step down here a minute, Fred? I could use a bit of legal aid."

"Got a problem, Throat?"

Dibbler scratched his nose.

"Well, Fred . . . Is it a crime to be given something? I mean, without you knowing it?"

"Someone been giving you things, Throat?"

Throat nodded. "Dunno. You know I keep merchandise down here?" he said.

"Yeah."

"You see, I just come down to do a bit of stock-taking, and . . ." He waved a hand helplessly. "Well . . . take a look . . ."

He opened the cellar door.

In the darkness something went *plop*.

Windle Poons lurched aimlessly along a dark alley in the Shades, arms extended in front of him, hands hanging down at the wrists. He didn't know why. It just seemed the right way to go about it.

Jumping off a building? No, that wouldn't work, either. It was hard enough to walk as it was, and two broken legs wouldn't help. Poison? He imagined it would be like having a very bad stomach ache. Noose? Hanging around would probably be more boring than sitting on the bottom of the river.

He reached a noisome courtyard where several alleys met. Rats

40

scampered away from him. A cat screeched and scurried off over the rooftops.

As he stood wondering where he was, why he was, and what ought to happen next, he felt the point of a knife against his backbone.

"Okay, grandad," said a voice behind him, "it's your money or your life."

In the darkness Windle Poons' mouth formed a horrible grin.

"I'm not playing about, old man," said the voice.

"Are you Thieves' Guild?" said Windle, without turning around.

"No, we're . . . freelances. Come on, let's see the colour of your money."

"Haven't got any," said Windle. He turned around. There were two more muggers behind him.

"Ye gods, look at his *eyes*," said one of them.

Windle raised his arms above his head.

"Ooooooooh," he moaned.

The muggers backed away. Unfortunately, there was a wall behind them. They flattened themselves against it.

"OoooOOOOooooobuggeroffoooOOOooo," said Windle, who hadn't realised that the only way of escape lay through him. He rolled his eyes for better effect.

Maddened by terror, the would-be attackers dived under his arms, but not before one of them had sunk his knife up to the hilt in Windle's pigeon chest.

He looked down at it.

"Hey! That was my best robe!" he said. "I wanted to be buried in – will you look at it? You know how difficult it is to darn silk? Come back here this – Look at it, right where it shows – "

He listened. There was no sound but the distant and retreating scurry of footsteps.

Windle Poons removed the knife.

"Could have killed me," he muttered, tossing it away.

In the cellar, Sergeant Colon picked up one of the objects that lay in huge drifts on the floor.

"There must be thousands of 'em," said Throat, behind him. "What I want to know is, who put them there?"*

Sergeant Colon turned the object round and round in his hands.

"Never seen one of these before," he said. He gave it a shake. His face lit up. "Pretty, ain't they?"

"The door was locked and everything," said Throat. "And I'm paid up with the Thieves' Guild."

Colon shook the thing again.

"Nice," he said.

"Fred?"

Colon, fascinated, watched the little snowflakes fall inside the tiny glass globe. "Hmm?"

"What am I supposed to *do*?"

"Dunno. I suppose they're yours, Throat. Can't imagine why anyone'd want to get rid of 'em, though."

He turned towards the door. Throat stepped into his path.

"Then that'll be twelve pence," he said smoothly.

"What?"

"For the one you just put in your pocket, Fred."

Colon fished the globe out of his pocket.

"Come *on*!" he protested. "You just found them here! They didn't cost you a penny!"

"Yes, but there's storage . . . packing . . . handling . . ."

"Tuppence," said Colon desperately.

"Tenpence."

"Threepence."

"Sevenpence – and that's cutting my own throat, mark you."

"Done," said the sergeant, reluctantly. He gave the globe another shake.

"Nice, ain't they?" he said.

---

* Although not common on the Discworld there are, indeed, such things as anti-crimes, in accordance with the fundamental law that everything in the multiverse has an opposite. They are, obviously, rare. Merely giving someone something is not the opposite of robbery; to be an anti-crime, it has to be done in such a way as to cause *outrage and/or humiliation to the victim*. So there is breaking-and-decorating, proffering-with-embarrassment (as in most retirement presentations) and whitemailing (as in threatening to reveal to his enemies a mobster's secret donations, for example, to charity). Anti-crimes have never really caught on.

"Worth every penny," said Dibbler. He rubbed his hands together hopefully. "Should sell like hot cakes," he said, picking up a handful and shoving them into a box.

He locked the door behind them when they left.

In the darkness something went *plop*.

Ankh-Morpork has always had a fine tradition of welcoming people of all races, colours and shapes, if they have money to spend and a return ticket.

According to the Guild of Merchants' famous publication, *Wellcome to Ankh-Morporke, Citie of One Thousand Surprises*, "you the visitor will be asurred of a Warm Wellcome in the countles Ins and hostelries of this Ancient Citie, where many specsialise in catoring for the taste of guest from distant part. So if you a Manne, Trolle, Dwarfe, Goblin or Gnomm, Annk-Morporke will raise your Glass convivial and say: Cheer! Here looking, you Kid! Up, You Bottom!"

Windle Poons didn't know where undead went for a good time. All he knew, and he knew it for a certainty, was that if they could have a good time anywhere then they could probably have it in Ankh-Morpork.

His laboured footsteps led him deeper into the Shades. Only they weren't so laboured now.

For more than a century Windle Poons had lived inside the walls of Unseen University. In terms of accumulated years, he may have lived a long time. In terms of experience, he was about thirteen.

He was seeing, hearing and smelling things he'd never seen, heard or smelled before.

The Shades was the oldest part of the city. If you could do a sort of relief map of sinfulness, wickedness and all-round immorality, rather like those representations of the gravitational field around a Black Hole, then even in Ankh-Morpork the Shades would be represented by a shaft. In fact the Shades was remarkably like the aforesaid well-known astronomical phenomenon: it had a certain strong attraction, no light escaped from it, and it could indeed become a gateway to another world. The next one.

The Shades was a city within a city.

The streets were thronged. Muffled figures slunk past on errands of their own. Strange music wound up from sunken stairwells. So did sharp and exciting smells.

Poons passed goblin delicatessens and dwarf bars, from which came the sounds of singing and fighting, which dwarfs traditionally did at the same time. And there were trolls, moving through the crowds like . . . like big people moving among little people. They weren't shambling, either.

Windle had hitherto seen trolls only in the more select parts of the city,* where they moved with exaggerated caution in case they accidentally clubbed someone to death and ate them. In the Shades they strode, unafraid, heads held so high they very nearly rose above their shoulder-blades.

Windle Poons wandered through the crowds like a random shot on a pinball table. Here a blast of smoky sound from a bar spun him back into the street, there a discreet doorway promising unusual and forbidden delights attracted him like a magnet. Windle Poons' life hadn't included even very many usual and approved delights. He wasn't even certain what they were. Some sketches outside one pink-lit, inviting doorway left him even more mystified but incredibly anxious to learn.

He turned around and around in pleased astonishment.

This place! Only ten minutes' walk or fifteen minutes' lurch from the University! And he'd never known it was there! All these people! All this noise! All this *life*!

Several people of various shapes and species jostled him. One or two started to say something, shut their mouths quickly, and hurried off.

They were thinking . . . his eyes! Like gimlets!

And then a voice from the shadows said: "Hallo, big boy. You want a nice time?"

"Oh, *yes*!" said Windle Poons, lost in wonder. "Oh, yes! Yes!"

He turned around.

"Bloody hell!" There was the sound of someone hurrying away down an alley.

* i.e., everywhere outside the Shades.

44

Windle's face fell.

Life, obviously, was only for the living. Perhaps this back-to-your-body business had been a mistake after all. He'd been a fool to think otherwise.

He turned and, hardly bothering to keep his own heart beating, went back to the University.

Windle trudged across the quad to the Great Hall. The Archchancellor would know what to do —

"There he is!"

"It's him!"

"Get him!"

Windle's train of thought ran over a cliff. He looked around at five red, worried, and above all familiar faces.

"Oh, hallo, Dean," he said, unhappily. "And is that the Senior Wrangler? Oh, and the Archchancellor, this is — "

"Grab his arm!"

"Don't look at his eyes!"

"Grab his other arm!"

"This is for your own good, Windle!"

"It's not Windle! It's a creature of the Night!"

"I assure you — "

"Have you got his legs?"

"Grab his leg!"

"Grab his other leg!"

"Have you grabbed everything?" roared the Archchancellor.

The wizards nodded.

Mustrum Ridcully reached into the massive recesses of his robe.

"Right, fiend in human shape," he growled, "what d'you think of *this*, then? Ah-*ha*!"

Windle squinted at the small object that was thrust triumphantly under his nose.

"Well, er . . ." he said diffidently, "I'd say . . . yes . . . hmm . . . yes, the smell is very distinctive, isn't it . . . yes, quite definitely. *Allium sativum*. The common domestic garlic. Yes?"

The wizards stared at him. They stared at the little white clove. They stared at Windle again.

"I am right, aren't I?" he said, and made an attempt at a smile.

"Er," said the Archchancellor. "Yes. Yes, that's right." Ridcully cast around for something to add. "Well done," he said.

"Thank you for trying," said Windle. "I really appreciate it." He stepped forward. The wizards might as well have tried to hold back a glacier.

"And now I'm going to have a lie down," he said. "It's been a long day."

He lurched into the building and creaked along the corridors until he reached his room. Someone else seemed to have moved some of their stuff into it, but Windle dealt with that by simply picking it all up in one sweep of his arms and throwing it out into the corridor.

Then he lay down on the bed.

Sleep. Well, he was tired. That was a start. But sleeping meant letting go of control, and he wasn't too certain that all the systems were fully functional yet.

Anyway, when you got right down to it, did he have to sleep at all? After all, he was dead. That was supposed to be just like sleeping, only even more so. They said that dying was just like going to sleep, although of course if you weren't careful bits of you could rot and drop off.

What were you supposed to do when you slept, anyway? Dreaming . . . wasn't that all to do with sorting out your memories, or something? How did you go about it?

He stared at the ceiling.

"I never thought being dead would be so much trouble," he said aloud.

After a while a faint but insistent squeaking noise made him turn his head.

Over the fireplace was an ornamental candlestick, fixed to a bracket on the wall. It was such a familiar piece of furniture that Windle hadn't really seen it for fifty years.

It was coming unscrewed. It spun around slowly, squeaking once a turn. After half a dozen turns it fell off and clattered to the floor.

Inexplicable phenomena were not in themselves unusual on the

Discworld.* It was just that they normally had more point, or at least were a bit more interesting.

Nothing else seemed to be about to move. Windle relaxed, and went back to organising his memories. There was stuff in there he'd completely forgotten about.

There was a brief whispering outside, and then the door burst open —

"Get his legs! Get his legs!"

"Hold his arms!"

Windle tried to sit up. "Oh, hallo, everyone," he said. "What's the matter?"

The Archchancellor, standing at the foot of the bed, fumbled in a sack and produced a large, heavy object.

He held it aloft.

"Ah-*ha*!" he said.

Windle peered at it.

"Yes?" he said, helpfully.

"Ah-*ha*," said the Archchancellor again, but with slightly less conviction.

"It's a symbolic double-handled axe from the cult of Blind Io," said Windle.

The Archchancellor gave him a blank look.

"Er, yes," he said, "that's right." He threw it over his shoulder, almost removing the Dean's left ear, and fished in the sack again.

"Ah-*ha*!"

"That's a rather fine example of the Mystic Tooth of Offler the Crocodile God," said Windle.

"Ah-ha!"

"And that's a . . . let me see now . . . yes, that's the matched set of sacred Flying Ducks of Ordpor the Tasteless. I say, this is fun!"

"Ah-ha."

"That's . . . don't tell me, don't tell me . . . that's the holy *linglong* of the notorious Sootee cult, isn't it?"

---

* Rains of fish, for example, were so common in the little landlocked village of Pine Dressers that it had a flourishing smoking, canning and kipper-filleting industry. And in the mountain regions of Syrrit many sheep, left out in the fields all night, would be found in the morning to *be facing the other way*, without the apparent intervention of any human agency.

"Ah-ha?"

"I think that one's the three-headed fish of the Howanda three-headed fish religion," said Windle.

"This is *ridiculous*," said the Archchancellor, dropping the fish.

The wizards sagged. Religious objects weren't such a surefire undead cure after all.

"I'm really sorry to be such a nuisance," said Windle.

The Dean suddenly brightened up.

"Daylight!" he said excitedly. "That'll do the trick!"

"Get the curtain!"

"Get the other curtain!"

"One, two, three . . . *now!*"

Windle blinked in the invasive sunlight.

The wizards held their breath.

"I'm sorry," he said. "It doesn't seem to work."

They sagged again.

"Don't you feel *anything*?" said Ridcully.

"No sensation of crumbling into dust and blowing away?" said the Senior Wrangler hopefully.

"My nose tends to peel if I'm out in the sun too long," said Windle. "I don't know if that's any help." He tried to smile.

The wizards looked at one another and shrugged.

"Get out," said the Archchancellor. They trooped out.

Ridcully followed them. He paused at the door and waved a finger at Windle.

"This uncooperative attitude, Windle, is not doing you *any* good," he said, and slammed the door behind him.

After a few seconds the four screws holding the door handle very slowly unscrewed themselves. They rose up and orbited near the ceiling for a while, and then fell.

Windle thought about this for a while.

Memories. He had lots of them. One hundred and thirty years of memories. When he was alive he hadn't been able to remember one-hundredth of the things he knew but now he was dead, his mind uncluttered with everything except the single silver thread of his thoughts, he could feel them all there. Everything he'd ever read, everything he'd ever seen, everything he'd ever heard. All there, ranged in ranks. Nothing forgotten. Everything in its place.

Three inexplicable phenomena in one day. Four, if you included the fact of his continued existence. That was really inexplicable.

It needed explicating.

Well, that was someone else's problem. Everything was someone else's problem now.

The wizards crouched outside the door of Windle's room.

"Got everything?" said Ridcully.

"Why can't we get some of the servants to do it?" muttered the Senior Wrangler. "It's undignified."

"Because I want it done properly and with dignity," snapped the Archchancellor. "If anyone's going to bury a wizard at a crossroads with a stake hammered through him, then wizards ought to do it. After all, we're his friends."

"What is this thing, anyway?" said the Dean, inspecting the implement in his hands.

"It's called a shovel," said the Senior Wrangler. "I've seen the gardeners use them. You stick the sharp end in the ground. Then it gets a bit technical."

Ridcully squinted through the keyhole.

"He's lying down again," he said. He got up, brushing the dust off his knees, and grasped the door handle. "Right," he said. "Take your time from me. One . . . two . . ."

Modo the gardener was trundling a barrow load of hedge trimmings to a bonfire behind the new High Energy Magic research building when about half a dozen wizards went past at, for wizards, high speed. Windle Poons was being borne aloft between them.

Modo heard him say, "Really, Archchancellor, are you quite *sure* this one will work – ?"

"We've got your best interests at heart," said Ridcully.

"I'm sure, but – "

"We'll soon have you feeling your old self again," said the Bursar.

"No, we won't," hissed the Dean. "That's the whole point!"

"We'll soon have you not feeling your old self again, that's the whole point," stuttered the Bursar, as they rounded the corner.

Modo picked up the handles of the barrow again and pushed it thoughtfully towards the secluded area where he kept his bonfire,

49

his compost heaps, his leafmould pile, and the little shed he sat in when it rained.

He used to be assistant gardener at the palace, but this job was a lot more interesting. You really got to see life.

Ankh-Morpork society is street society. There is always something interesting going on. At the moment, the driver of a two-horse fruit wagon was holding the Dean six inches in the air by the scruff of the Dean's robe and was threatening to push the Dean's face through the back of the Dean's head.

"It's peaches, right?" he kept bellowing. "You know what happens to peaches what lies around too long? They get *bruised*. Lots of things round here are going to get *bruised*."

"I am a wizard, you know," said the Dean, his pointy shoes dangling. "If it wasn't for the fact that it would be against the rules for me to use magic in anything except a purely defensive manner, you would definitely be in a lot of trouble."

"What you doing, anyway?" said the driver, lowering the Dean so he could look suspiciously over his shoulder.

"Yeah," said a man trying to control the team pulling a lumber wagon, "what's going on? There's people here being paid by the hour, you know!"

"Move along at the front there!"

The lumber driver turned in his seat and addressed the queue of carts behind him. "I'm trying to," he said. "It's not my fault, is it? There's a load of wizards digging up the godsdamn *street*!"

The Archchancellor's muddy face peered over the edge of the hole.

"Oh, for heaven's sake, Dean," he said, "I told you to sort things out!"

"Yes, I was just asking this gentleman to back up and go another way," said the Dean, who was afraid he was beginning to choke.

The fruiterer turned him around so that he could see along the crowded streets. "Ever tried to back up sixty carts all at once?" he demanded. "It's not easy. *Especially* when everyone can't move because you guys have got it so's the carts are backed up all round the block and no one can move because everyone's in someone else's way, right?"

The Dean tried to nod. He had wondered himself about the wisdom of digging the hole at the junction of the Street of Small Gods and Broad Way, two of the busiest streets in Ankh-Morpork. It had seemed logical at the time. Even the most persistent undead ought to stay decently buried under that amount of traffic. The only problem was that no one had thought seriously about the difficulty of digging up a couple of main streets during the busy time of day.

"All right, all right, what's going on here?"

The crowd of spectators opened to admit the bulky figure of Sergeant Colon of the Watch. He moved through the people unstoppably, his stomach leading the way. When he saw the wizards, waist deep in a hole in the middle of the road, his huge red face brightened up.

"What's this, then?" he said. "A gang of international crossroads thieves?"

He was overjoyed. His long-term policing strategy was paying off!

The Archchancellor tipped a shovelful of Ankh-Morpork loam over his boots.

"Don't be stupid, man," he snapped. "This is vitally important."

"Oh, yes. That's what they all say," said Sergeant Colon, not a man to be easily steered from a particular course of thought once he'd got up to mental speed. "I bet there's hundreds of villages in heathen places like Klatch that'd pay good money for a nice prestigious crossroads like this, eh?"

Ridcully looked up at him with his mouth open.

"What are you gabbling about, officer?" he said. He pointed irritably to his pointy hat. "Didn't you hear me? We're wizards. This is wizard business. So if you could just sort of direct the traffic around us, there's a good chap – "

"– these peaches bruise as soon as you even *look* at 'em – " said a voice behind Sergeant Colon.

"The old idiots have been holding us up for half an hour," said a cattle drover who had long ago lost control of forty steers now wandering aimlessly around the nearby streets. "I wants 'em arrested."

51

It dawned on the sergeant that he had inadvertently placed himself centre stage in a drama involving hundreds of people, some of them wizards and all of them angry.

"What are you doing, then?" he said weakly.

"We're burying our colleague. What does it look like?" said Ridcully.

Colon's eyes swivelled to an open coffin by the side of the road. Windle Poons gave him a little wave.

"But . . . he's not dead . . . is he?" he said, his forehead wrinkling as he tried to get ahead of the situation.

"Appearances can be deceptive," said the Archchancellor.

"But he just waved to me," said the sergeant, desperately.

"So?"

"Well, it's not normal for — "

"It's all right, sergeant," said Windle.

Sergeant Colon sidled closer to the coffin.

"Didn't I see you throw yourself into the river last night?" he said, out of the corner of his mouth.

"Yes. You were very helpful," said Windle.

"And then you threw yourself sort of out again," said the sergeant.

"I'm afraid so."

"But you were down there for ages."

"Well, it was very dark, you see. I couldn't find the steps."

Sergeant Colon had to concede the logic of this.

"Well, I suppose you must be dead, then," he said. "No one could stay down there who wasn't dead."

"This is it," Windle agreed.

"Only why are you waving and talking?" said Colon.

The Senior Wrangler poked his head out of the hole.

"It's not unknown for a dead body to move and make noises after death, Sergeant," he volunteered. "It's all down to involuntary muscular spasms."

"Actually, Senior Wrangler is right," said Windle Poons. "I read that somewhere."

"Oh." Sergeant Colon looked around. "Right," he said, uncertainly. "Well . . . fair enough, I suppose . . ."

"Okay, we're done," said the Archchancellor, scrambling out of the hole, "it's deep enough. Come on, Windle, down you go."

"I really am very touched, you know," said Windle, lying back in the coffin. It was quite a good one, from the mortuary in Elm Street. The Archchancellor had let him choose it himself.

Ridcully picked up a mallet.

Windle sat up again.

"Everyone's going to so much trouble – "

"Yes, right," said Ridcully, looking around. "Now – who's got the stake?"

Everyone looked at the Bursar.

The Bursar looked unhappy.

He fumbled in a bag.

"I couldn't get any," he said.

The Archchancellor put his hand over his eyes.

"All right," he said quietly. "You know, I'm not surprised? Not surprised at all. What did you get? Lamb chops? A nice piece of pork?"

"Celery," said the Bursar.

"It's his nerves," said the Dean, quickly.

"Celery," said the Archchancellor, his self-control rigid enough to bend horseshoes around. "Right."

The Bursar handed him a soggy green bundle. Ridcully took it.

"Now, Windle," he said, "I'd like you to imagine that what I have in my hand – "

"It's quite all right," said Windle.

"I'm not actually sure I can hammer – "

"I don't mind, I assure you," said Windle.

"You don't?"

"The principle is sound," said Windle. "If you just hand me the celery but *think* hammering a stake, that's probably sufficient."

"That's very decent of you," said Ridcully. "That shows a very proper spirit."

"Esprit de corpse," said the Senior Wrangler.

Ridcully glared at him, and thrust the celery dramatically towards Windle.

"Take that!" he said.

"Thank you," said Windle.

"And now let's put the lid on and go and have some lunch," said

Ridcully. "Don't worry, Windle. It's bound to work. Today is the last day of the rest of your life."

Windle lay in the darkness, listening to the hammering. There was a thump and a muffled imprecation against the Dean for not holding the end properly. And then the patter of soil on the lid, getting fainter and more distant.

After a while a distant rumbling suggested that the commerce of the city was being resumed. He could even hear muffled voices.

He banged on the coffin lid.

"Can you keep it down?" he demanded. "There's people down here trying to be dead!"

He heard the voices stop. There was the sound of feet hurrying away.

Windle lay there for some time. He didn't know how long. He tried stopping all functions, but that just made things uncomfortable. Why was dying so difficult? Other people seemed to manage it, even without practice.

Also, his leg itched.

He tried to reach down to scratch it, and his hand touched something small and irregularly shaped. He managed to get his fingers around it.

It felt like a bundle of matches.

In a coffin? Did anyone think he'd smoke a quiet cigar to pass the time?

After a certain amount of effort he managed to push one boot off with the other boot and ease it up until he could just grasp it. This gave him a rough surface to strike the match on –

Sulphurous light filled his tiny oblong world.

There was a tiny scrap of cardboard pinned to the inside of the lid.

He read it.

He read it again.

The match went out.

He lit another one, just to check that what he had read really did exist.

The message was still as strange, even third time round:

The second match went out, taking the last of the oxygen with it.

Windle lay in the dark for a while, considering his next move and finishing off the celery.

Who'd have thought it?

And it suddenly dawned on the late Windle Poons that there was no such thing as somebody else's problem, and that just when you thought the world had pushed you aside it turned out to be full of strangeness. He knew from experience that the living never found out half of what was really happening, because they were too busy *being* the living. The onlooker sees most of the game, he told himself.

It was the living who ignored the strange and wonderful, because life was too full of the boring and mundane. But it *was* strange. It had things in it like screws that unscrewed themselves, and little written messages to the dead.

He resolved to find out what was going on. And then . . . if Death wasn't going to come to him, he'd go to Death. He had his rights, after all. Yeah. He'd lead the biggest missing-person hunt of all time.

Windle grinned in the darkness.

Missing – believed Death.

Today was the *first* day of the rest of his life.

And Ankh-Morpork lay at his feet. Well, metaphorically. The only way was up.

He reached up, felt for the card in the dark, and pulled it free. He stuck it between his teeth.

Windle Poons braced his feet against the end of the box, pushed his hands past his head, and heaved.

The soggy loam of Ankh-Morpork moved slightly.

55

Windle paused out of habit to take a breath, and realised that there was no point. He pushed again. The end of the coffin splintered.

Windle pulled it towards him and tore the solid pine like paper. He was left with a piece of plank which would have been a totally useless spade for anyone with un-zombie-like strength.

Turning onto his stomach, tucking the earth around him with his impromptu spade and ramming it back with his feet, Windle Poons dug his way towards a fresh start.

Picture a landscape, a plain with rolling curves.

It's late summer in the octarine grass country below the towering peaks of the high Ramtops, and the predominant colours are umber and gold. Heat sears the landscape. Grasshoppers sizzle, as in a frying pan. Even the air is too hot to move. It's the hottest summer in living memory and, in these parts, that's a long, long time.

Picture a figure on horseback, moving slowly along a road that's an inch deep in dust between fields of corn that already promise an unusually rich harvest.

Picture a fence of baked, dead wood. There's a notice pinned to it. The sun has faded the letters, but they are still readable.

Picture a shadow, falling across the notice. You can almost hear it reading both the words.

There's a track leading off the road, towards a small group of bleached buildings.

Picture dragging footsteps.

Picture a door, open.

Picture a cool, dark room, glimpsed through the open doorway. This isn't a room that people live in a lot. It's a room for people who live outdoors but have to come inside sometimes, when it gets dark. It's a room for harnesses and dogs, a room where oilskins are hung up to dry. There's a beer barrel by the door. There are flagstones on the floor and, along the ceiling beams, hooks for bacon. There's a scrubbed table that thirty hungry men could sit down at.

There are no men. There are no dogs. There is no beer. There is no bacon.

*

There was silence after the knocking, and then the flap-flap of slippers on flagstones. Eventually a skinny old woman with a face the colour and texture of a walnut peered around the door.

"Yes?" she said.

THE NOTICE SAID "MAN WANTED".

"Did it? Did it? That's been up there since before last winter!"

I AM SORRY? YOU NEED NO HELP?

The wrinkled face looked at him thoughtfully.

"I can't pay more'n sixpence a week, mind," it said.

The tall figure looming against the sunlight appeared to consider this.

YES, it said, eventually.

"I wouldn't even know where to start you workin', either. We haven't had any proper help here for three years. I just hire the lazy goodfor-nothin's from the village when I want 'em."

YES?

"You don't mind, then?"

I HAVE A HORSE.

The old woman peered around the stranger. In the yard was the most impressive horse she'd ever seen. Her eyes narrowed.

"And that's *your* horse, is it?"

YES.

"With all that silver on the harness and everything?"

YES.

"And you want to work for sixpence a week?"

YES.

The old woman pursed her lips. She looked from the stranger to the horse to the dilapidation around the farm. She appeared to reach a decision, possibly on the lines that someone who owned no horses probably didn't have much to fear from a horse thief.

"You're to sleep in the barn, understand?" she said.

SLEEP? YES. OF COURSE. YES, I WILL HAVE TO SLEEP.

"Couldn't have you in the house anyway. It wouldn't be right."

THE BARN WILL BE QUITE ADEQUATE, I ASSURE YOU.

"But you can come into the house for your meals."

THANK YOU.

"My name's Miss Flitworth."

YES.

She waited.

"I expect you have a name, too," she prompted.

YES. THAT'S RIGHT.

She waited again.

"Well?"

I'M SORRY?

"What is your name?"

The stranger stared at her for a moment, and then looked around wildly.

"Come on," said Miss Flitworth. "I ain't employing no one without no name. Mr . . .?"

The figure stared upwards.

MR SKY?

"No one's called Mr Sky."

MR . . . DOOR?

She nodded.

"Could be. Could be Mr Door. There was a chap called Doors I knew once. Yeah. Mr Door. And your first name? Don't tell me you haven't got one of those, too. You've got to be a Bill or a Tom or a Bruce or one of those names."

YES.

"WHAT?"

ONE OF THOSE.

"Which one?"

ER. THE FIRST ONE?

"You're a Bill?"

YES?

Miss Flitworth rolled her eyes.

"All right, Bill Sky . . ." she said.

DOOR.

"Yeah. Sorry. All right, Bill Door . . ."

CALL ME BILL.

"And you can call me Miss Flitworth. I expect you want some dinner?"

I WOULD? AH. YES. THE MEAL OF THE EVENING. YES.

"You look half starved, to tell the truth. More than half, really." She squinted at the figure. Somehow it was very hard to be certain what Bill Door looked like, or even remember the exact sound of his voice. Clearly he *was* there, and clearly he had spoken – otherwise why did you remember anything at all?

"There's a lot of people in these parts as don't use the name they were born with," she said. "I always say there's nothing to be gained by going around asking pers'nal questions. I suppose you *can* work, Mr Bill Door? I'm still getting the hay in off the high meadows and there'll be a lot of work come harvest. Can you use a scythe?"

Bill Door seemed to meditate on the question for some time. Then he said, I THINK THE ANSWER TO THAT IS A DEFINITE "YES", MISS FLITWORTH.

Cut-Me-Own-Throat Dibbler also never saw the sense in asking personal questions, at least insofar as they applied to him and were on the lines of "Are these things yours to sell?" But no one appeared to be coming forward to berate him for selling off their property, and that was good enough for him. He'd sold more than a thousand of the little globes this morning, and he'd had to employ a troll to keep up a flow from the mysterious source of supply in the cellar.

People loved them.

The principle of operation was laughably simple and easily graspable by the average Ankh-Morpork citizen after a few false starts.

If you gave the globe a shake, a cloud of little white snowflakes swirled up in the liquid inside and settled, delicately, on a tiny model of a famous Ankh-Morpork landmark. In some globes it was the University, or the Tower of Art, or the Brass Bridge, or the Patrician's Palace. The detail was amazing.

And then there were no more left. Well, thought Throat, that's a shame. Since they hadn't technically belonged to him – although *morally*, of course, *morally* they were his – he couldn't actually complain. Well, he *could* complain, of course, but only under his breath and not to anybody specific. Maybe it was all for the best, come to think of it. Stack 'em high, sell 'em cheap. Get 'em off your hands – it made it much easier to spread them in a gesture of injured innocence when you said "Who, me?"

They were really pretty, though. Except, strangely enough, for the writing. It was on the bottom of each globe, in shaky, amateurish letters, as if done by someone who had never seen writing before and was trying to copy some down. On the bottom of every globe, below the intricate little snowflake-covered building, were the words:

a Pre ent from

ankh-morpork

Mustrum Ridcully, Archchancellor of Unseen University, was a shameless autocondimentor.* He had his own special cruet put in front of him at every meal. It consisted of salt, three types of pepper, four types of mustard, four types of vinegar, fifteen different kinds of chutney and his special favourite: Wow-Wow Sauce, a mixture of mature scumble, pickled cucumbers, capers, mustard, mangoes, figs, grated wahooni, anchovy essence, asafetida and, significantly, sulphur and saltpetre for added potency. Ridcully inherited the formula from his uncle who, after half a pint of sauce on a big meal one evening, had a charcoal biscuit to settle his stomach, lit his pipe and *disappeared in mysterious circumstances*, although his shoes were found on the roof the following summer.

There was cold mutton for lunch. Mutton went well with Wow-Wow Sauce; on the night of Ridcully senior's death, for example, it had gone at least three miles.

Mustrum tied his napkin behind his neck, rubbed his hands together, and reached out.

The cruet moved.

He reached out again. It slid away.

Ridcully sighed.

"All right, you fellows," he said. "No magic at Table, you know the rules. Who's playing silly buggers?"

The other senior wizards stared at him.

"I, I, I don't think we can play it any more," said the Bursar, who

---

* Someone who will put certainly salt and probably pepper on any meal you put in front of them *whatever it is and regardless of how much it's got on it already and regardless of how it tastes*. Behavioural psychiatrists working for fast-food outlets around the universe have saved billions of whatever the local currency is by noting the autocondimenting phenomenon and advising their employers to leave seasoning out in the first place. This is really true.

at the moment was only occasionally bouncing off the sides of sanity, "I, I, I think we lost some of the pieces . . ."

He looked around, giggled, and went back to trying to cut his mutton with a spoon. The other wizards were keeping knives out of his way at present.

The entire cruet floated up into the air and started to spin slowly. Then it exploded.

The wizards, dripping vinegar and expensive spices, watched it owlishly.

"It was probably the sauce," the Dean ventured. "It was definitely going a bit critical last night."

Something dropped on his head and landed in his lunch. It was a black iron screw, several inches long.

Another one mildly concussed the Bursar.

After a second or two, a third landed point down on the table by the Archchancellor's hand and stuck there.

The wizards turned their eyes upwards.

The Great Hall was lit in the evenings by one massive chandelier, although the word so often associated with glittering prismatic glassware seemed inappropriate for the huge, heavy, black, tallow-encrusted thing that hung from the ceiling like a threatening overdraft. It could hold a thousand candles. It was directly over the senior wizards' table.

Another screw tinkled onto the floor by the fireplace.

The Archchancellor cleared his throat.

"Run?" he suggested.

The chandelier dropped.

Bits of table and crockery smashed into the walls. Lumps of lethal tallow the size of a man's head whirred through the windows. A whole candle, propelled out of the wreckage at a freak velocity, was driven several inches into a door.

The Archchancellor disentangled himself from the remains of his chair.

"Bursar!" he yelled.

The Bursar was exhumed from the fireplace.

"Um, yes, Archchancellor?" he quavered.

"What was the meanin' of *that*?"

Ridcully's hat rose from his head.

It was a basic floppy-brimmed, pointy wizarding hat, but adapted to the Archchancellor's outgoing lifestyle. Fishing flies were stuck in it. A very small pistol crossbow was shoved in the hatband in case he saw something to shoot while out jogging, and Mustrum Ridcully had found that the pointy bit was just the right size for a small bottle of Bentinck's Very Old Peculiar Brandy. He was quite attached to his hat.

But it was no longer attached to him.

It drifted gently across the room. There was a faint but distinct gurgling noise.

The Archchancellor leapt to his feet. "Bugger *that*," he roared. "That stuff's nine dollars a fifth!" He made a leap for the hat, missed, and kept on going until he drifted to a halt several feet above the ground.

The Bursar raised a hand, nervously.

"Possibly woodworm?" he said.

"If there is any more of this," growled Ridcully, "any more at all, d'you hear, I shall get very angry!"

He was dropped to the floor at the same time as the big doors opened. One of the college porters bustled in, followed by a squad of the Patrician's palace guard.

The guard captain looked the Archchancellor up and down with the expression of one to whom the word "civilian" is pronounced in the same general tones as "cockroach".

"You the head chap?" he said.

The Archchancellor smoothed his robe and tried to straighten his beard.

"I am the Archchancellor of this university, yes," he said.

The guard captain looked curiously around the hall. The students were all cowering down the far end. Splashed food covered most of the walls to ceiling height. Bits of furniture lay around the wreckage of the chandelier like trees around ground zero of a meteor strike.

Then he spoke with all the distaste of someone whose own further education had stopped at age nine, but who'd heard stories . . .

"Indulging in a bit of youthful high spirits, were we?" he said. "Throwin' a few bread rolls around, that kind of thing?"

"May I ask the meaning of this intrusion?" said Ridcully, coldly.

The guard captain leaned on his spear.

"Well," he said, "it's like this. The Patrician is barricaded in his bedroom on account of the furniture in the palace is zooming around the place like you wouldn't believe, the cooks won't even go back in the kitchen on account of what's happening in there . . ."

The wizards tried not to look at the spear's head. It was starting to unscrew itself.

"Anyway," the captain went on, oblivious to the faint metallic noises, "the Patrician calls through the keyhole, see, and says to me, 'Douglas, I wonder if you wouldn't mind nipping down to the University and asking the head man if he would be so good as to step up here, if he's not too busy?' But I can always go back and tell him you're engagin' in a bit of student humour, if you like."

The spearhead was almost off the shaft.

"You listening to me?" said the captain suspiciously.

"Hmm? What?" said the Archchancellor, tearing his eyes away from the spinning metal. "Oh. Yes. Well, I can assure you, my man, that we are not the cause of – "

"Aargh!"

"Pardon?"

"The *spearhead* fell on my *foot!*"

"Did it?" said Ridcully, innocently.

The guard captain hopped up and down.

"Listen, are you bloody hocus-pocus merchants coming or not?" he said, between bounces. "The boss is not very happy. Not very happy at all."

A great formless cloud of Life drifted across the Discworld, like water building up behind a dam when the sluice gates are shut. With no Death to take the life force away when it was finished with, it had nowhere else to go.

Here and there it earthed itself in random poltergeist activity, like flickers of summer lightning before a big storm.

Everything that exists, yearns to live. That's what the cycle of life is all about. That's the engine that drives the great biological pumps of evolution. Everything tries to inch its way up the tree, clawing or tentacling or sliming its way up to the next niche until it

63

gets to the very top – which, on the whole, never seems to have been worth all that effort.

Everything that exists, yearns to live. Even things that are not alive. Things that have a kind of sub-life, a metaphorical life, an *almost* life. And now, in the same way that a sudden hot spell brings forth unnatural and exotic blooms . . .

There was something about the little globes. You had to pick them up and give them a shake, watch the pretty snowflakes swirl and glitter. And then take them home and put them on the mantelpiece.

And then forget about them.

The relationship between the University and the Patrician, absolute ruler and nearly benevolent dictator of Ankh-Morpork, was a complex and subtle one.

The wizards held that, as servants of a higher truth, they were not subject to the mundane laws of the city.

The Patrician said that, indeed, this was the case, but they would bloody well pay their taxes like everyone else.

The wizards said that, as followers of the light of wisdom, they owed allegiance to no mortal man.

The Patrician said that this may well be true but they also owed a city tax of two hundred dollars per head per annum, payable quarterly.

The wizards said that the University stood on magical ground and was therefore exempt from taxation and anyway you couldn't put a tax on knowledge.

The Patrician said you could. It was two hundred dollars per capita; if per capita was a problem, decapita could be arranged.

The wizards said that the University had never paid taxes to the civil authority.

The Patrician said he was not proposing to remain civil for long.

The wizards said, what about easy terms?

The Patrician said he was *talking* about easy terms. They wouldn't want to know about the hard terms.

The wizards said that there was a ruler back in, oh, it would be the Century of the Dragonfly, who had tried to tell the University what to do. The Patrician could come and have a look at him if he liked.

The Patrician said that he would. He truly would.

In the end it was agreed that while the wizards of course paid no taxes, they would nevertheless make an entirely voluntary donation of, oh, let's say two hundred dollars per head, without prejudice, *mutatis mutandis*, no strings attached, to be used strictly for non-militaristic and environmentally-acceptable purposes.

It was this dynamic interplay of power blocs that made Ankh-Morpork such an interesting, stimulating and above all bloody dangerous place in which to live.*

Senior wizards did not often get out and about on what *Wellcome to Ankh-Morporke* probably called the thronged highways and intimate byways of the city, but it was instantly obvious that something was wrong. It wasn't that cobblestones didn't sometimes fly through the air, but usually someone had thrown them. They didn't normally float by themselves.

A door burst open and a suit of clothes came out, a pair of shoes dancing along behind it, a hat floating a few inches above the empty collar. Close behind them came a skinny man endeavouring to do with a hastily-snatched flannel what normally it took a whole pair of trousers to achieve.

"You come back here!" he screamed, as they rounded the corner. "I still owe seven dollars for you!"

A second pair of trousers scurried out into the street and hurried after them.

The wizards clustered together like a frightened animal with five pointed heads and ten legs, wondering who was going to be the first to comment.

"That's bloody amazing!" said the Archchancellor.

"Hmm?" said the Dean, trying to imply that he saw more amaz-

---

* Many songs have been written about the bustling metropolis, the most famous of course being: "Ankh-Morpork! Ankh-Morpork! So good they named it Ankh-Morpork!", but others have included "Carry Me Away From Old Ankh-Morpork", "I Fear I'm Going Back to Ankh-Morpork" and the old favourite, "Ankh-Morpork Malady".

ing things than that all the time, and that in drawing attention to mere clothing running around by itself the Archchancellor was letting down the whole tone of wizardry.

"Oh, come *on*. I don't know many tailors round here who'd throw in a second pair of pants for a seven dollar suit," said Ridcully.

"Oh," said the Dean.

"If it comes past again, try to trip it up so's I can have a look at the label."

A bedsheet squeezed through an upper window and flapped away across the rooftops.

"Y'know," said the Lecturer in Recent Runes, trying to keep his voice calm and relaxed, "I don't think this is magic. It doesn't *feel* like magic."

The Senior Wrangler fished in one of the deep pockets of his robe. There was a muffled clanking and rustling and the occasional croak. Eventually he produced a dark blue glass cube. It had a dial on the front.

"You carry one of *them* around in your pocket?" said the Dean. "A valuable instrument like that?"

"What the hell is it?" said Ridcully.

"Amazingly sensitive magical measuring device," said the Dean. "Measures the density of a magical field. A thaumometer."

The Senior Wrangler proudly held the cube aloft and pressed a button on the side.

A needle on the dial wobbled around a little bit and stopped.

"See?" said the Senior Wrangler. "Just natural background, representing no hazard to the public."

"Speak up," said the Archchancellor. "I can't hear you above the noise."

Crashes and screams rose from the houses on either side of the street.

Mrs Evadne Cake was a medium, verging on small.

It wasn't a demanding job. Not many people who died in Ankh-Morpork showed much inclination to chat to their surviving relatives. Put as many mystic dimensions between you and them as possible, that was their motto. She filled in between engagements with dressmaking and church work – any church. Mrs Cake was very keen on religion, at least on Mrs Cake's terms.

Evadne Cake was not one of those bead-curtain-and-incense mediums, partly because she didn't hold with incense but mainly because she was actually very good at her profession. A good conjuror can astound you with a simple box of matches and a perfectly ordinary deck of cards, if you would care to examine them, sir, you will see they are a perfectly ordinary deck of cards – he doesn't need the finger-nipping folding tables and complicated collapsible top hats of lesser prestidigitators. And, in the same way, Mrs Cake didn't need much in the way of props. Even the industrial-grade crystal ball was only there as a sop to her customers. Mrs Cake could actually read the future in a bowl of porridge.* She could have a revelation in a panful of frying bacon. She had spent a lifetime dabbling in the spirit world, except that in Evadne's case dabbling wasn't really apposite. She wasn't the dabbling kind. It was more a case of stamping into the spirit world and demanding to see the manager.

And, while making her breakfast and cutting up dogfood for Ludmilla, she started to hear voices.

They were very faint. It wasn't that they were on the verge of hearing, because they were the kind of voices that ordinary ears can't hear. They were inside her head.

. . . *watch what you're doing . . . where am I . . . quit shoving, there . . .*

And then they faded again.

They were replaced by a squeaking noise from the next room. She pushed aside her boiled egg and waddled through the bead curtain.

The sound was coming from under the severe, no-nonsense hessian cover of her crystal ball.

Evadne went back into the kitchen and selected a heavy frying pan. She waved it through the air once or twice, getting the heft of it, and then crept towards the crystal under its hood.

Raising the pan ready to swat anything unpleasant, she twitched aside the cover.

The ball was turning slowly round and round on its stand.

* It would say, for example, that you would shortly undergo a painful bowel movement.

67

Evadne watched it for a while. Then she drew the curtains, eased her weight down on the chair, took a deep breath and said, "Is there anybody there?"

Most of the ceiling fell in.

After several minutes and a certain amount of struggle Mrs Cake managed to get her head free.

"Ludmilla!"

There were soft footsteps in the passageway and then something came in from the back yard. It was clearly, even attractively female, in general shape, and wore a perfectly ordinary dress. It was also apparently suffering from a case of superfluous hair that not all the delicate pink razors in the world could erase. Also, teeth and fingernails were being worn long this season. You expected the whole thing to growl, but it spoke in a pleasant and definitely human voice.

"Mother?"

"Oi'm under 'ere."

The fearsome Ludmilla lifted up a huge joist and tossed it lightly aside. "What happened? Didn't you have your premonition switched on?"

"Oi turned it off to speak to the baker. Cor, that gave me a turn."

"I'll make you a cup of tea, shall I?"

"Now then, you know you always crushes teacups when it's your Time."

"I'm getting better at it," said Ludmilla.

"There's a good girl, but I'll do it myself, thanks all the same."

Mrs Cake stood up, brushed the plaster dust off her apron, and said: "They shouted! They shouted! All at once!"

Modo the University gardener was weeding a rose bed when the ancient, velvet lawn beside him heaved and sprouted a hardy perennial Windle Poons, who blinked in the light.

"Is that you, Modo?"

"That's right, Mr Poons," said the dwarf. "Shall I give you a hand up?"

"I think I can manage, thank you."

"I've got a shovel in the shed, if you like."

"No, it's perfectly all right." Windle pulled himself out of the grass and brushed the soil off the remains of his robe. "Sorry about your lawn," he added, looking down at the hole.

"Don't mention it, Mr Poons."

"Did it take long to get it looking like that?"

"About five hundred years, I think."

"Gosh, I am sorry. I was aiming for the cellars, but I seem to have lost my bearings."

"Don't you worry about that, Mr Poons," said the dwarf cheerfully. "Everything's growing like crazy anyway. I'll fill it in this afternoon and put some more seed down and five hundred years will just zoom past, you wait and see."

"The way things are going, I probably will," said Windle moodily. He looked around. "Is the Archchancellor here?" he said.

"I saw them all going up to the palace," said the gardener.

"Then I think I'll just go and have a quick bath and a change of clothes. I wouldn't want to disturb anyone."

"I heard you wasn't just dead but buried too," said the gardener, as Windle lurched off.

"That's right."

"Can't keep a good man down, eh?"

Windle turned back.

"By the way . . . where's Elm Street?"

Modo scratched an ear. "Isn't it that one off Treacle Mine Road?"

"Oh, yes. I remember."

Modo went back to his weeding.

The circular nature of Windle Poons' death didn't bother him much. After all, trees looked dead in the winter, burst forth again every spring. Dried up old seeds went in the ground, fresh young plants sprang up. Practically nothing ever died for long. Take compost, for example.

Modo believed in compost with the same passion that other people believed in gods. His compost heaps heaved and fermented and glowed faintly in the dark, perhaps because of the mysterious and possibly illegal ingredients Modo fed them, although nothing had ever been proved and, anyway, no one was about to dig into one to see what was in it.

All dead stuff, but somehow alive. And it certainly grew roses.

The Senior Wrangler had explained to Modo that his roses grew so big because it was a miracle of existence, but Modo privately thought that they just wanted to get as far away from the compost as possible.

The heaps were in for a treat tonight. The weeds were really doing well. He'd never known plants to grow so fast and luxuriantly. It must be all the compost, Modo thought.

By the time the wizards reached the palace it was in uproar. Pieces of furniture were gliding across the ceiling. A shoal of cutlery, like silvery minnows in mid-air, flashed past the Archchancellor and dived away down a corridor. The place seemed to be in the grip of a selective and tidy-minded hurricane.

Other people had already arrived. They included a group dressed very like the wizards in many ways, although there were important differences to the trained eye.

"Priests?" said the Dean. "Here? Before *us*?"

The two groups began very surreptitiously to adopt positions that left their hands free.

"What good are they?" said the Senior Wrangler.

There was a noticeable drop in metaphorical temperature.

A carpet undulated past.

The Archchancellor met the gaze of the enormous Chief Priest of Blind Io who, as senior priest of the senior god in the Discworld's rambling pantheon, was the nearest thing Ankh-Morpork had to a spokesman on religious affairs.

"Credulous fools," muttered the Senior Wrangler.

"Godless tinkerers," said a small acolyte, peering out from behind the Chief Priest's bulk.

"Gullible idiots!"

"Atheistic scum!"

"Servile morons!"

"Childish conjurors!"

"Bloodthirsty priests!"

"Interfering wizards!"

Ridcully raised an eyebrow. The Chief Priest nodded very slightly.

They left the two groups hurling imprecations at each other from a safe distance and strolled nonchalantly towards a comparatively quiet part of the room where, beside a statue of one of the Patrician's predecessors, they turned and faced one another again.

"So . . . how are things in the godbothering business?" said Ridcully.

"We do our humble best. How is the dangerous meddling with things man was not meant to understand?"

"Pretty fair. Pretty fair." Ridcully removed his hat and fished inside the pointy bit. "Can I offer you a drop of something?"

"Alcohol is a snare for the spirit. Would you care for a cigarette? I believe you people indulge."

"Not me. If I was to tell you what that stuff does to your lungs – "

Ridcully unscrewed the very tip of his hat and poured a generous measure of brandy into it.

"So," he said, "what's happening?"

"We had an altar float up into the air and drop on us."

"A chandelier unscrewed itself. *Everything's* unscrewing itself. You know, I saw a suit of clothes run past on the way here? Two pairs of pants for seven dollars!"

"Hmm. Did you see the label?"

"Everything's throbbing, too. Notice the way everything's throbbing?"

"We thought it was you people."

"It's not magic. I suppose the gods aren't more than usually unhappy?"

"Apparently not."

Behind them, the priests and the wizards were screaming chin to chin.

The Chief Priest moved a little closer.

"I think I could be strong enough to master and defeat just a little snare," he said. "I haven't felt like this since Mrs Cake was one of my flock."

"Mrs Cake? What's a Mrs Cake?"

"You have . . . ghastly Things from the Dungeon Dimensions and things, yes? Terrible hazards of your ungodly profession?" said the Chief Priest.

"Yes."

"We have someone called Mrs Cake."

Ridcully gave him an enquiring look.

"Don't ask," said the priest, shuddering. "Just be grateful you'll never have to find out."

Ridcully silently passed him the brandy.

"Just between the two of us," said the priest, "have you got any ideas about all this? The guards are trying to dig his lordship out. You know he'll want answers. I'm not even certain I know the questions."

"Not magic and not gods," said Ridcully. "Can I have the snare back? Thank you. Not magic and not gods. That doesn't leave us much, does it?"

"I suppose there's not some kind of magic you don't know about?"

"If there is, we don't know about it."

"Fair enough," the priest conceded.

"I suppose it's not the gods up to a bit of ungodliness on the side?" said Ridcully, clutching at one last straw. "A couple of 'em had a bit of a tiff or something? Messing around with golden apples or something?"

"It's very quiet on the god front right now," said the Chief Priest. His eyes glazed as he spoke, apparently reading from a script inside his head. "Hyperopia, goddess of shoes, thinks that Sandelfon, god of corridors, is the long-lost twin brother of Grune, god of un-seasonal fruit. Who put the goat in the bed of Offler, the Crocodile God? Is Offler forging an alliance with Seven-handed Sek? Mean-while, Hoki the Jokester is up to his old tricks – "

"Yes, yes, all right," said Ridcully. "I've never been able to get interested in all that stuff, myself."

Behind them, the Dean was trying to prevent the Lecturer in Recent Runes from attempting to turn the priest of Offler the Crocodile God into a set of matching suitcases, and the Bursar had a bad nosebleed from a lucky blow with a thurible.

"What we've got to present here," said Ridcully, "is a united front. Right?"

"Agreed," said the Chief Priest.

"Right. For now."

A small rug sinewaved past at eye level. The Chief Priest handed back the brandy bottle.

"Incidentally, mother says you haven't written lately," he said.

"Yeah . . ." The other wizards would have been surprised at their Archchancellor's look of contrite embarrassment. "I've been busy. You know how it is."

"She said to be sure to remind you she's expecting both of us over for lunch on Hogswatchday."

"I haven't forgotten," said Ridcully, glumly. "I'm looking forward to it." He turned to the mêlée behind them.

"Cut it out, you fellows," he said.

"Brethren! Desist!" bellowed the Chief Priest.

The Senior Wrangler released his grip on the head of the high priest of the Cult of Hinki. A couple of curates stopped kicking the Bursar. There was a general adjustment of clothing, a finding of hats and a bout of embarrassed coughing.

"That's better," said Ridcully. "Now then, his Eminence the Chief Priest and myself have decided – "

The Dean glowered at a very small bishop.

"He kicked me! You kicked me!"

"Ooo! I never did, my son."

"You bloody well did," the Dean hissed. "Sideways, so they wouldn't see!"

" – *have decided* – " repeated Ridcully, glaring at the Dean, "to pursue a solution to the current disturbances in a spirit of brotherhood and goodwill *and that includes you, Senior Wrangler.*"

"I couldn't help it! He *pushed* me."

"Well! May you be forgiven!" said the Archdeacon of Thrume, stoutly.

There was a crash from above. A *chaise-longue* cantered down the stairs and smashed through the hall door.

"I think perhaps the guards are still trying to free the Patrician," said the High Priest. "Apparently even his secret passages locked themselves."

"All of them? I thought the sly devil had 'em everywhere," said Ridcully.

"All locked," said the High Priest. "All of them."

"Almost all of them," said a voice behind him.

Ridcully's tones did not change as he turned around, except that a slight extra syrup was added.

A figure had apparently stepped out of the wall. It was human, but only by default. Thin, pale, and clad all in dusty black, the Patrician always put Ridcully in mind of a predatory flamingo, if you could find a flamingo that was black and had the patience of a rock.

"Ah, Lord Vetinari," he said, "I am so glad you are unhurt."

"I will see you gentlemen in the Oblong Office," said the Patrician. Behind him, a panel in the wall slid back noiselessly.

"I, um, I believe there are a number of guards upstairs trying to free – " the Chief Priest began.

The Patrician waved a thin hand at him. "I wouldn't dream of stopping them," he said. "It gives them something to do and makes them feel important. Otherwise they just have to stand around all day looking fierce and controlling their bladders. Come this way."

The leaders of the other Ankh-Morpork Guilds turned up in ones and twos, gradually filling the room.

The Patrician sat gloomily staring at the paperwork on his desk as they argued.

"Well, it's not us," said the head of the Alchemists.

"Things are always flying through the air when you fellows are around," said Ridcully.

"Yes, but that's only because of unforeseen exothermic re-actions," said the alchemist.

"Things keep blowing up," translated the deputy head alchemist, without looking up.

"They may blow *up*, but they come down again. They don't flutter around and, e.g., start unscrewing themselves," said his chief, giving him a warning frown. "Anyway, why'd we do it to ourselves? I tell you, it's hell in my workshop! There's stuff whizzing every-where! Just before I came out, a huge and very expensive piece of glassware broke into splinters!"

"Marry, 'twas a sharp retort," said a wretched voice.

The press of bodies moved aside to reveal the General Secretary and Chief Butt of the Guild of Fools and Joculators. He flinched under the attention, but he generally flinched all the time anyway. He had the look of a man whose face has been Ground Zero for one custard pie too many, whose trousers have been too often awash with whitewash, whose nerves would disintegrate completely at the sound of just one more whoopee-cushion. The other Guild leaders tried to be nice to him, in the same way that people try to be kind to other people who are standing on the ledges of very high buildings.

"What do you mean, Geoffrey?" said Ridcully, as kindly as he could.

The Fool gulped. "Well, you see," he mumbled, "we have sharp as in splinters, and retort as in large glass alchemical vessel, and thus we get a pun on 'sharp retort' which also means, well, a scathing answer. Sharp retort. You see? It's a play on words. Um. It's not very good, is it."

The Archchancellor looked into eyes like two runny eggs.

"Oh, a *pun*," he said. "Of course. Hohoho." He waved a hand encouragingly at the others.

"Hohoho," said the Chief Priest.

"Hohoho," said the leader of the Assassins' Guild.

"Hohoho," said the head Alchemist. "And, you know, what makes it even funnier is that it was actually an alembic."

"So what you're telling me," said the Patrician, as considerate hands leds the Fool away, "is that none of you are responsible for these events?"

He gave Ridcully a meaningful look as he spoke.

The Archchancellor was about to answer when his eye was caught by a movement on the Patrician's desk.

There was a little model of the Palace in a glass globe. And next to it was a paperknife.

The paperknife was slowly bending.

"Well?" said the Patrician.

"Not us," said Ridcully, his voice hollow. The Patrician followed his gaze.

The knife was already curved like a bow.

The Patrician scanned the sheepish crowd until he found Captain Doxie of the City Guard Day Watch.

"Can't *you* do something?" he said.

"Er. Like what, sir? The knife? Er. I suppose I could arrest it for being bent."

Lord Vetinari threw his hands up in the air.

"So! It's not magic! It's not gods! It's not people! What *is* it? And who's going to stop it? Who am I going to call?"

Half an hour later the little globe had vanished. No one noticed. They never do.

Mrs Cake knew who she was going to call.

"You there, One-Man-Bucket?" she said.

Then she ducked, just in case.

A reedy and petulant voice oozed out of the air.

where have you been? can't move in here!

Mrs Cake bit her lip. Such a direct reply meant her spirit guide was worried. When he didn't have anything on his mind he spent five minutes talking about buffaloes and great white spirits, although if One-Man-Bucket had ever been near white spirit he'd drunk it and it was anyone's guess what he'd do to a buffalo. And he kept putting "ums" and "hows" into the conversation.

"What d'you mean?"

there been a catastrophe or something? some kind of ten-second plague?

"No. Don't think so."

there's real pressure here, you know. what's holding everything up?

"What do you mean?"

shutupshutupshutup I'm trying to talk to the lady! you lot over there, keep the noise down! oh yeah? sez you –

Mrs Cake was aware of other voices trying to drown him out.

"One-Man-Bucket!"

heathen savage, am I? so you know what this heathen savage says to you? yeah? listen, I've been over here for a hundred years, me! I don't have to take talk like that from someone who's still warm! right – that does it, you . . .

His voice faded.

Mrs Cake set her jaw.

His voice came back.

– oh yeah? oh yeah? well, maybe you was big when you was alive,

friend, but here and now you're just a bedsheet with holes in it! oh, so you don't like that, eh —

"He's going to start fighting again, mum," said Ludmilla, who was curled up by the kitchen stove. "He always calls people 'friend' just before he hits them."

Mrs Cake sighed.

"And it sounds as if he's going to fight a *lot* of people," said Ludmilla.

"Oh, all right. Go and fetch me a vase. A cheap one, mind."

It is widely suspected, but not generally *known*, that everything has an associated spirit form which, upon its demise, exists briefly in the draughty gap between the worlds of the living and the dead. This is important.

"No, not that one. That belonged to your granny."

This ghostly survival does not last for long without a consciousness to hold it together, but depending on what you have in mind it can last for just long enough.

"That one'll do. I never liked the pattern."

Mrs Cake took an orange vase with pink peonies on it from her daughter's paws.

"Are you still there, One-Man-Bucket?" she said.

— I'll make you regret the day you ever died, you whining —

"Catch."

She dropped the vase onto the stove. It smashed.

A moment later, there was a sound from the Other Side. If a discorporate spirit had hit another discorporate spirit with the ghost of a vase, it would have sounded just like that.

right, said the voice of One-Man-Bucket, *and there's more where that came from, okay?*

The Cakes, mother and hairy daughter, nodded at each other.

When One-Man-Bucket spoke again, his voice dripped with smug satisfaction.

just a bit of an altercation about seniority here, he said. *just sorting out a bit of personal space. got a lot of problems here, Mrs Cake. it's like a waiting room —*

There was a shrill clamour of other disembodied voices.

— could you get a message, please, to Mr —

— tell her there's a bag of coins on the ledge up the chimney —

– Agnes is not to have the silverware after what she said about our Molly –

– I didn't have time to feed the cat, could someone go –

shutupshutup! That was One-Man-Bucket again. *you've got no idea, have you? this is ghost talk, is it? feed the cat? whatever happened to "I am very happy here, and waiting for you to join me"?*

– listen, if anyone else joins us, we'll be standing on one another's heads –

that's not the point. that's not the point, that's all I'm saying. when you're a spirit, there's things you gotta say. Mrs Cake?

"Yes?"

you got to tell someone about this.

Mrs Cake nodded.

"Now you all go away," she said. "I'm getting one of my headaches."

The crystal ball faded.

"Well!" said Ludmilla.

"I ain't going to tell no priests," said Mrs Cake firmly.

It wasn't that Mrs Cake wasn't a religious woman. She was, as has already been hinted, a very religious woman indeed. There wasn't a temple, church, mosque or small group of standing stones anywhere in the city that she hadn't attended at one time or another, as a result of which she was more feared than an Age of Enlightenment; the mere sight of Mrs Cake's small fat body on the threshold was enough to stop most priests dead in the middle of their invocation.

Dead. That was the point. All the religions had very strong views about talking to the dead. And so did Mrs Cake. They held that it was sinful. Mrs Cake held that it was only common courtesy.

This usually led to a fierce ecclesiastical debate which resulted in Mrs Cake giving the chief priest what she called "a piece of her mind". There were so many pieces of Mrs Cake's mind left around the city now that it was quite surprising that there was enough left to power Mrs Cake but, strangely enough, the more pieces of her mind she gave away the more there seemed to be left.

There was also the question of Ludmilla. Ludmilla was a problem. The late Mr Cake, godsresthissoul, had never so much as even whistled at the full moon his whole life, and Mrs Cake had dark

78

suspicions that Ludmilla was a throwback to the family's distant past in the mountains, or maybe had contracted genetics as a child. She was pretty certain her mother had once alluded circumspectly to the fact that Great-uncle Erasmus sometimes had to eat his meals under the table. Either way, Ludmilla was a decent upright young woman for three weeks in every four and a perfectly well-behaved hairy wolf thing for the rest of the time.

Priests often failed to see it that way. Since by the time Mrs Cake fell out with whatever priests* were currently moderating between her and the gods, she had usually already taken over the flower arrangements, altar dusting, temple cleaning, sacrificial stone scrubbing, honorary vestigial virgining, hassock repairing and every other vital religious support role by sheer force of person- ality, her departure resulted in total chaos.

Mrs Cake buttoned up her coat.

"It won't work," said Ludmilla.

"I'll try the wizards. They ought to be tole," said Mrs Cake. She was quivering with self-importance, like a small enraged football.

"Yes, but you said they never listen," said Ludmilla.

"Got to try. Anyway, what are you doing out of your room?"

"Oh, mother. You know I hate that room. There's no need – "

"You can't be too careful. Supposin' you was to take it into your head to go and chase people's chickens? What would the neighbours say?"

"I've never felt the least urge to chase a chicken, mother," said Ludmilla wearily.

"Or run after carts, barkin'."

"That's *dogs*, mother."

"You just get back in your room and lock yourself in and get on with some sewing like a good girl."

"You know I can't hold the needles properly, mother."

"Try for your mother."

"*Yes*, mother," said Ludmilla.

----

* Mrs Cake was aware that some religions had priestesses. What Mrs Cake thought about the ordination of women was unprintable. The religions with priestesses in Ankh-Morpork tended to attract a large crowd of plain-clothes priests from other denominations who were looking for a few hours' respite somewhere where they wouldn't encounter Mrs Cake.

"And don't go near the window. We don't want people upset."

"Yes, mother. And you make sure you put your premonition on, mum. You know your eyesight isn't what it was."

Mrs Cake watched her daughter go upstairs. Then she locked the front door behind her and strode towards Unseen University where, she'd heard, there was too much nonsense of all sorts.

Anyone watching Mrs Cake's progress along the street would have noticed one or two odd details. Despite her erratic gait, no one bumped into her. They weren't avoiding her, she just wasn't where they were. At one point she hesitated, and stepped into an alley-way. A moment later a barrel rolled off a cart that was unloading outside a tavern and smashed on the cobbles where she would have been. She stepped out of the alley and over the wreckage, grumbling to herself.

Mrs Cake spent a lot of the time grumbling. Her mouth was constantly moving, as if she was trying to dislodge a troublesome pip from somewhere in the back of her teeth.

She reached the high black gates of the University and hesitated again, as if listening to some inner voice.

Then she stepped aside and waited.

Bill Door lay in the darkness of the hayloft and waited. Below, he could hear the occasional horsey sounds of Binky – a soft movement, the champ of a jaw.

Bill Door. So now he had a name. Of course, he'd always had a name, but he'd been named for what he embodied, not for who he was. Bill Door. It had a good solid ring to it. Mr Bill Door. William Door, Esq. Billy D– no. Not Billy.

Bill Door eased himself further into the hay. He reached into his robe and pulled out the golden timer. There was, quite perceptibly, less sand in the top bulb. He put it back.

And then there was this "sleep". He knew what it was. People did it for quite a lot of the time. They lay down and ˉleep happened. Presumably it served some purpose. He was watching out for it with interest. He would have to subject it to analysis.

*

Night drifted across the world, coolly pursued by a new day.

There was a stirring in the henhouse across the yard.

"Cock-a-doo . . . er."

Bill Door stared at the roof of the barn.

"Cock-a-doodle . . . er."

Grey light was filtering in between the cracks.

Yet only moments ago there had been the red light of sunset!

Six hours had vanished.

Bill hauled out the timer. Yes. The level was definitely down. While he had been waiting to experience sleep, something had stolen part of his . . . of his *life*. He'd completely missed it, too –

"Cock . . . cock-a . . . er . . ."

He climbed down from the loft and stepped out into the thin mist of dawn.

The elderly chickens watched him cautiously as he peered into their house. An ancient and rather embarrassed-looking cockerel glared at him and shrugged.

There was a clanging noise from the direction of the house. An old iron barrel hoop was hanging by the door, and Miss Flitworth was hitting it vigorously with a ladle.

He stalked over to investigate.

WHAT FOR ARE YOU MAKING THE NOISE, MISS FLITWORTH?

She spun around, ladle half-raised.

"Good grief, you must walk like a cat!" she said.

I MUST?

"I meant I didn't hear you." She stood back and looked him up and down.

"There's still something about you I can't put my finger on, Bill Door," she said. "Wish I knew what it was."

The seven-foot skeleton regarded her stoically. He felt there was nothing he could say.

"What do you want for breakfast?" said the old woman. "Not that it'll make any difference, 'cos it's porridge."

Later she thought: he must have eaten it, because the bowl is empty. Why can't I remember?

And then there was the matter of the scythe. He looked at it as if he'd never seen one before. She pointed out the grass nail and the handles. He looked at them politely.

81

How do you sharpen it, Miss Flitworth?

"It's sharp enough, for goodness sake."

How do you sharpen it more?

"You can't. Sharp's sharp. You can't get sharper than that."

He'd swished it aimlessly, and made a disappointed hissing noise.

And there was the grass, too.

The hay meadow was high on the hill behind the farm, overlooking the cornfield. She watched him for a while.

It was the most interesting technique she had ever witnessed. She wouldn't even have thought that it was technically possible.

Eventually she said: "It's good. You've got the swing and everything."

Thank you, Miss Flitworth.

"But why one blade of grass at a time?"

Bill Door regarded the neat row of stalks for some while.

There is another way?

"You can do lots in one go, you know."

No. No. One blade at a time. One time, one blade.

"You won't cut many *that* way," said Miss Flitworth.

Every last one, Miss Flitworth.

"Yes?"

Trust me on this.

Miss Flitworth left him to it and went back to the farmhouse. She stood at the kitchen window and watched the distant dark figure for a while, as it moved over the hillside.

I wonder what he did? she thought. He's got a Past. He's one of them Men of Mystery, I expect. Perhaps he did a robbery and is Lying Low.

He's cut a whole row already. One at a time, but somehow faster than a man cutting swathe by swathe . . .

Miss Flitworth's only reading matter was the *Farmer's Almanac and Seed Catalogue*, which could last a whole year in the privy if no one was ill. In addition to sober information about phases of the moon and seed sowings it took a certain grisly relish in recounting the various mass murders, vicious robberies and natural disasters that befell mankind, on the lines of "June 15, Year of the Impromptu Stoat: On this Day 150 yrs. since, a Man killed by Freak shower of Goulash in Quirm" or "14 die at hands of Chume, the Notorious Herring Thrower."

The important thing about all these was that they happened a long way away, possibly by some kind of divine intervention. The only things that usually happened locally were the occasional theft of a chicken, and the occasional wandering troll. Of course, there were also robbers and bandits in the hills but they got on well with the actual residents and were essential to the local economy. Even so, she felt she'd certainly feel safer with someone else about the place.

The dark figure on the hillside was well into the second row. Behind it, the cut grass withered in the sun.

I HAVE FINISHED, MISS FLITWORTH.

"Go and feed the pig, then. She's called Nancy."

NANCY, said Bill, turning the word around in his mouth as though he was trying to see it from all sides.

"After my mother."

I WILL GO AND FEED THE PIG NANCY, MISS FLITWORTH.

It seemed to Miss Flitworth that mere seconds went by.

I HAVE FINISHED, MISS FLITWORTH.

She squinted at him. Then, slowly and deliberately, she wiped her hands on a cloth, stepped out into the yard and headed for the pigsty.

Nancy was eyeball-deep in the swill trough.

Miss Flitworth wondered exactly what comment she should make. Finally she said, "Very good. Very good. You, you, you certainly work . . . fast."

MISS FLITWORTH, WHY DOES NOT THE COCKEREL CROW PROPERLY?

"Oh, that's just Cyril. He hasn't got a very good memory. Ridiculous, isn't it? I wish he'd get it right."

Bill Door found a piece of chalk in the farm's old smithy, located a piece of board among the debris, and wrote very carefully for some time. Then he wedged the board in front of the henhouse and pointed Cyril towards it.

THIS YOU WILL READ, he said.

Cyril peered myopically at the "Cock-A-Doodle-Doo" in heavy gothic script. Somewhere in his tiny mad chicken mind a very distinct and chilly understanding formed that he'd better learn to read very, very quickly.

*

83

Bill Door sat back among the hay and thought about the day. It seemed to have been quite a full one. He'd cut hay and fed animals and mended a window. He'd found some old overalls hanging in the barn. They seemed far more appropriate for a Bill Door than a robe woven of absolute darkness, so he'd put them on. And Miss Flitworth had given him a broad-brimmed straw hat.

And he'd ventured the half-mile walk into the town. It wasn't even a one horse town. If anyone had a horse, they'd have eaten it. The residents appeared to make a living by stealing one another's washing.

There was a town square, which was ridiculous. It was really only an enlarged crossroads, with a clock tower. And there was a tavern. He'd gone inside.

After the initial pause while everyone's mind had refocused to allow him room, they'd been cautiously hospitable; news travels even faster on a vine with few grapes.

"You'd be the new man up at Miss Flitworth's," said the barman. "A Mr Door, I did hear."

CALL ME BILL.

"Ah? Used to be a tidy old farm, once upon a time. We never thought the old girl'd stay on."

"Ah," agreed a couple of old men by the fireplace.

AH.

"New to these parts, then?" said the barman.

The sudden silence of the other men in the bar was like a black hole.

NOT PRECISELY.

"Been here before, have you?"

JUST PASSING THROUGH.

"They say old Miss Flitworth's a loony," said one of the figures on the benches around the smoke-blackened walls.

"But sharp as a knife, mind," said another hunched drinker.

"Oh, yes. She's sharp all right. But still a loony."

"And they say she's got boxes full of treasure in that old parlour of hers."

"She'm tight with money, I know that."

"That proves it. Rich folk are always tight with money."

"All right. Sharp and *rich*. But still a loony."

"You can't be loony and rich. You've got to be eccentric if you're rich."

The silence returned and hovered. Bill Door sought desperately for something to say. He had never been very good at small talk. He'd never had much occasion to use it.

What did people say at times like this? Ah. Yes.

I WILL BUY EVERYONE A DRINK, he announced.

Later on they taught him a game that consisted of a table with holes and nets around the edge, and balls carved expertly out of wood, and apparently balls had to bounce off one another and into the holes. It was called Pond. He played it well. In fact, he played it perfectly. At the start, he didn't know how not to. But after he heard them gasp a few times he corrected himself and started making mistakes with painstaking precision; by the time they taught him darts he was getting really good at them. The more mistakes he made, the more people liked him. So he propelled the little feathery darts with cold skill, never letting one drop within a foot of the targets they urged on him. He even sent one ricocheting off a nail head and a lamp so that it landed in someone's beer, which made one of the older men laugh so much he had to be taken outside into the fresh air.

They'd called him Good Old Bill.

No one had ever called him that before.

What a strange evening.

There had been one bad moment, though. He'd heard a small voice say: "That man is a skelington," and had turned to see a small child in a nightdress watching him over the top of the bar, without terror but with a sort of fascinated horror.

The landlord, who by now Bill Door knew to be called Lifton, had laughed nervously and apologised.

"That's just her fancy," he said. "The things children say, eh? Get on with you back to bed, Sal. And say you're sorry to Mr Door."

"He's a skelington with clothes on," said the child. "Why doesn't all the drink fall through?"

He'd almost panicked. His intrinsic powers were fading, then. People could not normally see him – he occupied a blind spot in their senses, which they filled in somewhere inside their heads with something they preferred to encounter. But the adults' inability to see him clearly wasn't proof against this sort of insistent declaration, and he could feel the puzzlement around him. Then, just in time, its mother had come in from the back room and had taken the child away. There'd been muffled

85

complaints on the lines of " – a skelington, with all bones on – "
disappearing around the bend in the stairs.

And all the time the ancient clock over the fireplace had been ticking,
ticking, chopping seconds off his life. There'd seemed so many of them,
not long ago . . .

There was a faint knocking at the barn door, below the hayloft. He
heard it pushed open.

"Are you decent, Bill Door?" said Miss Flitworth's voice in the
darkness.

Bill Door analysed the sentence for meaning within context.

YES? he ventured.

"I've brought you a hot milk drink."

YES?

"Come on, quick now. Otherwise it'll go cold."

Bill Door cautiously climbed down the wooden ladder. Miss Flitworth
was holding a lantern, and had a shawl around her shoulders.

"It's got cinnamon on it. My Ralph always liked cinnamon." She
sighed.

Bill Door was aware of undertones and overtones in the same way that
an astronaut is aware of weather patterns below him; they're all visible,
all there, all laid out for study and all totally divorced from actual
experience.

THANK YOU, he said.

Miss Flitworth looked around.

"You've really made yourself at home here," she said brightly.

YES.

She pulled the shawl around her shoulders.

"I'll be getting back to the house, then," she said. "You can bring the
mug back in the morning."

She sped away into the night.

Bill Door took the drink up to the loft. He put it on a low beam and sat
and watched it long after it grew cold and the candle had gone out.

After a while he was aware of an insistent hissing. He took out the
golden timer and put it right at the other end of the loft, under a pile of
hay.

It made no difference at all.

*

Windle Poons peered at the house numbers – a hundred Counting Pines had died for this street alone – and then realised he didn't have to. He was being shortsighted out of habit. He improved his eyesight.

Number 668 took some while to find because it was in fact on the first floor above a tailor's shop. Entrance was via an alleyway. There was a wooden door at the end of the alley. On its peeling paintwork someone had pinned a notice which read, in optimistic lettering:

"Come in! Come in!! The Fresh Start Club.
Being Dead is only the Beginning!!!"

The door opened on to a flight of stairs that smelled of old paint and dead flies. They creaked even more than Windle's knees.

Someone had been drawing on the walls. The phraseology was exotic but the general tone was familiar enough: *Spooks of the world Arise, You have Nothing to lose but your Çhains* and *The Silent Majority want Dead Rights* and *End vitalism now!!!*

At the top was a landing, with one door opening off it. Once upon a time someone had hung an oil lamp from the ceiling, but it looked as though it had never been lit for thousands of years. An ancient spider, possibly living on the remains of the oil, watched him warily from its eyrie.

Windle looked at the card again, took a deep breath out of habit, and knocked.

The Archchancellor strode back into College in a fury, with the others trailing desperately behind him.

"Who is he going to call! *We're* the wizards around here!"

"Yes, but we don't actually know what's happening, do we?" said the Dean.

"So we're going to find out!" Ridcully growled. "I don't know who *he's* going to call, but I'm damn sure who *I'm* going to call."

He halted abruptly. The rest of the wizards piled into him.

"Oh, no," said the Senior Wrangler. "Please, not that!"

"Nothing to it," said Ridcully. "Nothing to worry about. Read up on it last night, 's'matterofact. You can do it with three bits of wood and – "

"Four cc of mouse blood," said the Senior Wrangler mournfully. "You don't even need that. You can use two bits of wood and an egg. It has to be a fresh egg, though."

"Why?"

"I suppose the mouse feels happier about it."

"No, I mean the egg."

"Oh, who knows how an egg feels?"

"*Anyway*," said the Dean, "it's dangerous. I've always felt that he only stays in the octogram for the look of the thing. I hate it when he peers at you and seems to be counting."

"Yes," said the Senior Wrangler. "We don't need to do that. We get over most things. Dragons, monsters. Rats. Remember the rats last year? Seemed to be everywhere. Lord Vetinari wouldn't listen to us, oh no. He paid that glib bugger in the red and yellow tights a thousand gold pieces to get rid of 'em."

"It worked, though," said the Lecturer in Recent Runes.

"Of course it bloody worked," said the Dean. "It worked in Quirm and Sto Lat as well. He'd have got away with it in Pseudopolis as well if someone hadn't recognised him. Mr so-called Amazing Maurice and His Educated Rodents!"

"It's no good trying to change the subject," said Ridcully. "We're going to do the Rite of AshKente. Right?"

"And summon Death," said the Dean. "Oh, dear."

"Nothing wrong with Death," said Ridcully. "Professional fellow. Job to do. Fair and square. Play a straight bat, no problem. He'll know what's happening."

"Oh, dear," said the Dean again.

They reached the gateway. Mrs Cake stepped forward, blocking the Archchancellor's path.

Ridcully raised his eyebrows.

The Archchancellor was not the kind of man who takes a special pleasure in being brusque and rude to women. Or, to put it another way, he was brusque and rude to absolutely everyone, regardless of sex, which was equality of a sort. And if the following conversation had *not* been taking place between someone who listened to what people said several seconds before they said it, and someone who didn't listen to what people said at all, everything might have been a lot different. Or perhaps it wouldn't.

Mrs Cake led with an answer.

"I'm not your good woman!" she snapped.

"And who are you, my good woman?" said the Archchancellor.

"Well, that's no way to talk to a respectable person," said Mrs Cake.

"There's no need to be offended," said Ridcully.

"Oh blow, is that what I'm doin'?" said Mrs Cake.

"Madam, why are you answering me before I've even said something?"

"What?"

"What d'you mean?"

"What do *you* mean?"

"What?"

They stared at one another, fixed in an unbreakable conversational deadlock. Then Mrs Cake realised.

"Oi'm prematurely premoniting again," she said. She stuck a finger in her ear and wiggled it around with a squelching noise. "It's all orlright now. Now, the reason – "

But Ridcully had had enough.

"Bursar," he said, "give this woman a penny and send her about her business, will you?"

"What?" said Mrs Cake, suddenly enraged beyond belief.

"There's too much of this sort of thing these days," said Ridcully to the Dean, as they strolled away.

"It's the pressures and stresses of living in a big city," said the Senior Wrangler. "I read that somewhere. It takes people in a funny way."

They stepped through the wicket gate in one of the big doors and the Dean shut it in Mrs Cake's face.

"He might not come," said the Senior Wrangler, as they crossed the quadrangle. "He didn't come for poor old Windle's farewell party."

"He'll come for the Rite," said Ridcully. "It doesn't just send him an invitation, it puts a bloody RSVP on it!"

"Oh, good. I like sherry," said the Bursar.

"Shut up, Bursar."

*

89

There was an alley, somewhere in the Shades, which was the most alley-ridden part of an alley-ridden city.

Something small and shiny rolled into it, and vanished in the darkness.

After a while, there were faint metallic noises.

The atmosphere in the Archchancellor's study was very cold.

Eventually the Bursar quavered: "Maybe he's busy?"

"Shut up," said the wizards, in unison.

Something was happening. The floor inside the chalked magic octogram was going white with frost.

"It's never done that before," said the Senior Wrangler.

"This is all wrong, you know," said the Dean. "We should have some candles and some cauldrons and some stuff bubbling in crucibles and some glitter dust and some coloured smoke – "

"The Rite doesn't need any of that stuff," said Ridcully sharply.

"*It* might not need them, but I do," muttered the Dean. "Doing it without the right paraphernalia is like taking all your clothes off to have a bath."

"That's what I do," said Ridcully.

"Humph. Well, each to his own, of course, but some of us like to think that we're maintaining *standards*."

"Perhaps he's on holiday?" said the Bursar.

"Oh, yes," sneered the Dean. "On a beach somewhere? A few iced drinks and a Kiss Me Quick hat?"

"Hold on. Hold on. Someone's coming," hissed the Senior Wrangler.

The faint outlines of a hooded figure appeared above the octogram. It wavered constantly, as if it was being seen through superheated air.

"That's him," said the Dean.

"No it isn't," said the Lecturer in Recent Runes. "It's just a grey ro– there's nothing in – "

He stopped.

It turned, slowly. It was filled out, suggesting a wearer, but at the same time had a feeling of hollowness, as if it was merely a shape for something with no shape of its own. The hood was empty.

The emptiness watched the wizards for a few seconds and then focused on the Archchancellor.

It said, Who are you?

Ridcully swallowed. "Er. Mustrum Ridcully. Archchancellor."

The hood nodded. The Dean stuck a finger in his ear and waggled it around. The robe wasn't talking. Nothing was being heard. It was just that, afterwards, you had a sudden memory of what had just failed to be said and no knowledge of how it had got there.

The hood said, You are a superior being on this world?

Ridcully looked at the other wizards. The Dean glared.

"Well . . . you know . . . yes . . . first among equals and all that sort of thing . . . yes . . ." Ridcully managed.

He was told, We bring good news.

"Good news? Good news?" Ridcully squirmed under the gazerless gaze. "Oh, *good*. That *is* good news."

He was told, Death has retired.

"Pardon?"

He was told, Death has retired.

"Oh? That is . . . news . . ." said Ridcully uncertainly. "Uh. How? Exactly . . . how?"

He was told, We apologise for the recent lapse in standards.

"Lapse?" said the Archchancellor, now totally mystified. "Well, uh, I'm not sure there's been a . . . I mean, of course the fella was always knockin' around, but most of the time we hardly . . ."

He was told, It has all been most irregular.

"It has? Has it? Oh, well, can't have irregularity," said the Archchancellor.

He was told, It must have been terrible.

"Well, I . . . that is . . . I suppose we . . . I'm not sure . . . must it?"

He was told, But now the burden is removed. Rejoice. That is all. There will be a short transitional period before a suitable candidate presents itself, and then normal service will be resumed. In the meantime, we apologise for any unavoidable inconvenience caused by superfluous life effects.

The figure wavered and began to fade.

The Archchancellor waved his hands desperately.

"Wait!" he said. "You can't just go like that! I command you to stay! What service? What does it all mean? Who are you?"

91

The hood turned back towards him and said, We are nothing.

"That's no help! What is your name?"

We are oblivion.

The figure vanished.

The wizards fell silent. The frost in the octogram began to sublime back into air.

"Oh-oh," said the Bursar.

"Short transitional period? Is that what this is?" said the Dean.

The floor shook.

"Oh-oh," said the Bursar again.

"That doesn't explain why everything is living a life of its own," said the Senior Wrangler.

"Hold on . . . hold on," said Ridcully, "If people are coming to the end of their life and leaving their bodies and everything, but Death isn't taking them away — "

"Then that means they're queueing up here," said the Dean.

"With nowhere to go."

"Not just people," said the Senior Wrangler. "It must be everything. Every thing that dies."

"Filling up the world with life force," said Ridcully. The wizards were speaking in a monotone, everyone's mind running ahead of the conversation to the distant horror of the conclusion.

"Hanging around with nothing to do," said the Lecturer in Recent Runes.

"Ghosts."

"Poltergeist activity."

"Good grief."

"Hang on, though," said the Bursar, who had managed to catch up with events. "Why should that worry us? We don't have anything to fear from the dead, do we? After all, they're just people who are dead. They're just ordinary people. People like us."

The wizards thought about this. They looked at one another. They started to shout, all at once.

No one remembered the bit about suitable candidates.

Belief is one of the most powerful organic forces in the multiverse. It may not be able to move mountains, exactly. But it can create someone who can.

People get exactly the wrong idea about belief. They think it works back to front. They think the sequence is, first object, then belief. In fact, it works the other way.

Belief sloshes around in the firmament like lumps of clay spiralling into a potter's wheel. That's how gods get created, for example. They clearly must be created by their own believers, because a brief résumé of the lives of most gods suggests that their origins certainly couldn't be divine. They tend to do exactly the things people would do if only they could, especially when it comes to nymphs, golden showers, and the smiting of your enemies.

Belief creates other things.

It created Death. Not death, which is merely a technical term for a state caused by prolonged absence of life, but Death, the personality. He evolved, as it were, along with life. As soon as a living thing was even dimly aware of the concept of suddenly becoming a non-living thing, there was Death. He was Death long before humans ever considered him; they only added the shape and all the scythe and robe business to a personality that was already millions of years old.

And now he had gone. But belief doesn't stop. Belief goes right on believing. And since the focal point of belief had been lost, new points sprang up. Small as yet, not very powerful. The private deaths of every species, no longer united but specific.

In the stream, black-scaled, swam the new Death of Mayflies. In the forests, invisible, a creature of sound only, drifted the chop-chop-chop of the Death of Trees.

Over the desert a dark and empty shell moved purposefully, half an inch above the ground . . . the Death of Tortoises.

The Death of Humanity hadn't been finished yet. Humans can believe some very complex things.

It's like the difference between off-the-peg and bespoke.

The metallic sounds stopped coming from the alley.

Then there was a silence. It was the particularly wary silence of something making no noise.

And, finally, there was a very faint jangling sound, disappearing into the distance.

*

93

"Don't stand in the doorway, friend. Don't block up the hall. Come on in."

Windle Poons blinked in the gloom.

When his eyes became accustomed to it, he realised that there was a semi-circle of chairs in an otherwise rather bare and dusty room. They were all occupied.

In the centre – at the focus, as it were, of the half circle – was a small table at which someone had been seated. They were now advancing towards him, with their hand out and a big smile on their face.

"Don't tell me, let me guess," they said. "You're a zombie, right?"

"Er." Windle Poons had never seen anyone with such a pallid skin, such as there was of it, before. Or wearing clothes that looked as if they'd been washed in razor blades and smelled as though someone had not only died in them but was *still* in them. Or sporting a Glad To Be Grey badge.

"I don't know," he said. "I suppose so. Only they buried me, you see, and there was this card – " He held it out, like a shield.

"'Course there was. *'Course* there was," said the figure.

He's going to want me to shake hands, Windle thought. If I do, I just know I'm going to end up with more fingers than I started with. Oh, my goodness. Will I end up like that?

"And I'm dead," he said, lamely.

"And fed up with being pushed around, eh?" said the greenish-skinned one. Windle shook his hand very carefully.

"Well, not exactly fed – "

"Shoe's the name. Reg Shoe."

"Poons. Windle Poons," said Windle. "Er – "

"Yeah, it's always the same," said Reg Shoe bitterly. "Once you're dead, people just don't want to know, right? They act as if you've got some horrible disease. Dying can happen to anyone, right?"

"Everyone, I should have thought," said Windle. "Er, I – "

"Yeah, I know what it's like. Tell someone you're dead and they look at you as if they've seen a ghost," Mr Shoe went on.

Windle realised that talking to Mr Shoe was very much like talking to the Archchancellor. It didn't actually matter what you said, because he wasn't listening. Only in Mustrum Ridcully's case it was because he just wasn't bothering, while Reg Shoe was in fact supplying your side of the conversation somewhere inside his own head.

"Yeah, right," said Windle, giving in.

"We were just finishing off, in fact," said Mr Shoe. "Let me introduce you. Everyone, this is – " He hesitated.

"Poons. Windle Poons."

"Brother Windle," said Mr Shoe. "Give him a big Fresh Start welcome!"

There was an embarrassed chorus of "hallos". A large and rather hairy young man at the end of the row caught Windle's eye and rolled his own yellow eyes in a theatrical gesture of fellow feeling.

"This is Brother Arthur Winkings – "

"*Count Notfaroutoe*," said a female voice sharply.

"And Sister Doreen – I mean Countess Notfaroutoe, of course – "

"Charmed, I'm sure," said the female voice, as the small dumpy woman sitting next to the small dumpy shape of the Count extended a beringed hand. The Count himself gave Windle a worried grin. He seemed to be wearing opera dress designed for a man several sizes larger.

"And Brother Schleppel – "

The chair was empty. But a deep voice from the darkness underneath it said, "Evenin'."

"And Brother Lupine." The muscular, hairy young man with the long canines and pointy ears gave Windle's hand a hearty shake.

"And Sister Drull. And Brother Gorper. And Brother Ixolite."

Windle shook a number of variations on the theme of hand.

Brother Ixolite handed him a small piece of yellow paper. On it was written one word: OoooEeeeOoooEeeeOoooEEEee.

"I'm sorry there aren't more here tonight," said Mr Shoe. "I do my best, but I'm afraid some people just don't seem prepared to make the effort."

"Er . . . dead people?" said Windle, still staring at the note.

"Apathy, I call it," said Mr Shoe, bitterly. "How can the movement make progress if people are just going to lie around the whole time?"

Lupine started making frantic "don't get him started" signals

95

behind Mr Shoe's head, but Windle wasn't able to stop himself in time.

"What movement?" he said.

"Dead Rights," said Mr Shoe promptly. "I'll give you one of my leaflets."

"But, surely, er, dead people don't have rights?" said Windle. In the corner of his vision he saw Lupine put his hand over his eyes.

"You're dead right there," said Lupine, his face absolutely straight. Mr Shoe glared at him.

"Apathy," he repeated. "It's always the same. You do your best for people, and they just ignore you. Do you know people can say what they like about you *and* take away your property, just because you're dead? And they – "

"I thought that most people, when they died, just . . . you know . . . *died*," said Windle.

"It's just laziness," said Mr Shoe. "They just don't want to make the effort."

Windle had never seen anyone look so dejected. Reg Shoe seemed to shrink several inches.

"How long have you been undead, Vindle?" said Doreen, with brittle brightness.

"Hardly any time at all," said Windle, relieved at the change of tone. "I must say it's turning out to be different than I imagined."

"You get used to it," said Arthur Winkings, alias Count Notfaroutoe, gloomily. "That's the thing about being undead. It's as easy as falling off a cliff. We're all undead here."

Lupine coughed.

"Except Lupine," said Arthur.

"I'm more what you might call honorary undead," said Lupine.

"Him being a werewolf," explained Arthur.

"I thought he was a werewolf as soon as I saw him," said Windle, nodding.

"Every full moon," said Lupine. "Regular."

"You start howling and growing hair," said Windle.

They all shook their heads.

"Er, no," said Lupine. "I more sort of *stop* howling and some of my hair temporarily falls out. It's bloody embarrassing."

"But I thought at the full moon your basic werewolf always – "

96

"Lupine's problem," said Doreen, "is that he approaches it from ze ozzer way, you see."

"I'm technically a wolf," said Lupine. "Ridiculous, really. Every full moon I turn into a wolfman. The rest of the time I'm just a . . . wolf."

"Good grief," said Windle. "That must be a terrible problem."

"The trousers are the worst part," said Lupine.

"Er . . . they are?"

"Oh, yeah. See, it's all right for human werewolves. They just keep their own clothes on. I mean, they might get a bit ripped, but at least they've got them handy on, right? Whereas if I see the full moon, next minute I'm walking and talking and I'm definitely in big trouble on account of being very deficient in the trousery vicinity. So I have to keep a pair stashed somewhere. Mr Shoe – "

" – call me Reg – "

" – lets me keep a pair where he works."

"*I* work at the mortuary on Elm Street," said Mr Shoe. "I'm not ashamed. It's worth it to save a brother or sister."

"Sorry?" said Windle. "Save?"

"It's me that pins the card on the bottom of the lid," said Mr Shoe. "You never know. It has to be worth a try."

"Does it often work?" said Windle. He looked around the room. His tone must have suggested that it was a reasonably large room, and had only eight people in it; nine if you included the voice from under the chair, which presumably belonged to a person.

Doreen and Arthur exchanged glances.

"It vorked for Artore," said Doreen.

"Excuse me," said Windle, "I couldn't help wondering . . . are you two . . . er . . . vampires, by any chance?"

"'S'right," said Arthur. "More's the pity."

"Hah! You should not tvalk like zat," said Doreen haughtily. "You should be prout of your noble lineage."

"Prout?" said Arthur.

"Did you get bitten by a bat or something?" said Windle quickly, anxious not to be the cause of any family friction.

"No," said Arthur, "by a lawyer. I got this letter, see? With a posh blob of wax on it and everything. Blahblahblah . . . great-great-uncle . . . blahblahblah . . . only surviving relative . . .

97

blahblahblah . . . may we be the first to offer our heartiest . . . blahblahblah. One minute I'm Arthur Winkings, a coming man in the wholesale fruit and vegetable business, next minute I find I'm Arthur, Count Notfaroutoe, owner of fifty acres of cliff face a goat'd fall off of and a castle that even the cockroaches have abandoned and an invitation from the burgomaster to drop in down at the village one day and discuss three hundred years of back taxes."

"I hate lawyers," said the voice from under the chair. It had a sad, hollow sound. Windle tried to move his legs a little closer to his own chair.

"It voss quite a good castle," said Doreen.

"A bloody heap of mouldering stone is what it was," said Arthur.

"It had nice views."

"Yeah, through every wall," said Arthur, dropping a portcullis into that avenue of conversation. "I should have known even before we went to look at it. So I turned the carriage around, right? I thought, well, that's four days wasted, right in the middle of our busy season. I don't think any more about it. Next thing, I wake up in the dark, I'm in a box, I finally find these matches, I light one, there's this card six inches from my nose. It said – "

"'You Don't Have to Take this Lying Down'," said Mr Shoe proudly. "That was one of my first ones."

"It vasn't my fault," said Doreen, stiffly. "You had been lyink rigid for tree dace."

"It gave the priest a shock, I can tell you," said Arthur.

"Huh! Priests!" said Mr Shoe. "They're all the same. Always telling you that you're going to live again after you're dead, but you just try it and see the look on their faces!"

"Don't like priests, either," said the voice from under the chair. Windle wondered if anyone else was hearing it.

"I won't forget the look on the Reverend Welegare's face in a hurry," said Arthur gloomily. "I've been going to that temple for thirty years. I was respected in the community. Now if I even *think* of setting foot in a religious establishment I get a pain all down my leg."

"Yes, but there was no need for him to say what he said when you pushed the lid off," said Doreen. "And him a priest, too. They shouldn't know those kind of words."

"I enjoyed that temple," said Arthur, wistfully. "It was something to do on a Wednesday."

It dawned on Windle Poons that Doreen had miraculously acquired the ability to use her double-yous.

"And you're a vampire too, Mrs Win . . . I do beg your pardon . . . *Countess* Notfaroutoe?" he enquired politely.

The Countess smiled. "My vord, yes," she said.

"By marriage," said Arthur.

"Can you do that? I thought you had to be bitten," said Windle.

The voice under the chair sniggered.

"I don't see why I should have to go around biting my wife after thirty years of marriage, and that's flat," said the Count.

"Every voman should share her husband's hobbies," said Doreen. "It iss vot keeps a marriage intervesting."

"Who wants an interesting marriage? I never said I wanted an interesting marriage. That's what's wrong with people today, expecting things like marriage to be interesting. And it's not a hobby, anyway," moaned Arthur. "This vampiring's not all it's cracked up to be, you know. Can't go out in daylight, can't eat garlic, can't have a decent shave – "

"Why can't you have a – " Windle began.

"Can't use a *mirror*," said Arthur. "I thought the turning-into-a-bat bit would be interesting, but the owls round here are *murder*. And as for the . . . you know . . . with the blood . . . well . . ." His voice trailed off.

"Artore's never been very good at meetink people," said Doreen.

"And the worst part is having to wear evening dress the whole time," said Arthur. He gave Doreen a sideways glance. "I'm sure it's not really compulsory."

"It iss very important to maintain standerts," said Doreen. Doreen, in addition to her here-one-minute-and-gone-the-next vampire accent, had decided to complement Arthur's evening dress with what she considered appropriate for a female vampire: figure-hugging black dress, long dark hair cut into a widow's peak, and very pallid makeup. Nature had designed her to be small and plump with frizzy hair and a hearty complexion. There were definite signs of conflict.

"I should have stayed in that coffin," said Arthur.

"Oh, no," said Mr Shoe. "That's taking the easy way out. The movement needs people like you, Arthur. We had to set an example. Remember our motto."

"Which motto is that, Reg?" said Lupine wearily. "We have so many."

"'Undead yes – unperson no!'" Reg said.

"You see, he means well," said Lupine, after the meeting had broken up.

He and Windle were walking back through the grey dawn. The Notfaroutoes had left earlier to be back home before daylight heaped even more troubles on Arthur, and Mr Shoe had gone off, he said, to address a meeting.

"He goes down to the cemetery behind the Temple of Small Gods and shouts," Lupine explained. "He calls it consciousness raising but I don't reckon he's on to much of a certainty."

"Who was it under the chair?" said Windle.

"That was Schleppel," said Lupine. "We think he's a bogeyman."

"Are bogeymen undead?"

"He won't say."

"You've never seen him? I thought bogeymen hid under things and, er, behind things and sort of leapt out at people."

"He's all right on the hiding. I don't think he likes the leaping out," said Lupine.

Windle thought about this. An agoraphobic bogeyman seemed to complete the full set.

"Fancy that," he said, vaguely.

"We only go along to the club to keep Reg happy," said Lupine. "Doreen said it'd break his heart if we stopped. You know the worst bit?"

"Go on," said Windle.

"Sometimes he brings a guitar along and makes us sing songs like 'The Streets of Ankh-Morpork' and 'We Shall Overcome'.* It's terrible."

"Can't sing, eh?" said Windle.

---

* A song which, in various languages, is common on every known world in the multiverse. It is always sung by the same people, viz., the people who, when they grow up, will be the people who the next generation sing "We Shall Overcome" at.

"Sing? Never mind sing. Have you ever seen a zombie try to play a guitar? It's helping him find his fingers afterwards that's so embarrassing." Lupine sighed. "By the way, Sister Drull is a ghoul. If she offers you any of her meat patties, don't accept."

Windle remembered a vague, shy old lady in a shapeless grey dress.

"Oh, dear," he said. "You mean she makes them out of human flesh?"

"What? Oh. No. She just can't cook very well."

"Oh."

"And Brother Ixolite is probably the only banshee in the *world* with a speech impediment, so instead of sitting on roofs and screaming when people are about to die he just writes them a note and slips it under the door – "

Windle recalled a long, sad face. "He gave me one, too."

"We try to encourage him," said Lupine. "He's very self-conscious."

His arm shot out and flung Windle against a wall.

"Quiet!"

"What?"

Lupine's ears swivelled. His nostrils flared.

Motioning Windle to remain where he was, the wereman slunk silently along the alley until he reached its junction with another, even smaller and nastier one. He paused for a moment, and then thrust a hairy hand around the corner.

There was a yelp. Lupine's hand came back holding a struggling man. Huge hairy muscles moved under Lupine's torn shirt as the man was hoisted up to fang level.

"You were waiting to attack us, weren't you," said Lupine.

"Who, me – ?"

"I could smell you," said Lupine, evenly.

"I never – "

Lupine sighed. "Wolves don't do this sort of thing, you know," he said.

The man dangled.

"Hey, is that a fact," he said.

"It's all head-on combat, fang against fang, claw against claw,"

101

said Lupine. "You don't find wolves lurking behind rocks ready to mug a passing badger."

"Get away?"

"Would you like me to tear your throat out?"

The man stared eye to yellow eye. He estimated his chances against a seven-foot man with teeth like that.

"Do I get a choice?" he said.

"My friend here," said Lupine, indicating Windle, "is a zombie—"

"Well, I don't know about actual *zombie*, I think you have to eat some sort of fish and root to be a zom—"

" – and you know what zombies do to people, don't you?"

The man tried to nod, even though Lupine's fist was right under his neck.

"Yeggg," he managed.

"Now, he's going to take a very good look at you, and if he ever sees you again – "

"I say, hang on," murmured Windle.

" – he'll come after you. Won't you, Windle?"

"Eh? Oh, yes. That's right. Like a shot," said Windle, unhappily. "Now run along, there's a good chap. Okay?"

"OggAy," said the prospective mugger. He was thinking: Ig eyes! Ike imlets!

Lupine let go. The man hit the cobbles, gave Windle one last terrified glance, and ran for it.

"Er, what *do* zombies do to people?" said Windle. "I suppose I'd better know."

"They tear them apart like a sheet of dry paper," said Lupine.

"Oh? Right," said Windle. They strolled on in silence. Windle was thinking: why me? Hundreds of people must die in this city every day. I bet they don't have this trouble. They just shut their eyes and wake up being born as someone else, or in some sort of heaven or, I suppose, possibly some sort of hell. Or they go and feast with the gods in their hall, which has never seemed a particularly great idea – gods are all right in their way, but not the kind of people a decent man would want to have a meal with. The Yen buddhists think you just become very rich. Some of the Klatchian religions say you go to a lovely garden full of young women, which doesn't sound very religious to *me* . . .

102

Windle found himself wondering how you applied for Klatchian nationality after death.

And at that moment the cobblestones came up to meet him.

This is usually a poetic way of saying that someone fell flat on their face. In this case, the cobblestones really came up to meet him. They fountained up, circled silently in the air above the alley for a moment, and then dropped like stones.

Windle stared at them. So did Lupine.

"That's something you don't often see," said the wereman, after a while. "I don't think I've ever seen stones flying before."

"Or dropping like stones," said Windle. He nudged one with the toe of his boot. It seemed perfectly happy with the role gravity had chosen for it.

"You're a wizard – "

"*Were* a wizard," said Windle.

"You were a wizard. What caused all that?"

"I think it was probably an inexplicable phenomenon," said Windle. "There's a lot of them about, for some reason. I wish I knew why."

He prodded a stone again. It showed no inclination to move.

"I'd better be getting along," said Lupine.

"What's it like, being a wereman?" said Windle.

Lupine shrugged. "Lonely," he said.

"Hmm?"

"You don't fit in, you see. When I'm a wolf I remember what it's like to be a man, and vice versa. Like . . . I mean . . . sometimes . . . sometimes, right, when I'm wolf-shaped, I run up into the hills . . . in the winter, you know, when there's a crescent moon in the sky and a crust on the snow and the hills go on for ever . . . and the other wolves, well, they *feel* what it's like, of course, but they don't *know* like I do. To feel and know at the same time. No one else knows what that's like. No one else in the whole world could know what that's like. That's the bad part. Knowing there's no one else . . ."

Windle became aware of teetering on the edge of a pit of sorrows. He never knew what to say in moments like this.

Lupine brightened up. "Come to that . . . what's it like, being a zombie?"

"It's okay. It's not too bad."

Lupine nodded.

"See you around," he said, and strode off.

The streets were beginning to fill up as the population of Ankh-Morpork began its informal shift change between the night people and the day people. All of them avoided Windle. People didn't bump into a zombie if they could help it.

He reached the University gates, which were now open, and made his way to his bedroom.

He'd need money, if he was moving out. He'd saved quite a lot over the years. Had he made a will? He'd been fairly confused the past ten years or so. He might have made one. Had he been confused enough to leave all his money to himself? He hoped so. There'd been practically no known cases of anyone successfully challenging their own will –

He levered up the floorboard by the end of his bed, and lifted out a bag of coins. He remembered he'd been saving up for his old age.

There was his diary. It was a five-year diary, he recalled, so in a technical sense Windle had wasted about – he did a quick calculation – yes, about three-fifths of his money.

Or more, when you came to think about it. After all, there wasn't much on the pages. Windle hadn't done anything worth writing down for years, or at least anything he'd been able to remember by the evening. There were just phases of the moon, lists of religious festivals, and the occasional sweet stuck to a page.

There was something else down there under the floor, too. He fumbled around in the dusty space and found a couple of smooth spheres. He pulled them out and stared at them, mystified. He shook them, and watched the tiny snowfalls. He read the writing, noting how it wasn't so much writing as a drawing of writing. He reached down and picked up the third object; it was a little bent metal wheel. Just one little metal wheel. And, beside it, a broken sphere.

Windle stared at them.

Of course, he had been a bit non-compos mentis in his last thirty years or so, and maybe he'd worn his underwear outside his clothes and dribbled a bit, but . . . he'd collected souvenirs? And little wheels?

There was a cough behind him.

Windle dropped the mysterious objects back into the hole and looked around. The room was empty, but there seemed to be a shadow behind the open door.

"Hallo?" he said.

A deep, rumbling, but very diffident voice said, "'S'only me, Mr Poons."

Windle wrinkled his forehead with the effort of recollection.

"Schleppel?" he said.

"That's right."

"The bogeyman?"

"That's right?"

"Behind *my* door?"

"That's right."

"Why?"

"It's a friendly door."

Windle walked over to the door and gingerly shut it. There was nothing behind it but old plaster, although he did fancy that he felt an air movement.

"I'm under the bed now, Mr Poons," said Schleppel's voice from, yes, under the bed. "You don't mind, do you?"

"Well, no. I suppose not. But shouldn't you be in a closet somewhere? That's where bogeymen used to hide when I was a lad."

"A good closet is hard to find, Mr Poons."

Windle sighed. "All right. The underside of the bed's yours. Make yourself at home, or whatever."

"I'd prefer going back to lurking behind the door, Mr Poons, if it's all the same to you."

"Oh, all right."

"Do you mind shutting your eyes a moment?"

Windle obediently shut his eyes.

There was another movement of air.

"You can look now, Mr Poons."

Windle opened his eyes.

"Gosh," said Schleppel's voice, "you've even got a coat hook and everything behind here."

Windle watched the brass knobs on the end of his bedstead unscrew themselves.

A tremor shook the floor.

105

"What's going on, Schleppel?" he said.

"Build up of life force, Mr Poons."

"You mean you *know*?"

"Oh, yes. Hey, wow, there's a lock and a handle and a brass finger plate and *everything* behind here – "

"What do you mean, a build up of life force?"

" – and the hinges, there's a really good rising butts here, never had a door with – "

"Schleppel!"

"Just life force, Mr Poons. You know. It's a kind of force what you get in things that are alive? I thought you wizards knew about this sort of thing."

Windle Poons opened his mouth to say something like "Of course we do," before proceeding diplomatically to find out what the hell the bogeyman was talking about, and then remembered that he didn't have to act like that now. That's what he would have done if he was alive, but despite what Reg Shoe proclaimed, it was quite hard to be proud when you were dead. A bit stiff, perhaps, but not proud.

"Never heard of it," he said. "What's it building up for?"

"Don't know. Very unseasonal. It ought to be dying down around now," said Schleppel.

The floor shook again. Then the loose floorboard that had concealed Windle's little fortune creaked, and started to put out shoots.

"What do you mean, unseasonal?" he said.

"You get a lot of it in the spring," said the voice from behind the door. "Shoving the daffodils up out of the ground and that kind of stuff."

"Never heard of it," said Windle, fascinated.

"I thought you wizards knew everything about everything."

Windle looked at his wizarding hat. Burial and tunnelling had not been kind to it, but after more than a century of wear it hadn't been the height of *haute couture* to start with.

"There's always something new to learn," he said.

It was another dawn. Cyril the cockerel stirred on his perch.

The chalked words glowed in the half light.

He concentrated.

He took a deep breath.

"Dock-a-loodle-fod!"

Now that the memory problem was solved, there was only the dyslexia to worry about.

Up in the high fields the wind was strong and the sun was close and strong. Bill Door strode back and forth through the stricken grass of the hillside like a shuttle across a green weave.

He wondered if he'd ever felt wind and sunlight before. Yes, he'd felt them, he must have done. But he'd never *experienced* them like this; the way wind pushed at you, the way the sun made you hot. The way you could feel Time passing.

Carrying you with it.

There was a timid knocking at the barn door.

YES?

"Come on down here, Bill Door."

He climbed down in the darkness and opened the door cautiously.

Miss Flitworth was shielding a candle with one hand.

"Um," she said.

I AM SORRY?

"You can come into the house, if you like. For the evening. Not for the night, of course. I mean, I don't like to think of you all alone out here of an evening, when I've got a fire and everything."

Bill Door was no good at reading faces. It was a skill he'd never needed. He stared at Miss Flitworth's frozen, worried, pleading smile like a baboon looking for meaning in the Rosetta Stone.

THANK YOU, he said.

She scuttled off.

When he arrived at the house she wasn't in the kitchen. He followed a rustling, scraping noise out into a narrow hallway and through a low doorway. Miss Flitworth was down on her hands and knees in the little room beyond, feverishly lighting the fire.

She looked up, flustered, when he rapped politely on the open door.

"Hardly worth putting a match to it for one," she mumbled, by way of embarrassed explanation. "Sit down. I'll make us some tea."

107

Bill Door folded himself into one of the narrow chairs by the fire, and looked around the room.

It was an unusual room. Whatever its functions were, being lived in wasn't apparently one of them. Whereas the kitchen was a sort of roofed-over outside space and the hub of the farm's activities, this room resembled nothing so much as a mausoleum.

Contrary to general belief, Bill Door wasn't very familiar with funereal decor. Deaths didn't normally take place *in* tombs, except in rare and unfortunate cases. The open air, the bottoms of rivers, halfway down sharks, any amount of bedrooms, yes – tombs, no.

His business was the separation of the wheatgerm of the soul from the chaff of the mortal body, and that was usually concluded long before any of the rites associated with, when you got right down to it, a reverential form of garbage disposal.

But this room looked like the tombs of those kings who wanted to take it all with them.

Bill Door sat with his hands on his knees, looking around.

First, there were the ornaments. More teapots than one might think possible. China dogs with staring eyes. Strange cake stands. Miscellaneous statues and painted plates with cheery little messages on them: A Present from Quirm, Long Life and Happiness. They covered every flat surface in a state of total democracy, so that a rather valuable antique silver candlestick was next to a bright coloured china dog with a bone in its mouth and an expression of culpable idiocy.

Pictures hid the walls. Most of them were painted in shades of mud and showed depressed cattle standing on wet moorland in a fog.

In fact the ornaments almost concealed the furniture, but this was no loss. Apart from two chairs groaning under the weight of accumulated antimacassars, the rest of the furniture seemed to have no use whatsoever apart from supporting ornaments. There were spindly tables everywhere. The floor was layered in rag rugs. Someone had really liked making rag rugs. And, above all, and around all, and permeating all, was the smell.

It smelled of long, dull afternoons.

On a cloth-draped sideboard were two small wooden chests flanking a larger one. They must be the famous boxes full of treasure, he thought.

He became aware of ticking.

There was a clock on the wall. Someone had once had what they must have thought was the jolly idea of making a clock like an owl. When the pendulum swung, the owl's eyes went backwards and forwards in what the seriously starved of entertainment probably imagined was a humorous way. After a while, your own eyes started to oscillate in sympathy.

Miss Flitworth bustled in with a loaded tray. There was a blur of activity as she performed the alchemical ceremony of making tea, buttering scones, arranging biscuits, hooking sugar tongs on the basin . . .

She sat back. Then, as if she had been in a state of repose for twenty minutes, she trilled slightly breathlessly: "Well . . . isn't this nice."

YES, MISS FLITWORTH.

"Don't often have occasion to open up the parlour these days."

NO.

"Not since I lost my dad."

For a moment Bill Door wondered if she'd lost the late Mr Flitworth in the parlour. Perhaps he'd taken a wrong turning among the ornaments. Then he recalled the funny little ways humans put things.

AH.

"He used to sit in that very chair, reading the almanac."

Bill Door searched his memory.

A TALL MAN, he ventured. WITH A MOUSTACHE? MISSING THE TIP OF THE LITTLE FINGER ON HIS LEFT HAND?

Miss Flitworth stared at him over the top of her cup.

"You knew him?" she said.

I THINK I MET HIM ONCE.

"He never mentioned you," said Miss Flitworth archly. "Not by name. Not as Bill Door."

I DON'T THINK HE WOULD HAVE MENTIONED ME, said Bill Door slowly.

"It's all right," said Miss Flitworth. "I know all about it. Dad used to do a bit of smuggling, too. Well, this isn't a big farm. It's not what you'd call a living. He always said a body has to do what it can. I expect you were in his line of business. I've been watching you. That was your business, right enough."

Bill Door thought deeply.

GENERAL TRANSPORTATION, he said.

"That sounds like it, yes. Have you got any family, Bill?"

A DAUGHTER.

"That's nice."

109

I'M AFRAID WE'VE LOST TOUCH.

"That's a shame," said Miss Flitworth, and sounded as though she meant it. "We used to have some good times here in the old days. That was when my young man was alive, of course."

YOU HAVE A SON? said Bill, who was losing track.

She gave him a sharp look.

"I invite you to think hard about the word 'Miss'," she said. "We takes things like that seriously in these parts."

MY APOLOGIES.

"No, Rufus was his name. He was a smuggler, like dad. Not as good, though. I got to admit that. He was more artistic. He used to give me all sorts of things from foreign parts, you know. Bits of jewelry and suchlike. And we used to go dancing. He had very good calves, I remember. I like to see good legs on a man."

She stared at the fire for a while.

"See . . . he never come back one day. Just before we were going to be wed. Dad said he never should have tried to run the mountains that close to winter, but I know he wanted to do it so's he could bring me a proper present. And he wanted to make some money and impress dad, because dad was against – "

She picked up the poker and gave the fire a more ferocious jab than it deserved.

"*Anyway*, some folk said he ran away to Farferee or Ankh-Morpork or somewhere, but I know he wouldn't have done something like that."

The penetrating look she gave Bill Door nailed him to the chair.

"What do you think, Bill Door?" she said sharply.

He felt quite proud of himself for spotting the question within the question.

MISS FLITWORTH, THE MOUNTAINS CAN BE VERY TREACHEROUS IN THE WINTER.

She looked relieved. "That's what I've always said," she said. "And do you know what, Bill Door? Do you know what I thought?"

NO, MISS FLITWORTH.

"It was the day before we were going to be wed, like I said. And then one of his pack ponies came back by itself and then the men went and found the avalanche . . . and you know what I thought? I thought, that's ridiculous. That's *stupid*. Terrible, isn't it? Oh, I thought other things afterwards, naturally, but the first thing was that the world shouldn't act as if it was some kind of book. Isn't that a terrible thing to have thought?"

I MYSELF HAVE NEVER TRUSTED DRAMA, MISS FLITWORTH.

She wasn't really listening.

"And I thought, what life expects me to do now is moon around the place in the wedding dress for years and go completely doolally. That's what it *wants* me to do. Hah! Oh, yes! So I put the dress in the ragbag and we still invited everyone to the wedding breakfast, because it's a crime to let good food go to waste."

She attacked the fire again, and then gave him another megawatt stare.

"I think it's always very important to see what's really real and what isn't, don't you?"

MISS FLITWORTH?

"Yes?"

DO YOU MIND IF I STOP THE CLOCK?

She glanced up at the boggle-eyed owl.

"What? Oh. Why?"

I AM AFRAID IT GETS ON MY NERVES.

"It's not very loud, is it?"

Bill Door wanted to say that every tick was like the hammering of iron clubs on bronze pillars.

IT'S JUST RATHER ANNOYING, MISS FLITWORTH.

"Well, stop it if you want to, I'm sure. I only keep it wound up for the company."

Bill Door got up thankfully, stepped gingerly through the forest of ornaments, and grabbed the pine-cone shaped pendulum. The wooden owl glared at him and the ticking stopped, at least in the realm of common sound. He was aware that, elsewhere, the pounding of Time continued none the less. How could people endure it? They allowed Time in their houses, as though it was a *friend*.

He sat down again.

Miss Flitworth had started to knit, ferociously.

The fire rustled in the grate.

Bill Door leaned back in the chair and stared at the ceiling.

"Your horse enjoying himself?"

PARDON?

"Your horse. He seems to be enjoying himself in the meadow," prompted Miss Flitworth.

111

OH. YES.

"Running around as if he's never seen grass before."

HE LIKES GRASS.

"And you like animals. I can tell."

Bill Door nodded. His reserves of small talk, never very liquid, had dried up.

He sat silently for the next couple of hours, hands gripping the arms of the chair, until Miss Flitworth announced that she was going to bed. Then he went back to the barn, and slept.

Bill Door hadn't been aware of it coming. But there it was, a grey figure floating in the darkness of the barn.

Somehow it had got hold of the golden timer.

It told him, Bill Door, there has been a mistake.

The glass shattered. Fine golden seconds glittered in the air, for a moment, and then settled.

It told him, Return. You have work to do. *There has been a mistake.* The figure faded.

Bill Door nodded. Of course there had been a mistake. Anyone could see there had been a mistake. He'd known all along it had been a mistake.

He tossed the overalls in a corner and took up the robe of absolute blackness.

Well, it had been an experience. And, he had to admit, one that he didn't want to relive. He felt as though a huge weight had been removed.

Was that what it was really like to be alive? The feeling of darkness dragging you forward?

How could they live with it? And yet they did, and even seemed to find enjoyment in it, when surely the only sensible course would be to despair. Amazing. To feel you were a tiny living thing, sandwiched between two cliffs of darkness. How could they stand to be alive?

Obviously it was something you had to be born to.

Death saddled his horse and rode out and up over the fields. The corn rippled far below, like the sea. Miss Flitworth would have to find someone else to help her gather in the harvest.

That was odd. There was a feeling there. Regret? Was that it? But it was Bill Door's feeling, and Bill Door was . . . dead. Had never lived. He was his old self again, safe where there were no feelings and no regrets.

112

Never any regrets.

And now he was in his study, and that was odd, because he couldn't quite remember how he'd got there. One minute on horseback, the next in the study, with its ledgers and timers and instruments.

And it was bigger than he remembered. The walls lurked on the edge of sight.

That was Bill Door's doing. Of course it would seem big to Bill Door, and there was probably just a bit of him still hanging on. The thing to do was keep busy. Throw himself into his work.

There were already some lifetimers on his desk. He didn't remember putting them there, but that didn't matter, the important thing was to get on with the job . . .

He picked up the nearest one, and read the name.

"Lod-a-foodle-wok!"

Miss Flitworth sat up in bed. On the edge of dreams she'd heard another noise, which must have woken the cockerel.

She fiddled with a match until she got a candle alight, and then felt under the bed and her fingers found the hilt of a cutlass that had been much employed by the late Mr Flitworth during his business trips across the mountains.

She hurried down the creaking stairs and out into the chill of the dawn.

She hesitated at the barn door, and then pulled it open just enough to slip inside.

"Mr Door?"

There was a rustle in the hay, and then an alert silence.

MISS FLITWORTH?

"Did you call out? I'm sure I heard someone shout my name."

There was another rustle, and Bill Door's head appeared over the edge of the loft.

MISS FLITWORTH?

"Yes. Who did you expect? Are you all right?"

ER. YES. YES, I BELIEVE SO.

"You sure you're all right? You woke up Cyril."

YES. YES. IT WAS JUST A – I THOUGHT THAT – YES.

She blew out the candle. There was already enough pre-dawn light to see by.

"Well, if you're sure . . . Now I'm up I may as well put the porridge on."

Bill Door lay back on the hay until he felt he could trust his legs to carry him, and then climbed down and tottered across the yard to the farmhouse.

He said nothing while she ladled porridge into a bowl in front of him, and drowned it with cream. Finally, he couldn't contain himself any longer. He didn't know how to ask the questions, but he really needed the answers.

MISS FLITWORTH?

"Yes?"

WHAT IS IT . . . IN THE NIGHT . . . WHEN YOU SEE THINGS, BUT THEY ARE NOT THE REAL THINGS?

She stood, porridge pot in one hand and ladle in the other.

"You mean dreaming?" she said.

IS THAT WHAT DREAMING IS?

"Don't you dream? I thought everyone dreamed."

ABOUT THINGS THAT ARE GOING TO HAPPEN?

"That's premonitions, that is. I've never believed in 'em myself. You're not telling me you don't know what dreams are?"

NO. NO. OF COURSE NOT.

"What's worrying you, Bill?"

I SUDDENLY KNOW THAT WE ARE GOING TO DIE.

She watched him thoughtfully.

"Well, so does everyone," she said. "And that's what you've been dreaming about, is it? Everyone feels like this sometimes. I wouldn't worry about it, if I was you. The best thing to do is keep busy and act cheerful, I always say."

BUT WE WILL COME TO AN END!

"Oh, I don't know about that," said Miss Flitworth. "It all depends on what kind of life you've led, I suppose."

I'M SORRY?

"Are you a religious man?"

YOU MEAN THAT WHAT HAPPENS TO YOU WHEN YOU DIE IS WHAT YOU *BELIEVE* WILL HAPPEN?

"It would be nice if that was the case, wouldn't it?" she said brightly.

BUT, YOU SEE, I KNOW WHAT *I* BELIEVE. I BELIEVE . . . NOTHING.

"We *are* gloomy this morning, aren't we?" said Miss Flitworth. "Best thing you could do right now is finish off that porridge. It's good for you. They say it builds healthy bones."

Bill Door looked down at the bowl.

CAN I HAVE SOME MORE?

Bill Door spent the morning chopping wood. It was pleasantly monotonous.

Get tired. That was important. He must have slept before last night, but he must have been so tired that he didn't dream. And he was determined not to dream again. The axe rose and fell on the logs like clockwork.

No! Not like clockwork!

Miss Flitworth had several pots on the stove when he came in.

IT SMELLS GOOD, Bill volunteered. He reached for a wobbling pot lid. Miss Flitworth spun around.

"Don't touch it! You don't want that stuff! It's for the rats."

DO RATS NOT FEED THEMSELVES?

"You bet they do. That's why we're going to give them a little extra something before the harvest. A few dollops of this around the holes and – no more rats."

It took a little while for Bill Door to put two and two together, but when this took place it was like megaliths mating.

THIS IS POISON?

"Essence of spikkle, mixed with oatmeal. Never fails."

AND THEY DIE?

"Instantly. Straight over and legs in the air. We're having bread and cheese," she added. "I ain't doing big cooking twice in one day, and we're having chicken tonight. Talking of chicken, in fact . . . come on . . ."

She took a cleaver off the rack and went out into the yard. Cyril the cockerel eyed her suspiciously from the top of the midden. His harem of fat and rather elderly hens, who had been scratching up the dust, bounded unsteadily towards Miss Flitworth in the broken-knicker-elastic run of hens everywhere. She reached down quickly and picked one up.

It regarded Bill Door with bright, stupid eyes.

"Do you know how to pluck a chicken?" said Miss Flitworth.

Bill looked from her to the hen.

BUT WE FEED THEM, he said helplessly.

"That's right. And then they feed us. This one's been off lay for months. That's how it goes in the chicken world. Mr Flitworth used to wring their necks but I never got the knack of that; the cleaver's messy and they run around a bit afterwards, but they're dead all right, and they know it."

Bill Door considered his options. The chicken had focused one beady eye on him. Chickens are a lot more stupid than humans, and don't have the sophisticated mental filters that prevent them seeing what is truly there. It knew where it was and who was looking at it.

He looked into its small and simple life and saw the last few seconds pouring away.

He'd never killed. He'd taken life, but only when it was finished with. There was a difference between theft and stealing by finding.

NOT THE CLEAVER, he said wearily. GIVE ME THE CHICKEN.

He turned his back for a moment, then handed the limp body to Miss Flitworth.

"Well done," she said, and went back to the kitchen.

Bill Door felt Cyril's accusing gaze on him.

He opened his hand. A tiny spot of light hovered over his palm.

He blew on it, gently, and it faded away.

After lunch they put down the rat poison. He felt like a murderer.

A lot of rats died.

Down in the runs under the barn – in the deepest one, one tunnelled long ago by long-forgotten ancestral rodents – something appeared in the darkness.

It seemed to have difficulty deciding what shape it was going to be.

It began as a lump of highly-suspicious cheese. This didn't seem to work.

Then it tried something that looked very much like a small, hungry terrier. This was also rejected.

For a moment it was a steel-jawed trap. This was clearly unsuitable.

It cast around for fresh ideas and much to its surprise one arrived smoothly, as if travelling from no distance at all. Not so much a shape as a memory of a shape.

It tried it and found that, while totally wrong for the job, in some deeply satisfying way it was the only shape it could possibly be.

It went to work.

*

116

That evening the men were practising archery on the green. Bill Door had carefully ensured a local reputation as the worst bowman in the entire history of toxophily; it had never occurred to anyone that putting arrows through the hats of bystanders behind him must logically take a lot more skill than merely sending them through a quite large target a mere fifty yards away.

It was amazing how many friends you could make by being bad at things, provided you were bad enough to be funny.

So he was allowed to sit on a bench outside the inn, with the old men.

Next door, sparks poured from the chimney of the village smithy and spiralled up into the dusk. There was a ferocious hammering from behind its closed doors. Bill Door wondered why the smithy was always shut. Most smiths worked with their doors open, so that their forge became an unofficial village meeting room. This one was keen on his work –

"Hallo, skelington."

He swivelled round.

The small child of the house was watching him with the most penetrating gaze he had ever seen.

"You are a skelington, aren't you," she said. "I can tell, because of the bones."

YOU ARE MISTAKEN, SMALL CHILD.

"You are. People turn into skelingtons when they're dead. They're not supposed to walk around afterwards."

HA. HA. HA. WILL YOU HARK AT THE CHILD.

"Why are you walking around, then?"

Bill Door looked at the old men. They appeared engrossed in the sport.

I'LL TELL YOU WHAT, he said desperately, IF YOU WILL GO AWAY, I WILL GIVE YOU A HALF-PENNY.

"I've got a skelington mask for when we go trickle-treating on Soul Cake Night," she said. "It's made of paper. You get given sweets."

Bill Door made the mistake millions of people had tried before with small children in slightly similar circumstances. He resorted to reason.

LOOK, he said, IF I WAS REALLY A SKELETON, LITTLE GIRL, I'M SURE THESE OLD GENTLEMEN HERE WOULD HAVE SOMETHING TO SAY ABOUT IT.

She regarded the old men at the other end of the bench.

"They're nearly skelingtons anyway," she said. "I shouldn't think they'd want to see another one."

117

He gave in.

I HAVE TO ADMIT THAT YOU ARE RIGHT ON THAT POINT.

"Why don't you fall to bits?"

I DON'T KNOW. I NEVER HAVE.

"I've seen skelingtons of birds and things and they all fall to bits."

PERHAPS IT IS BECAUSE THEY ARE WHAT SOMETHING *WAS*, WHEREAS THIS IS WHAT I AM.

"The apothecary who does medicine over in Chambly's got a skelington on a hook with all wire to hold the bones together," said the child, with the air of one imparting information gained after diligent research.

I DON'T HAVE WIRES.

"There's a difference between alive skelingtons and dead ones?"

YES.

"It's a dead skelington he's got then, is it?"

YES.

"What was inside someone?"

YES.

"Ur. Yuk."

The child stared distantly at the landscape for a while and then said, "I've got new socks."

YES?

"You can look, if you like."

A grubby foot was extended for inspection.

WELL, WELL. FANCY THAT. NEW SOCKS.

"My mum knitted them out of sheep."

MY WORD.

The horizon was given another inspection.

"D'you know," she said, "d'you know . . . it's Friday."

YES.

"I found a spoon."

Bill Door found he was waiting expectantly. He was not familiar with people who had an attention span of less than three seconds.

"You work along of Miss Flitworth's?"

YES.

"My dad says you've got your feet properly under the table there."

Bill Door couldn't think of an answer to this because he didn't know what it meant. It was one of those many flat statements humans made that were really just a disguise for something more subtle, which was often

118

conveyed merely by the tone of voice or a look in the eyes, neither of which was being done by the child.

"My dad says she said she's got boxes of treasure."

HAS SHE?

"I've got tuppence."

MY GOODNESS.

"Sal!"

They both looked up as Mrs Lifton appeared on the doorstep.

"Bedtime for you. Stop worrying Mr Door."

OH, I ASSURE YOU SHE IS NOT –

"Say goodnight, now."

"How do skelingtons go to sleep? They can't close their eyes because –"

He heard their voices, muffled, inside the inn.

"You mustn't call Mr Door that just because . . . he's . . . very . . . he's very thin . . ."

"It's all right. He's not the dead sort."

Mrs Lifton's voice had the familiar worried tones of someone who can't bring themselves to believe the evidence of their own eyes. "Perhaps he's just been very ill."

"I should think he's just about been as ill as he can be ever."

Bill Door walked back home thoughtfully.

There was a light on in the farmhouse kitchen, but he went straight to the barn, climbed the ladder to the hayloft, and lay down.

He could put off dreaming, but he couldn't escape remembering.

He stared at the darkness.

After a while he was aware of the pattering of feet. He turned.

A stream of pale rat-shaped ghosts skipped along the roof beam above his head, fading as they ran so that soon there was nothing but the sound of the scampering.

They were followed by a . . . shape.

It was about six inches high. It wore a black robe. It held a small scythe in one skeletal paw. A bone-white nose with brittle grey whiskers protruded from the shadowy hood.

Bill Door reached out and picked it up. It didn't resist, but stood on the palm of his hand and eyed him as one professional to another.

Bill Door said: AND YOU ARE – ?

The Death of Rats nodded.

SQUEAK.

I REMEMBER, said Bill Door, WHEN YOU WERE A PART OF ME.

The Death of Rats squeaked again.

Bill Door fumbled in the pockets of his overall. He'd put some of his lunch in there. Ah, yes.

I EXPECT, he said, THAT YOU COULD MURDER A PIECE OF CHEESE?

The Death of Rats took it graciously.

Bill Door remembered visiting an old man once – only once – who had spent almost his entire life locked in a cell in a tower for some alleged crime or other, and had tamed little birds for company during his life sentence. They crapped on his bedding and ate his food, but he tolerated them and smiled at their flight in and out of the high barred windows. Death had wondered, at the time, why anyone would do something like that.

I WON'T DELAY YOU, he said. I EXPECT YOU'VE GOT THINGS TO DO, RATS TO SEE. I KNOW HOW IT IS.

And now he understood.

He put the figure back on the beam, and lay down in the hay.

DROP IN ANY TIME YOU'RE PASSING.

Bill Door stared at the darkness again.

Sleep. He could feel her prowling around. Sleep, with a pocketful of dreams.

He lay in the darkness and fought back.

Miss Flitworth's shouting jolted him upright and, to his momentary relief, still went on.

The barn door slammed open.

"Bill! Come down quick!"

He swung his legs onto the ladder.

WHAT IS HAPPENING, MISS FLITWORTH?

"Something's on fire!"

They ran across the yard and out onto the road. The sky over the village was red.

"Come on!"

BUT IT IS NOT OUR FIRE.

"It's going to be everyone's! It spreads like crazy on thatch!"

They reached the apology for a town square. The inn was already well alight, the thatch roaring starwards in a million twisting sparks.

"Look at everyone standing around," snarled Miss Flitworth. "There's the pump, buckets are everywhere, why don't people *think*?"

There was a scuffle a little way away as a couple of his customers tried to stop Lifton from running into the building. He was screaming at them.

"The girl's still in there," said Miss Flitworth. "Is that what he said?"

YES.

Flames curtained every upper window.

"There's got to be some way," said Miss Flitworth. "Maybe we could find a ladder – "

WE SHOULD NOT.

"What? We've got to try. We can't leave people in there!"

YOU DON'T UNDERSTAND, said Bill Door. TO TINKER WITH THE FATE OF ONE INDIVIDUAL COULD DESTROY THE WHOLE WORLD.

Miss Flitworth looked at him as if he had gone mad.

"What kind of garbage is that?"

I MEAN THAT THERE IS A TIME FOR EVERYONE TO DIE.

She stared. Then she drew her hand back, and gave him a ringing slap across the face.

He was harder than she'd expected. She yelped and sucked at her knuckles.

"You leave my farm *tonight*, Mr Bill Door," she growled. "Understand?" Then she turned on her heel and ran towards the pump.

Some of the men had brought long hooks to drag the burning thatch off the roof. Miss Flitworth organised a team to get a ladder up to one of the bedroom windows but, by the time a man was persuaded to climb it behind the steaming protection of a damp blanket, the top of the ladder was already smouldering.

Bill Door watched the flames.

He reached into his pocket and pulled out the golden timer. The firelight glowed redly on the glass. He put it away again.

Part of the roof fell in.

SQUEAK.

Bill Door looked down. A small robed figure marched between his legs and strutted into the flaming doorway.

Someone was yelling something about barrels of brandy.

Bill Door reached back into his pocket and took out the timer again. Its hissing drowned out the roar of the flames. The future flowed into the past, and there was a lot more past than there was future, but he was struck by the fact that what it flowed through all the time was *now*.

He replaced it carefully.

Death knew that to tinker with the fate of one individual could destroy the whole world. He knew this. The knowledge was built into him.

To Bill Door, he realised, it was so much horse elbows.

OH, DAMN, he said.

And walked into the fire.

"Um. It's me, Librarian," said Windle, trying to shout through the keyhole. "Windle Poons."

He tried hammering some more.

"Why won't he answer?"

"Don't know," said a voice behind him.

"Schleppel?"

"Yes, Mr Poons."

"Why are you behind me?"

"I've got to be behind something, Mr Poons. That's what being a bogeyman is all about."

"Librarian?" said Windle, hammering some more.

"Oook."

"Why won't you let me in?"

"Oook."

"But I need to look something up."

"Oook oook!"

"Well, yes. I am. What's that got to do with it?"

"Oook!"

"That's – that's unfair!"

"What's he saying, Mr Poons?"

"He won't let me in because I'm dead!"

"That's typical. That's the sort of thing Reg Shoe is always going on about, you know."

"Is there anyone else that knows about life force?"

"There's always Mrs Cake, I suppose. But she's a bit weird."

"Who's Mrs Cake?" Then Windle realised what Schleppel had just said. "Anyway, you're a *bogeyman*."

"You never heard of Mrs Cake?"

"No."

"I don't suppose she's interested in magic . . . Anyway, Mr Shoe says we shouldn't talk to her. She exploits dead people, he says."

"How?"

"She's a medium. Well, more a small."

"Really? All right, let's go and see her. And . . . Schleppel?"

"Yes?"

"It's creepy, feeling you standing behind me the whole time."

"I get very upset if I'm not behind something, Mr Poons."

"Can't you lurk behind something else?"

"What do you suggest, Mr Poons?"

Windle thought about it. "Yes, it might work," he said quietly, "if I can find a screwdriver."

Modo the gardener was on his knees mulching the dahlias when he heard a rhythmic scraping and thumping behind him, such as might be made by someone trying to move a heavy object.

He turned his head.

"'Evening, Mr Poons. Still dead, I see."

"'Evening, Modo. You've got the place looking very nice."

"There's someone moving a door along behind you, Mr Poons."

"Yes, I know."

The door edged cautiously along the path. As it passed Modo it pivoted awkwardly, as if whoever was carrying it was trying to keep as much behind it as possible.

"It's a kind of security door," said Windle.

He paused. There was something wrong. He couldn't quite be certain what it was, but there was suddenly a lot of wrongness about, like hearing one note out of tune in an orchestra. He audited the view in front of him.

"What's that you're putting the weeds into?" he said.

Modo glanced at the thing beside him.

"Good, isn't it?" he said. "I found it by the compost heaps. My wheelbarrow'd broke, and I looked up, and there – "

"I've never seen anything like it before," said Windle. "Who'd want to make a big basket out of wire? And those wheels don't look big enough."

123

"But it pushes along well by the handle," said Modo. "I'm amazed that anyone would want to throw it away. Why would anyone want to throw away something like this, Mr Poons?"

Windle stared at the trolley. He couldn't escape the feeling that it was watching him.

He heard himself say, "Maybe it got there by itself."

"That's right, Mr Poons! It wanted a bit of peace, I expect!" said Modo. "You are a one!"

"Yes," said Windle, unhappily. "It rather looks that way."

He stepped out into the city, aware of the scraping and thumping of the door behind him.

If someone had told me a month ago, he thought, that a few days after I died I'd be walking along the road followed by a bashful bogeyman hiding behind a door . . . why, I'd have laughed at them.

No, I wouldn't. I'd have said "eh?" and "what?" and "speak up!" and wouldn't have understood anyway.

Beside him, someone barked.

A dog was watching him. It was a very large dog. In fact, the only reason it could be called a dog and not a wolf was that everyone knew you didn't get wolves in cities.

It winked. Windle thought: no full moon last night.

"Lupine?" he ventured.

The dog nodded.

"Can you talk?"

The dog shook its head.

"So what do you do now?"

Lupine shrugged.

"Want to come with me?"

There was another shrug that almost vocalised the thought: why not? What else have I got to do?

If someone had told me a month ago, Windle thought, that a few days after I died I'd be walking along the road followed by a bashful bogeyman hiding behind a door and accompanied by a kind of negative version of a werewolf . . . why, I probably *would* have laughed at them. After they'd repeated themselves a few times, of course. In a loud voice.

*

124

The Death of Rats rounded up the last of his clients, many of whom had been in the thatch, and led the way through the flames towards wherever it was that good rats went.

He was surprised to pass a burning figure forcing its way through the incandescent mess of collapsed beams and crumbling floorboards. As it mounted the blazing stairs it removed something from the disintegrating remains of its clothing and held it carefully in its teeth.

The Death of Rats did not wait to see what happened next. While it was, in some respects, as ancient as the first proto-rat, it was also less than a day old and still feeling its way as a Death, and it was possibly aware that a deep, thumping noise that was making the building shake was the sound of brandy starting to boil in its barrels.

The thing about boiling brandy is that it doesn't boil for long.

The fireball dropped bits of the inn half a mile away. White-hot flames erupted from the holes where the doors and windows had been. The walls exploded. Burning rafters whirred overhead. Some buried themselves in neighbouring roofs, starting more fires.

What was left was just an eye-watering glow.

And then little pools of shadow, within the glow.

They moved and ran together and formed the shape of a tall figure striding forward, carrying something in front of it.

It passed through the blistered crowd and trudged up the cool dark road towards the farm. The people picked themselves up and followed it, moving through the dusk like the tail of a dark comet.

Bill Door climbed the stairs to Miss Flitworth's bedroom and laid the child on the bed.

SHE SAID THERE WAS AN APOTHECARY SOMEWHERE NEAR HERE.

Miss Flitworth pushed her way through the crowd at the top of the stairs.

"There's one in Chambly," she said. "But there's a witch over Lancre way."

NO WITCHES. NO MAGIC. SEND FOR HIM. AND EVERYONE ELSE, GO AWAY.

It wasn't a suggestion. It wasn't even a command. It was simply an irrefutable statement.

Miss Flitworth waved her skinny arms at the people.

"Come on, it's all over! Shoo! You're all in my bedroom! Go on, get out!"

"How'd he do it?" said someone at the back of the crowd. "No one could have got out of there alive! We saw it all blow up!"

Bill Door turned around slowly.

WE HID, he said, IN THE CELLAR.

"There! See?" said Miss Flitworth. "In the cellar. Makes sense."

"But the inn hasn't got – " the doubter began, and stopped. Bill Door was glaring at him.

"In the cellar," he corrected himself. "Yeah. Right. Clever."

"*Very* clever," said Miss Flitworth. "Now get along with the lot of you."

He heard her shoo them down the stairs and back into the night. The door slammed. He didn't hear her come back up the stairs with a bowl of cold water and a flannel. Miss Flitworth could walk lightly, too, when she had a mind to.

She came in and shut the door behind her.

"Her parents'll want to see her," she said. "Her mum's in a faint and Big Henry from the mill knocked her dad out when he tried to run into the flames, but they'll be here directly."

She bent down and ran the flannel over the girl's forehead.

"Where was she?"

SHE WAS HIDING IN A CUPBOARD.

"From a fire?"

Bill Door shrugged.

"I'm amazed you could find anyone in all that heat and smoke," she said.

I SUPPOSE YOU WOULD CALL IT A KNACK.

"And not a mark on her."

Bill Door ignored the question in her voice.

DID YOU SEND SOMEONE FOR THE APOTHECARY?

"Yes."

HE MUST NOT TAKE ANYTHING AWAY.

"What do you mean?"

STAY HERE WHEN HE COMES. YOU MUST NOT TAKE ANYTHING OUT OF THIS ROOM.

"That's silly. Why should he take anything? What would he want to take?"

126

IT IS VERY IMPORTANT. AND NOW I MUST LEAVE YOU.

"Where are you going?"

TO THE BARN. THERE ARE THINGS I MUST DO. THERE MAY NOT BE MUCH TIME NOW.

Miss Flitworth stared at the small figure on the bed. She felt far out of her depth, and all she could do was tread water.

"She just looks as if she's sleeping," she said helplessly. "What's wrong with her?"

Bill Door paused at the top of the stairs.

SHE IS LIVING ON BORROWED TIME, he said.

There was an old forge behind the barn. It hadn't been used for years. But now red and yellow light spilled out into the yard, pulsing like a heart.

And like a heart, there was a regular thumping. With every crash the light flared blue.

Miss Flitworth sidled through the open doorway. If she was the kind of person who would swear, she would have sworn that she made no noise that could possibly be heard above the crackle of the fire and the hammering, but Bill Door spun around in a half-crouch, holding a curved blade in front of him.

"It's me!"

He relaxed, or at least moved into a different level of tension.

"What the hell are you doing?"

He looked at the blade in his hands as if he was seeing it for the first time.

I THOUGHT I WOULD SHARPEN THIS SCYTHE, MISS FLITWORTH.

"At one o'clock in the morning?"

He looked at it blankly.

IT'S JUST AS BLUNT AT NIGHT, MISS FLITWORTH.

Then he slammed it down on the anvil.

AND I CAN'T SHARPEN IT ENOUGH!

"I think perhaps the heat has got to you," she said, and reached out and took his arm.

"Besides, it looks sharp enough to – " she began, and paused. Her fingers moved on the bone of his arm. They pulled away for a moment, and then closed again.

Bill Door shivered.

127

Miss Flitworth didn't hesitate for long. In seventy-five years she had dealt with wars, famine, innumerable sick animals, a couple of epidemics and thousands of tiny, everyday tragedies. A depressed skeleton wasn't even in the top ten Worst Things she had seen.

"So it *is* you," she said.

MISS FLITWORTH, I –

"I always knew you would come one day."

I THINK PERHAPS THAT –

"You know, I spent most of my life waiting for a knight on a white charger." Miss Flitworth grinned. "The joke's on me, eh?"

Bill Door sat down on the anvil.

"The apothecary came," she said. "He said he couldn't do anything. He said she was fine. We just couldn't wake her up. And, you know, it took us ages to get her hand open. She had it closed so tightly."

I SAID NOTHING WAS TO BE TAKEN!

"It's all right. It's all right. We left her holding it."

GOOD.

"What was it?"

MY TIME.

"Sorry?"

MY TIME. THE TIME OF MY LIFE.

"It looks like an eggtimer for very expensive eggs."

Bill Door looked surprised. YES. IN A WAY. I HAVE GIVEN HER SOME OF MY TIME.

"How come you need time?"

EVERY LIVING THING NEEDS TIME. AND WHEN IT RUNS OUT, THEY DIE. WHEN IT RUNS OUT, SHE WILL DIE. AND I WILL DIE, TOO. IN A FEW HOURS.

"But *you* can't – "

I CAN. IT'S HARD TO EXPLAIN.

"Move up."

WHAT?

"I said move up. I want to sit down."

Bill Door made space on the anvil. Miss Flitworth sat down.

"So you're going to die," she said.

YES.

"And you don't want to."

NO.

"Why not?"

He looked at her as if she was mad.

BECAUSE THEN THERE WILL BE NOTHING. BECAUSE I WON'T EXIST.

"Is that what happens for humans, too?"

I DON'T THINK SO. IT'S DIFFERENT FOR YOU. YOU HAVE IT ALL BETTER ORGANISED.

They both sat watching the fading glow of the coals in the forge.

"So what were you working on the scythe blade for?" said Miss Flitworth.

I THOUGHT PERHAPS I COULD . . . FIGHT BACK . . .

"Has it ever worked? With you, I mean."

NOT USUALLY. SOMETIMES PEOPLE CHALLENGE ME TO A GAME. FOR THEIR LIVES, YOU KNOW.

"Do they ever win?"

NO. LAST YEAR SOMEONE GOT THREE STREETS AND ALL THE UTILITIES.

"What? What sort of game is that?"

I DON'T RECALL. "EXCLUSIVE POSSESSION", I THINK. I WAS THE BOOT.

"Just a moment," said Miss Flitworth. "If *you're* you, who will be coming for you?"

DEATH. LAST NIGHT *THIS* WAS PUSHED UNDER THE DOOR.

Death opened his hand to reveal a small grubby piece of paper, on which Miss Flitworth could read, with some difficulty, the word: OOoooEEEeeOOOoooEEeeeOOOoooEEeee.

I HAVE RECEIVED THE BADLY-WRITTEN NOTE OF THE BANSHEE.

Miss Flitworth looked at him with her head on one side.

"But . . . correct me if I'm wrong, but . . ."

THE *NEW* DEATH.

Bill Door picked up the blade.

HE WILL BE TERRIBLE.

The blade twisted in his hands. Blue light flickered along its edge.

I WILL BE THE FIRST.

Miss Flitworth stared at the light as if fascinated.

"Exactly how terrible?"

HOW TERRIBLE CAN YOU IMAGINE?

"Oh."

EXACTLY AS TERRIBLE AS THAT.

The blade tilted this way and that.

"And for the child, too," said Miss Flitworth.

YES.

"I don't reckon I owe you any favours, Mr Door. I don't reckon anyone in the whole world owes you any favours."

YOU MAY BE RIGHT.

"Mind you, life's got one or two things to answer for too. Fair's fair."

I CANNOT SAY.

Miss Flitworth gave him another long, appraising look.

"There's a pretty good grindstone in the corner," she said.

I'VE USED IT.

"And there's an oilstone in the cupboard."

I'VE USED THAT, TOO.

She thought she could hear a sound as the blade moved. A sort of faint whine of tensed air.

"And it's still not sharp enough?"

Bill Door sighed. IT MAY NEVER BE SHARP ENOUGH.

"Come on, man. No sense in giving in," said Miss Flitworth. "Where there's life, eh?"

WHERE THERE'S LIFE EH WHAT?

"There's hope?"

IS THERE?

"Right enough."

Bill Door ran a bony finger along the edge.

HOPE?

"Got anything else left to try?"

Bill shook his head. He'd tried a number of emotions, but this was a new one.

COULD YOU FETCH ME A STEEL?

It was an hour later.

Miss Flitworth sorted through her rag-bag.

"What next?" she said.

WHAT HAVE WE HAD SO FAR?

"Let's see . . . hessian, calico, linen . . . how about satin? Here's a piece."

Bill Door took the rag and wiped it gently along the blade.

130

Miss Flitworth reached the bottom of the bag, and pulled out a swatch of white cloth.

YES?

"Silk," she said softly. "Finest white silk. The real stuff. Never worn."

She sat back and stared at it.

After a while he took it tactfully from her fingers.

THANK YOU.

"Well now," she said, waking up. "That's it, isn't it?"

When he turned the blade, it made a noise like *whommmm*. The fires of the forge were barely alive now, but the blade glowed with razor light.

"Sharpened on silk," said Miss Flitworth. "Who'd believe it?"

AND STILL BLUNT.

Bill Door looked around the dark forge, and then darted into a corner.

"What have you found?"

COBWEB.

There was a long thin whine, like the torturing of ants.

"Any good?"

STILL TOO BLUNT.

She watched Bill Door stride out of the forge, and scuttled after him. He went and stood in the middle of the yard, holding the scythe blade edge-on to the faint, dawn breeze.

It hummed.

"How sharp can a blade get, for goodness' sake?"

IT CAN GET SHARPER THAN THIS.

Down in his henhouse, Cyril the cockerel awoke and stared blearily at the treacherous letters chalked on the board. He took a deep breath.

"Floo-a-cockle-dod!"

Bill Door glanced at the rimward horizon and then, speculatively, at the little hill behind the house.

He jerked forward, legs clicking over the ground.

The new daylight sloshed onto the world. Discworld light is old, slow and heavy; it roared across the landscape like a cavalry charge. The occasional valley slowed it for a moment and, here and there, a mountain range banked it up until it poured over the top and down the far slope.

It moved across a sea, surged up the beach and accelerated over the plains, driven by the lash of the sun.

On the fabled hidden continent of Xxxx, somewhere near the rim, there is a lost colony of wizards who wear corks around their pointy hats and live on nothing but prawns. There, the light is still wild and fresh as it rolls in from space, and they surf on the boiling interface between night and day.

If one of them had been carried thousands of miles inland on the dawn, he might have seen, as the light thundered over the high plains, a stick figure toiling up a low hill in the path of the morning.

It reached the top a moment before the light arrived, took a breath, and then spun around in a crouch, grinning.

It held a long blade upright between extended arms.

Light struck . . . split . . . slid . . .

Not that the wizard would have paid much attention, because he'd be too busy worrying about the five-thousand-mile walk back home.

Miss Flitworth panted up as the new day streamed past. Bill Door was absolutely still, only the blade moving between his fingers as he angled it against the light.

Finally he seemed satisfied.

He turned around and swished it experimentally through the air.

Miss Flitworth stuck her hands on her hips. "Oh, come *on*," she said, "No one can / /any- / /on *day*/
/ sharpen / /thing / /*light*."

She paused.

He waved the blade again.

"Go / /ief."
/ od gr/

Down in the yard, Cyril stretched his bald neck for another go. Bill Door grinned, and swung the blade towards the sound.

"Sud / /oodle-f/
/ -a-n/ /od!"

Then he lowered the blade.

THAT'S SHARP.

His grin faded, or at least faded as much as it was able to.

Miss Flitworth turned, following the line of his gaze until it intersected a faint haze over the cornfields.

It looked like a pale grey robe, empty but still somehow maintaining

132

the shape of its wearer, as if a garment on a washing line was catching the breeze.

It wavered for a moment, and then vanished.

"I saw it," said Miss Flitworth.

THAT WASN'T IT. THAT WAS THEM.

"Them who?"

THEY'RE LIKE – Bill Door waved a hand vaguely – SERVANTS. WATCHERS. AUDITORS. INSPECTORS.

Miss Flitworth's eyes narrowed.

"Inspectors? You mean like the Revenoo?" she said.

I SUPPOSE SO –

Miss Flitworth's face lit up.

"Why didn't you *say*?"

I'M SORRY?

"My father always made me promise *never* to help the Revenoo. Even just thinking about the Revenoo, he said, made him want to go and have a lie down. He said that there was death and taxes, and taxes was worse, because at least death didn't happen to you every year. We had to go out of the room when he really got started about the Revenoo. *Nasty* creatures. Always poking around asking what you've got hidden under the woodpile and behind the secret panels in the cellar and other stuff which is no concern whatsoever of anyone."

She sniffed.

Bill Door was impressed. Miss Flitworth could actually give the word "revenue", which had two vowels and one diphthong, all the peremptoriness of the word "scum".

"You should have said that they were after you right from the start," said Miss Flitworth. "The Revenoo aren't popular in these parts, you know. In my father's day, any Revenooer came around here prying around by himself, we used to tie weights to their feet and heave 'em into the pond."

BUT THE POND IS ONLY A FEW INCHES DEEP, MISS FLITWORTH.

"Yeah, but it was fun watching 'em find out. You should have said. Everyone thought you were to do with taxes."

NO. NOT TAXES.

"Well, well. I didn't know there was a Revenoo Up There, too."

YES. IN A WAY.

She sidled closer.

"When will he come?"

TONIGHT. I CANNOT BE EXACT. TWO PEOPLE ARE LIVING ON THE SAME TIMER. IT MAKES THINGS UNCERTAIN.

"I didn't know people could give people some of their life."

IT HAPPENS ALL THE TIME.

"And you're sure about tonight?"

YES.

"And that blade will work, will it?"

I DON'T KNOW. IT'S A MILLION TO ONE CHANCE.

"Oh." She seemed to be considering something. "So you've got the rest of the day free, then?"

YES?

"Then you can start getting the harvest in."

WHAT?

"It'll keep you busy. Keep your mind off things. Besides, I'm paying you sixpence a week. And sixpence is sixpence."

Mrs Cake's house was also in Elm Street. Windle knocked on the door.

After a while a muffled voice called out, "Is there anybody there?"

"Knock once for yes," Schleppel volunteered.

Windle levered open the letter-box.

"Excuse me? Mrs Cake?"

The door opened.

Mrs Cake wasn't what Windle had expected. She was big, but not in the sense of being fat. She was just built to a scale slightly larger than normal; the sort of person who goes through life crouching slightly and looking apologetic in case they inadvertently loom. And she had magnificent hair. It crowned her head and flowed out behind her like a cloak. She also had slightly pointed ears and teeth which, while white and quite beautiful, caught the light in a disturbing way. Windle was amazed at the speed at which his heightened zombie senses reached a conclusion. He looked down.

Lupine was sitting bolt upright, too excited even to wag his tail.

"I don't think *you* could be Mrs Cake," said Windle.

"You want mother," said the tall girl. "Mother! There's a gentleman!"

A distant muttering became a closer muttering, and then Mrs Cake appeared around the side of her daughter like a small moon emerging from planetary shadow.

"What d'yew want?" said Mrs Cake.

Windle took a step backwards. Unlike her daughter, Mrs Cake was quite short, and almost perfectly circular. And still unlike her daughter, whose whole stance was dedicated to making herself look small, she loomed tremendously. This was largely because of her hat, which he later learned she wore at all times with the dedication of a wizard. It was huge and black and had things on it, like bird wings and wax cherries and hatpins; Carmen Miranda could have worn that hat to the funeral of a continent. Mrs Cake travelled underneath it as the basket travels under a balloon. People often found themselves talking to her hat.

"Mrs Cake?" said Windle, fascinated.

"Oim down 'ere," said a reproachful voice.

Windle lowered his gaze.

"That's 'oo I am," said Mrs Cake.

"Am I addressing Mrs Cake?" said Windle.

"Yes, oi know," said Mrs Cake.

"My name's Windle Poons."

"Oi knew that, too."

"I'm a wizard, you see – "

"All right, but see you wipes your feet."

"May I come in?"

Windle Poons paused. He replayed the last few lines of conversation in the clicking control room of his brain. And then he smiled.

"That's right," said Mrs Cake.

"Are you by any chance a natural clairvoyant?"

"About ten seconds usually, Mr Poons."

Windle hesitated.

"You gotta ask the question," said Mrs Cake quickly. "I gets a migraine if people goes and viciously not asks questions after I've already foreseen 'em and answered 'em."

"How far into the future can you see, Mrs Cake?"

She nodded.

"Roight, then," she said, apparently mollified, and led the way through the hall into a tiny sitting-room. "And the bogey can come in, only he's got to leave 'is door outside and go in the cellar. I don't hold with bogeys wanderin' around the house."

"Gosh, it's ages since I've been in a proper cellar," said Schleppel.

"It's got spiders in it," said Mrs Cake.

"Wow!"

"And you'd like a cup of tea," said Mrs Cake to Windle. Someone else might have said "I expect you'd like a cup of tea", or "Do you want a cup of tea?" But this was a statement.

"Yes, please," said Windle. "I'd love a cup of tea."

"You shouldn't," said Mrs Cake. "That stuff rots your teeth."

Windle worked this one out.

"Two sugars, please," he said.

"It's all right."

"This is a nice place you have here, Mrs Cake," said Windle, his mind racing. Mrs Cake's habit of answering questions while they were still forming in your mind taxed the most active brain.

"He's been dead for ten years," she said.

"Er," said Windle, but the question was already there in his larynx, "I trust Mr Cake is in good health?"

"It's okay. Oi speaks to him occasional," said Mrs Cake.

"I'm sorry to hear that," said Windle.

"All right, if it makes you feel any better."

"Um, Mrs Cake? I'm finding it a little confusing. Could you . . . switch off . . . your precognition . . . ?"

She nodded.

"Sorry. Oi gets into the habit of leavin' it on," she said, "what with there only bein' me an' Ludmilla and One-Man-Bucket. He's a ghost," she added. "Oi knew you was goin' to ask that."

"Yes, I had heard that mediums have native spirit guides," said Windle.

"'Im? 'E's not a guide, 'e's a sort of odd-job ghost," said Mrs Cake. "I don't hold with all that stuff with cards and trumpets and Oo-jar boards, mind you. An' I think ectoplasm's disgustin'. Oi won't have it in the 'ouse. Oi won't. You can't get it out of the carpets, you know. Not even with vinegar."

"My word," said Windle Poons.

"Or wailin'. I don't hold with it. Or messin' around with the supernatural. It's unnatural, the supernatural. I won't have it."

136

"Um," said Windle cautiously. "There are those who might think that being a medium is a bit . . . you know . . . supernatural?"

"What? *What?* Nothing supernatural about dead people. Load of nonsense. Everyone dies sooner or later."

"I do hope so, Mrs Cake."

"So what is it you'd be wanting, Mr Poons? I'm not precognitin', so you have to tell me."

"I want to know what's happening, Mrs Cake."

There was a muted thump from under their feet and the faint, happy sound of Schleppel.

"Oh, wow! Rats, too!"

"I went up and tried to tell you wizards," said Mrs Cake, primly. "An' no one listened. I knew they weren't going to, but I 'ad to try, otherwise I wouldn't 'ave known."

"Who did you speak to?"

"The big one with the red dress and a moustache like he's trying to swaller a cat."

"Ah. The Archchancellor," said Windle, positively.

"And there was a huge fat one. Walks like a duck."

"He does, doesn't he? That was the Dean," said Windle.

"They called me their good woman," said Mrs Cake. "They told me to be about my business. Don't see why I should go around helpin' wizards who call me a good woman when I was only trying to help."

"I'm afraid wizards don't often listen," said Windle. "I never listened for one hundred and thirty years."

"Why not?"

"In case I heard what rubbish I was saying, I expect. What's happening, Mrs Cake? You can tell me. I may be a wizard, but I'm a dead one."

"Well . . ."

"Schleppel told me it was all due to life force."

"It's buildin' up, see?"

"What does that *mean*?"

"There's more'f it than there should be. You get" – she waved her hands vaguely – "when things are like in a scales only not the same on both sides . . ."

"Imbalance?"

Mrs Cake, who looked as though she was reading a distant script, nodded.

"One of them things, yeah . . . see, sometimes it just happens a little bit, and you get ghosts, because the life is not in the body any more but it hasn't gone . . . and you get less of it in the winter, because it sort of drains away, and it comes back in the spring . . . and some things concentrate it . . ."

Modo the University gardener hummed a little tune as he wheeled the strange trolley into his private little area between the Library and the High Energy Magic* building, with a load of weeds bound for composthood.

There seemed to be a lot of excitement around at the moment. It was certainly interesting, working with all these wizards.

Teamwork, that's what it was. They looked after the cosmic balance, the universal harmonies and the dimensional equilibriums, and he saw to it that the aphids stayed off the roses.

There was a metallic tinkle. He peered over the top of the heap of weeds.

"Another one?"

A gleaming metal wire basket on little wheels sat on the path. Maybe the wizards had bought it for him? The first one was quite

---

* The only building on the campus less than a thousand years old. The senior wizards have never bothered much about what the younger, skinnier and more bespectacled wizards get up to in there, treating their endless requests for funding for thaumic particle accelerators and radiation shielding as one treats pleas for more pocket money, and listening with amusement to their breathless accounts of the search for the elementary particles of magic itself. This may one day turn out to be a major error on the part of the senior wizards, especially if they *do* let the younger wizards build whatever that blasted thing is they keep wanting to build in the squash court.

The senior wizards know that the proper purpose of magic is to form a social pyramid with the wizards on top of it, eating big dinners, but in fact the HEM building has helped provide one of the rarest foods in the universe – antipasta. Ordinary pasta is prepared some hours before being eaten. Antipasta is created some hours *after* the meal, whereupon it then exists *backwards in time*, and if properly prepared should arrive on the taste buds at exactly the same moment, thus creating a true taste explosion. It costs five thousand dollars a forkful, or a little more if you include the cost of cleaning the tomato sauce off the walls afterwards.

useful, although it was a little bit hard to steer; the little wheels seemed to want to go in different directions. There was probably a knack.

Well, this one would be handy for carrying seed trays in. He pushed the second trolley aside and heard, behind him, a sound which, if it had to be written down, and if he could write, he would probably have written down as: glop.

He turned around, saw the biggest of the compost heaps pulsating in the dark, and said, "Look what I brought you for your tea!"

And then he saw that it was moving.

"Some places, too . . ." said Mrs Cake.

"But why should it build up?" said Windle.

"It's like a thunderstorm, see? You know how you get that prickly feelin' before a storm? That's what's happening now."

"Yes, but why, Mrs Cake?"

"Well . . . One-Man-Bucket says nothing's dying."

"What?"

"Daft, isn't it? He says lots of lives are ending, but not going away. They're just staying here."

"What, like ghosts?"

"Not just ghosts. Just – it's like puddles. When you get a lot of puddles, it's like the sea. Anyway, you only get ghosts from things like people. You don't get ghosts of cabbages."

Windle Poons sat back in his chair. He had a vision of a vast pool of life, a lake being fed by a million short-lived tributaries as living things came to the end of their span. And life force was leaking out as the pressure built up. Leaking out wherever it could.

"Do you think I could have a word with One – " he began, and then stopped.

He got up and lurched over to Mrs Cake's mantelpiece.

"How long have you had this, Mrs Cake?" he demanded, picking up a familiar glassy object.

"That? Bought it yesterday. Pretty, ain't it?"

Windle shook the globe. It was almost identical to the ones under his floorboards. Snowflakes whirled up and settled on an exquisite model of Unseen University.

It reminded him strongly of something. Well, the building obviously reminded him of the University, but the shape of the whole thing, there was a hint of, it made him think of . . .

. . . breakfast?

"Why is it happening?" he said, half to himself. "These damn things are turning up everywhere."

The wizards ran down the corridor.

"How can you kill ghosts?"

"How should I know? The question doesn't usually arise!"

"You exorcise them, I think."

"What? Jumpin' up and down, runnin' on the spot, that kind of thing?"

The Dean had been ready for this. "It's spelled with an 'O', Archchancellor. I don't think one is expected to subject them to, er, physical exertion."

"Should think not, man. We don't want a lot of healthy ghosts buzzin' around."

There was a blood-curdling scream. It echoed around the dark pillars and arches, and was suddenly cut off.

The Archchancellor stopped abruptly. The wizards cannoned into him.

"Sounded like a blood-curdlin' scream," he said. "Follow me!"

He ran around the corner.

There was a metallic crash, and a lot of swearing.

Something small and striped red and yellow, with tiny dripping fangs and three pairs of wings, flew around the corner and shot over the Dean's head making a noise like a miniature buzzsaw.

"Anyone know what that was?" said the Bursar, faintly. The thing orbited the wizards and then disappeared into the darkness of the roof. "And I wish he wouldn't *swear* so."

"Come on," said the Dean. "We'd better see what's happened to him."

"Must we?" said the Senior Wrangler.

They peered around the corner. The Archchancellor was sitting up, rubbing his ankle.

"What idiot left this here?" he said.

140

"Left what?" said the Dean.

"This blasted wire baskety wheely thing," said the Archchancellor. Beside him, a tiny purple spider-like creature materialised out of the air and scuttled towards a crevice. The wizards didn't notice it.

"What wire baskety wheely thing?" said the wizards, in unison.

Ridcully looked around him.

"I could have sworn – " he began.

There was another scream.

Ridcully scrambled to his feet.

"Come on, you fellows!" he said, limping heroically onwards.

"Why does *everyone* run towards a blood-curdling scream?" mumbled the Senior Wrangler. "It's contrary to all sense."

They trotted out through the cloisters and into the quadrangle.

A rounded, dark shape was squatting in the middle of the ancient lawn. Steam was coming out of it in little, noisome wisps.

"What is it?"

"It can't be a compost heap in the middle of the lawn, can it?"

"Modo will be very upset."

The Dean peered closer. "Er . . . especially because, I do believe, that's his feet poking out from under it . . ."

The heap swivelled towards the wizards and made a *glop, glop* noise.

Then it moved.

"Right, then," said Ridcully, rubbing his hands together hopefully, "which of you fellows has got a spell about them at the moment?"

The wizards patted their pockets in an embarrassed fashion.

"Then I shall attract its attention while the Bursar and the Dean try to pull Modo out," said Ridcully.

"Oh, good," said the Dean faintly.

"How can you attract a compost heap's attention?" said the Senior Wrangler. "I shouldn't think it's even got one."

Ridcully removed his hat and stepped gingerly forward.

"Load of rubbish!" he roared.

The Senior Wrangler groaned and put his hand over his eyes.

Ridcully flapped his hat in front of the heap.

"Biodegradable garbage!"

141

"Poor green trash?" said the Lecturer in Recent Runes helpfully.

"That's the ticket," said the Archchancellor. "Try to infuriate the bugger." (Behind him, a slightly different variety of mad waspy creature popped out of the air and buzzed away.)

The heap lunged at the hat.

"Midden!" said Ridcully.

"Oh, I say," said the Lecturer in Recent Runes, shocked.

The Dean and the Bursar crept forward, grabbed a gardener's foot each, and pulled. Modo slid out of the heap.

"It's eaten through his clothes!" said the Dean.

"But is he all right?"

"He's still breathing," said the Bursar.

"And if he's lucky, he's lost his sense of smell," said the Dean.

The heap snapped at Ridcully's hat. There was a *glop*. The point of the hat had vanished.

"Hey, there was still almost half a bottle in there!" Ridcully roared. The Senior Wrangler grabbed his arm.

"Come on, Archchancellor!"

The heap swivelled and lunged towards the Bursar.

The wizards backed away.

"It can't be intelligent, can it?" said the Bursar.

"All it's doing is moving around slowly and eating things," said the Dean.

"Put a pointy hat on it and it'd be a faculty member," said the Archchancellor.

The heap came after them.

"I wouldn't call that moving slowly," said the Dean.

They looked expectantly at the Archchancellor.

"Run!"

Portly though most of the faculty were, they hit a fair turn of speed up the cloisters, fought one another through the door, slammed it behind them and leaned on it. Very soon afterwards, there was a damp, heavy thud on the far side.

"We're well out of *that*," said the Bursar.

The Dean looked down.

"I think it's coming through the door, Archchancellor," he said, in a tiny voice.

"Don't be daft, man, we're all leanin' on it."

"I didn't mean through, I mean . . . *through* . . ."

The Archchancellor sniffed.

"What's burnin'?"

"Your boots, Archchancellor," said the Dean.

Ridcully looked down. A greenish-yellow puddle was spreading under the door. The wood was charring, the flagstones were hissing, and the leather soles of his boots were definitely in trouble. He could feel himself getting lower.

He fumbled with the laces, and then took a standing jump onto a dry flagstone.

"Bursar!"

"Yes, Archchancellor?"

"Give me your boots!"

"What?"

"Dammit, man, I command you to give me your blasted boots!"

This time, a long creature with four pairs of wings, two at each end, and three eyes, popped into existence over Ridcully's head and dropped onto his hat.

"But – "

"I am your Archchancellor!"

"Yes, but – "

"I think the hinges are going," said the Lecturer in Recent Runes.

Ridcully looked around desperately.

"We'll regroup in the Great Hall," he said. "We'll . . . strategically withdraw to previously prepared positions."

"Who prepared them?" said the Dean.

"We'll prepare them when we get there," said the Archchancellor through gritted teeth. "Bursar! Your boots! Now!"

They reached the double doors of the Great Hall just as the door behind them half-collapsed, half-dissolved. The Great Hall's doors were much sturdier. Bolts and bars were dragged into place.

"Clear the tables and pile them up in front of the door," snapped Ridcully.

"But it eats through wood," said the Dean.

There was a moan from the small body of Modo, which had been propped against a chair. He opened his eyes.

"Quick!" said Ridcully. "How can we kill a compost heap?"

"Um. I don't think you can, Mr Ridcully, sir," said the gardener.

143

"How about fire? I could probably manage a small fireball," said the Dean.

"It wouldn't work. Too soggy," said Ridcully.

"It's right outside! It's eating away at the door! It's eating away at the *door*," sang the Lecturer in Recent Runes.

The wizards backed further away down the length of the hall.

"I hope it doesn't eat *too* much wood," said the dazed Modo, radiating genuine concern. "They're a devil, excuse my Klatchian, if you get too much carbon in them. It's far too heating."

"You know, this is *exactly* the right time for a lecture on the dynamics of compost making, Modo," said the Dean.

Dwarfs do not know the meaning of the word "irony".

"Well, all right. Ahem. The correct balance of materials, correctly layered according to – "

"There goes the door," said the Lecturer in Recent Runes, lumbering towards the rest of them.

The mound of furniture started to move forward.

The Archchancellor stared desperately around the hall, at a loss. Then his eyes were drawn to a familiar, heavy bottle on one of the sideboards.

"Carbon," he said. "That's like charcoal, isn't it?"

"How should I know? I'm not an alchemist," sniffed the Dean.

The compost heap emerged from the debris. Steam poured off it.

The Archchancellor looked longingly at the bottle of Wow-Wow Sauce. He uncorked it. He took a deep sniff.

"The cooks here just can't make it properly, you know," he said. "It'll be weeks before I can get any more from home."

He tossed the bottle towards the advancing heap.

It vanished into the seething mass.

"Stinging nettles are always useful," said Modo, behind him. "They add iron. And comfrey, well, you can never get enough comfrey. For the minerals, you know. Myself, I've always reckoned that a small quantity of wild yarrow – "

The wizards peered over the top of an overturned table.

The heap had stopped moving.

"Is it just me, or is it getting bigger?" said the Senior Wrangler.

"And looking happier," said the Dean.

"It smells *awful*," said the Bursar.

144

"Oh, well. And that was nearly a full bottle of sauce, too," said the Archchancellor sadly. "I'd hardly opened it."

"Nature's a wonderful thing, when you come to think about it," said the Senior Wrangler. "You don't all have to glare at me like that, you know. I was only passing a remark."

"There are times when – " Ridcully began, and then the compost heap exploded.

It wasn't a bang or a boom. It was the dampest, most corpulent eruption in the history of terminal flatulence. Dark red flame, fringed with black, roared up to the ceiling. Pieces of heap rocketed across the hall and slapped wetly into the walls.

The wizards peered out from their barricade, which was now thick with tea-leaves.

A cabbage stalk dropped softly onto the Dean's head.

He looked at a small, bubbling patch on the flagstones.

His face split slowly into a grin.

"Wow," he said.

The other wizards unfolded themselves. Adrenalin backwash worked its seductive spell. They grinned, too, and started playfully punching one another on the shoulder.

"Eat hot sauce!" roared the Archchancellor.

"Up against the hedge, fermented rubbish!"

"Can we kick ass, or can we kick ass?" burbled the Dean happily.

"You mean can't the second time, not can. And I'm not sure that a compost heap can be said to *have* an – " the Senior Wrangler began, but the tide of excitement was flowing against him.

"That's one heap that won't mess with *wizards* again," said the Dean, who was getting carried away. "We're keen and mean and – "

"There's three more of them out there, Modo says," said the Bursar.

They fell silent.

"We could go and pick up our staffs, couldn't we?" said the Dean.

The Archchancellor prodded a piece of exploded heap with the toe of his boot.

"Dead things coming alive," he murmured. "I don't like that. What's next? Walking statues?"

The wizards looked up at the statues of dead Archchancellors that lined the Great Hall and, indeed, most of the corridors of the

145

University. The University had been in existence for thousands of years and the average Archchancellor remained in office for about eleven months, so there were plenty of statues.

"You know, I really wish you hadn't said that," said the Lecturer in Recent Runes.

"It was just a thought," said Ridcully. "Come on, let's have a look at the rest of those heaps."

"Yeah!" said the Dean, now in the grip of a wild, unwizardly machismo. "We're mean! Yeah! Are we mean?"

The Archchancellor raised his eyebrows, and then turned to the rest of the wizards.

"*Are* we mean?" he said.

"Er. I'm feeling *reasonably* mean," said the Lecturer in Recent Runes.

"I'm definitely very mean, I think," said the Bursar. "It's having no boots that does it," he added.

"I'll be mean if everyone else is," said the Senior Wrangler.

The Archchancellor turned back to the Dean.

"Yes," he said, "it appears that we are all mean."

"Yo!" said the Dean.

"Yo what?" said Ridcully.

"It's not a yo what, it's just a yo," said the Senior Wrangler, behind him. "It's a general street greeting and affirmative with convivial military ingroup and masculine bonding-ritual overtones."

"What? What? Like 'jolly good'?" said Ridcully.

"I *suppose* so," said the Senior Wrangler, reluctantly.

Ridcully was pleased. Ankh-Morpork had never offered very good prospects for hunting. He'd never thought it was possible to have so much fun in his own university.

"Right," he said. "Let's get those heaps!"

"Yo!"

"Yo!"

"Yo!"

"Yo-yo."

Ridcully sighed. "Bursar?"

"Yes, Archchancellor?"

"Just *try* to understand, all right?"

*

Clouds piled up over the mountains. Bill Door strode up and down the first field, using one of the ordinary farm scythes; the sharpest one had been temporarily stored at the back of the barn, in case it was blunted by air convection. Some of Miss Flitworth's tenants followed behind him, binding the sheaves and stacking them. Miss Flitworth had never employed more than one man full time, Bill Door learned; she bought in other help as she needed it, to save pennies.

"Never seen a man cut corn with a scythe before," said one of them. "It's a sickle job."

They stopped for lunch, and ate it under the hedge.

Bill Door had never paid a great deal of attention to the names and faces of people, beyond that necessary for business. Corn stretched over the hillside; it was made up of individual stalks, and to the eye of one stalk another stalk might be quite an impressive stalk, with a dozen amusing and distinctive little mannerisms that set it apart from all other stalks. But to the reaper man, all stalks start off as . . . just stalks.

Now he was beginning to recognise the little differences.

There was William Spigot and Gabby Wheels and Duke Bottomley. All old men, as far as Bill Door could judge, with skins like leather. There were young men and women in the village, but at a certain age they seemed to flip straight over to being old, without passing through any intermediate stage. And then they stayed old for a long time. Miss Flitworth had said that before they could start a graveyard in these parts they'd had to hit someone over the head with the shovel.

William Spigot was the one that sang when he worked, breaking into that long nasal whine which meant that folk song was about to be perpetrated. Gabby Wheels never said anything; this, Spigot had said, was why he had been called Gabby. Bill Door had failed to understand the logic of this, although it seemed transparent to the others. And Duke Bottomley had been named by parents with upwardly-mobile if rather simplistic ideas about class structure; his brothers were Squire, Earl and King.

Now they sat in a row under the hedge, putting off the moment when they'd need to start work again. A glugging noise came from the end of the row.

"It's not been a bad old summer, then," said Spigot. "And good harvest weather for a change."

"Ah . . . many a slip 'twixt dress and drawers," said Duke. "Last night I

147

saw a spider spinnin' its web backwards. That's a sure sign there's going to be a dretful storm."

"Don't see how spiders know things like that."

Gabby Wheels passed a big earthenware jug to Bill Door. Something sloshed.

WHAT IS THIS?

"Apple juice," said Spigot. The others laughed.

AH, said Bill Door. STRONG DISTILLED SPIRITS, GIVEN HUMOROUSLY TO THE UNSUSPECTING NEWCOMER, THUS TO AFFORD SIMPLE AMUSEMENT WHEN HE BECOMES INADVERTENTLY INEBRIATED.

"Cor," said Spigot. Bill Door took a long swig.

"And I saw swallows flying low," said Duke. "And partridges are heading for the woods. And there's a lot of big snails about. And – "

"I don't reckon any of them buggers knows the first thing about meteorology," said Spigot. "I reckon you goes around telling 'em. Eh, lads? Big storm comin', Mr Spider, so get on and do somethin' folklorish."

Bill Door took another drink.

WHAT IS THE NAME OF THE BLACKSMITH IN THE VILLAGE?

Spigot nodded. "That's Ned Simnel, down by the green. O'course, he's real busy about now, what with the harvest and all."

I HAVE SOME WORK FOR HIM.

Bill Door got up and strode away towards the gate.

"Bill?"

He stopped. YES?

"You can leave the brandy behind, then."

The village forge was dark and stifling in the heat. But Bill Door had very good eyesight.

Something moved among a complicated heap of metal. It turned out to be the lower half of a man. His upper body was somewhere in the machinery, from which came the occasional grunt.

A hand shot out as Bill Door approached.

"Right. Give me a three-eighths Gripley."

Bill looked around. A variety of tools were strewn around the forge.

"Come on, come *on*," said a voice from somewhere in the machine.

Bill Door selected a piece of shaped metal at random, and placed it in the hand. It was drawn inside. There was metallic noise, and a grunt.

"I said a *Gripley*. This isn't a" – there was the scringeing noise of a piece of metal giving way – "my *thumb*, my *thumb*, you made me" – there was a clang – "aargh. That was my *head*. Now look what you've made me do. And the ratchet spring's snapped off the trunnion armature again, do you realise?"

No. I am sorry.

There was a pause.

"Is that you, young Egbert?"

No. It is me, old Bill Door.

There was a series of thumps and twanging noises as the top half of the human extricated itself from the machinery, and turned out to belong to a young man with black curly hair, a black face, black shirt, and black apron. He wiped a cloth across his face, leaving a pink smear, and blinked the sweat out of his eyes.

"Who're you?"

Good old Bill Door? Working for Miss Flitworth?

"Oh, yes. The man in the fire? Hero of the hour, I heard. Put it there."

He extended a black hand. Bill Door looked at it blankly.

I am sorry. I still do not know what a three-eighths Gripley is.

"I mean your hand, Mr Door."

Bill Door hesitated, and then put his hand in the young man's palm. The oil-rimmed eyes glazed for a moment, as the brain overruled the sense of touch, and then the smith smiled.

"The name's Simnel. What do you think, eh?"

It's a good name.

"No, I mean the machine. Pretty ingenious, eh?"

Bill Door regarded it with polite incomprehension. It looked, at first sight, like a portable windmill that had been attacked by an enormous insect, and at second sight like a touring torture chamber for an Inquisition that wanted to get out and about a bit and enjoy the fresh air. Mysterious jointed arms stuck out at various angles. There were belts, and long springs. The whole thing was mounted on spiked metal wheels.

"Of course, you're not seeing it at its best when it's standing still," said Simnel. "It needs a horse to pull it. At the moment, anyway. I've got one or two rather radical ideas in that direction," he added dreamily.

IT IS A DEVICE OF SOME SORT?

Simnel looked mildly affronted.

"I prefer the term machine," he said. "It will revolutionise farming methods, and drag them kicking and screaming into the Century of the Fruitbat. My folk have had this forge for three hundred years, but Ned Simnel doesn't intend to spend the rest of *his* life nailing bits of bent metal onto horses, I call tell you."

Bill looked at him blankly. Then he bent down and glanced under the machine. A dozen sickles were bolted to a big horizontal wheel. Ingenious linkages took power from the wheels, via a selection of pulleys, to a whirligig arrangement of metal arms.

He began to experience a horrible feeling about the thing in front of him, but he asked anyway.

"Well, the heart of it all is this cam shaft," said Simnel, gratified at the interest. "The power comes up via the pulley *here*, and the cams move the swaging arms – that's these things – and the combing gate, which is operated by the reciprocating mechanism, comes down just as the gripping shutter drops in this slot *here*, and of course at the same time the two brass balls go round and round and the fletching sheets carry off the straw while the grain drops with the aid of gravity down the riffling screw and into the hopper. Simple."

AND THE THREE-EIGHTHS GRIPLEY?

"Good job you reminded me." Simnel fished around among the debris on the floor, picked up a small knurled object, and screwed it onto a protruding piece of the mechanism. "Very important job. It stops the elliptical cam gradually sliding up the beam shaft and catching on the flange rebate, with disastrous results as you can no doubt imagine."

Simnel stood back and wiped his hands on a cloth, making them slightly more oily.

"I'm calling it the Combination Harvester," he said.

Bill Door felt very old. In fact he was very old. But he'd never felt it as much as this. Somewhere in the shadow of his soul he felt he knew, without the blacksmith explaining, what it was that the Combination Harvester was supposed to do.

OH.

"We're going to give it a trial run this afternoon up in old Peedbury's big field. It looks very promising, I must say. What you're looking at now, Mr Door, is the future."

Yes.

Bill Door ran his hand over the framework.

AND THE HARVEST ITSELF?

"Hmm? What about it?"

WHAT WILL IT THINK OF IT? WILL IT KNOW?

Simnel wrinkled his nose. "Know? Know? It won't know anything. Corn's corn."

AND SIXPENCE IS SIXPENCE.

"Exactly." Simnel hesitated. "What was it you were wanting?"

The tall figure ran a disconsolate finger over the oily mechanism. "Mr Door?"

PARDON? OH. YES. I HAD SOMETHING FOR YOU TO DO –

He strode out of the forge and returned almost immediately with something wrapped in silk. He unwrapped it carefully.

He'd made a new handle for the blade – not a straight one, such as they used in the mountains, but the heavy double-curved handle of the plains.

"You want it beaten out? A new grass nail? Metalwork replacing?"

Bill Door shook his head.

I WANT IT KILLED.

"Killed?"

YES. TOTALLY. EVERY BIT DESTROYED. SO THAT IT IS ABSOL-UTELY DEAD.

"Nice scythe," said Simnel. "Seems a shame. You've kept a good edge on it – "

DON'T TOUCH IT!

Simnel sucked his finger.

"Funny," he said, "I could have sworn I didn't touch it. My hand was inches away. Well, it's sharp, anyway."

He swished it through the air. "Yes. Pre| |rp, I'd s|
                                       |tty sha| |ay."

He paused, stuck his little finger in his ear and swivelled it around a bit.

"You sure you know what you want?" he said.

Bill Door solemnly repeated his request.

Simnel shrugged. "Well, I suppose I could melt it down and burn the handle," he said.

YES.

"Well, okay. It's your scythe. And you're basically right, of course. This is old technology now. Redundant."

I FEAR YOU MAY BE RIGHT.

Simnel jerked a grimy thumb towards the Combination Harvester. Bill Door knew it was made only of metal and canvas, and therefore couldn't possibly lurk. But it *was* lurking. Moreover, it was doing so with a chilling, metallic smugness.

"You could get Miss Flitworth to buy you one of these, Mr Door. It'd be just the job for a one-man farm like that. I can see you now, up there, up in the breeze, with the belts clacking away and the sparge arms oscillating – "

NO.

"Go on. She could afford it. They say she's got boxes full of treasure from the old days."

NO!

"Er – " Simnel hesitated. The last "No" contained a threat more certain than the creak of thin ice on a deep river. It said that going any further could be the most foolhardy thing Simnel would ever do.

"I'm sure you know your own mind best," he mumbled.

YES.

"Then it'll just be, oh, call it a farthing for the scythe," Simnel gabbled. "Sorry about that, but it'll use a lot of coals, you see, and those dwarfs keep winding up the price of – "

HERE. IT MUST BE DONE BY TONIGHT.

Simnel didn't argue. Arguing would mean that Bill Door remained in the forge, and he was getting quite anxious that this should not be so.

"Fine, fine."

YOU UNDERSTAND?

"Right. Right."

FAREWELL, said Bill Door solemnly, and left.

Simnel shut the doors after him, and leaned against them. Whew. Nice man, of course, everyone was talking about him, it was just that after a couple of minutes in his presence you got a pins-and-needles sensation that someone was walking over your grave and it hadn't even been dug yet.

He wandered across the oily floor, filled the tea kettle and wedged it on a corner of the forge. He picked up a spanner to do some final adjustments to the Combination Harvester, and spotted the scythe leaning against the wall.

He tiptoed towards it, and realised that tiptoeing was an amazingly stupid thing to do. It wasn't alive. It couldn't hear. It just *looked* sharp.

He raised the spanner, and felt guilty about it. By Mr Door had said – well, Mr Door had said something very odd, using the wrong sort of words to use in talking about a mere implement. But he could hardly object to this.

Simnel brought the spanner down hard.

There was no resistance. He would have sworn, again, that the spanner sheared in two, as though it was made of bread, several inches from the edge of the blade.

He wondered if something could be so sharp that it began to possess, not just a sharp edge, but the very essence of sharpness itself, a field of absolute sharpness that actually extended beyond the last atoms of metal.

"Bloo / dy hell / ire!"

And then he remembered that this was sloppy and superstitious thinking for a man who knew how to bevel a three-eighths Gripley. You knew where you were with a reciprocating linkage. It either worked or it didn't. It certainly didn't present you with mysteries.

He looked proudly at the Combination Harvester. Of course, you needed a horse to pull it. That spoiled things a bit. Horses belonged to Yesterday; Tomorrow belonged to the Combination Harvester and its descendants, which would make the world a cleaner and better place. It was just a matter of taking the horse out of the equation. He'd tried clockwork, and that wasn't powerful enough. Maybe if he tried winding a –

Behind him, the kettle boiled over and put the fire out.

Simnel fought his way through the steam. That was the bloody trouble, every time. Whenever someone was trying to do a bit of sensible thinking, there was always some pointless distraction.

Mrs Cake drew the curtains.

"Who exactly is One-Man-Bucket?" said Windle.

She lit a couple of candles and sat down.

"'E belonged to one of them heathen Howondaland tribes," she said shortly.

"Very strange name, One-Man-Bucket," said Windle.

"It's not 'is full name," said Mrs Cake darkly. "Now, we've got to 'old 'ands." She looked at him speculatively. "We need someone else."

"I could call Schleppel," said Windle.

"I ain't 'aving no bogey under my table trying to look up me drawers," said Mrs Cake. "Ludmilla!" she shouted. After a moment or two the bead curtain leading into the kitchen was swept aside and the young woman who had originally opened the door to Windle came in.

"Yes, mother?"

"Sit down, girl. We need another one for the seancing."

"Yes, mother."

The girl smiled at Windle.

"This is Ludmilla," said Mrs Cake shortly.

"Charmed, I'm sure," said Windle. Ludmilla gave him the bright, crystalline smile perfected by people who had long ago learned not to let their feelings show.

"We have already met," said Windle. It must be at least a day since full moon, he thought. All the signs are nearly gone. Nearly. Well, well, well . . .

"She's my shame," said Mrs Cake.

"Mother, you do go on," said Ludmilla, without rancour.

"Join hands," said Mrs Cake.

They sat in the semi-darkness. Then Windle felt Mrs Cake's hand being pulled away.

"Oi forgot about the glass," she said.

"I thought, Mrs Cake, that you didn't hold with ouija boards and that sort of – " Windle began. There was a glugging noise from the sideboard. Mrs Cake put a full glass on the tablecloth and sat down again.

"Oi don't," she said.

Silence descended again. Windle cleared his throat nervously.

Eventually Mrs Cake said, "All right, One-Man-Bucket, oi knows you're there."

The glass moved. The amber liquid inside sloshed gently.

A bodiless voice quavered, *greetings, pale face, from the happy hunting ground* –

"You stop that," said Mrs Cake. "Everyone knows you got run

154

over by a cart in Treacle Street because you was drunk, One-Man-Bucket."

s'not my fault. not my fault. is it my fault my great-grandad moved here? by rights I should have been mauled to death by a mountain lion or a giant mammoth or something. I bin denied my deathright.

"Mr Poons here wants to ask you a question, One-Man-Bucket," said Mrs Cake.

she is happy here and waiting for you to join her, said One-Man-Bucket.

"Who is?" said Windle.

This seemed to fox One-Man-Bucket. It was a line that generally satisfied without further explanation.

who would you like? he asked cautiously. *can I have that drink now?*

"Not yet, One-Man-Bucket," said Mrs Cake.

well, I need it. it's bloody crowded in here.

"What?" said Windle quickly. "With ghosts, you mean?"

there's hundreds of 'em, said the voice of One-Man-Bucket.

Windle was disappointed.

"Only hundreds?" he said. "That doesn't sound a lot."

"Not many people become ghosts," said Mrs Cake. "To be a ghost, you got to have, like, serious unfinished business, or a terrible revenge to take, or a cosmic purpose in which you are just a pawn."

or a cruel thirst, said One-Man-Bucket.

"Will you hark at him," said Mrs Cake.

I wanted to stay in the spirit world. or even wine and beer. hngh. hngh. hngh.

"So what happens to the life force if things stop living?" said Windle. "Is that what's causing all this trouble?"

"You tell the man," said Mrs Cake, when One-Man-Bucket seemed reluctant to answer.

what trouble you talking about?

"Things unscrewing. Clothes running around by themselves. Everyone feeling more alive. That sort of thing."

that? that's nothing. see, the life force leaks back where it can. you don't need to worry about that.

Windle put his hand over the glass.

"But there's something I should be worrying about, isn't there," he said flatly. "It's to do with the little glass souvenirs."

don't like to say.

"Do tell him."

It was Ludmilla's voice – deep but, somehow, attractive. Lupine was watching her intently. Windle smiled. That was one of the advantages about being dead. You spotted things the living ignored.

One-Man-Bucket sounded shrill and petulant.

what's he going to do if I tell him, then? I could get into heap big trouble for that sort of thing.

"Well, can you tell me if I guess right?" said Windle.

ye-ess. maybe.

"You don't have to say anythin'," said Mrs Cake. "Just knock twice for yes and once for no, like in the old days."

oh, all right.

"Go on, Mr Poons," said Ludmilla. She had the kind of voice Windle wanted to stroke.

He cleared his throat.

"I think," he began, "that is, I think they're some sort of eggs. I thought . . . why breakfast? and then I thought . . . eggs . . ."

Knock.

"Oh. Well, perhaps it was a rather silly idea . . ."

sorry, was it once for yes or twice for yes?

"Twoice!" snapped the medium.

KNOCK. KNOCK.

"Ah," breathed Windle. "And they hatch into something with wheels on?"

twice for yes, was it?

"Roight!"

KNOCK. KNOCK.

"I *thought* so. I *thought* so! I found one under my floor that tried to hatch where there wasn't enough room!" crowed Windle. Then he frowned.

"But hatch into what?"

*

156

Mustrum Ridcully trotted into his study and took his wizard's staff from its rack over the fireplace. He licked his finger and gingerly touched the top of the staff. There was a small octarine spark and a smell of greasy tin.

He headed back for the door.

Then he turned around slowly, because his brain had just had time to analyse the study's cluttered contents and spot the oddity.

"What the hell's that doin' there?" he said.

He prodded it with the tip of the staff. It gave a jingling noise and rolled a little way.

It looked vaguely, but not very much, like the sort of thing the maids trundled around loaded with mops and fresh linen and whatever it was maids pushed around. Ridcully made a mental note to take it up with the housekeeper. Then he forgot about it.

"Damn wire wheely things are gettin' everywhere," he muttered.

Upon the word "damn", something like a large bluebottle with cat-sized dentures flopped out of the air, fluttered madly as it took stock of its surroundings, and then flew after the unheeding Archchancellor.

The words of wizards have power. And swearwords have power. And with life force practically crystallising out of the air, it had to find outlets wherever it could.

cities. said One-Man-Bucket. *I think they're city eggs.*

The senior wizards gathered again in the Great Hall. Even the Senior Wrangler was feeling a certain excitement. It was considered bad form to use magic against fellow wizards, and using it against civilians was unsporting. It did you good to have a really righteous zap occasionally.

The Archchancellor looked them over.

"Dean, why have you got stripes all over your face?" he enquired.

"Camouflage, Archchancellor."

"Camouflage, eh?"

"Yo, Archchancellor."

"Oh, well. So long as you feel happy in yourself, that's what matters."

They crept out towards the patch of ground that had been Modo's little territory. At least, most of them crept. The Dean advanced in a series of spinning leaps, occasionally flattening himself against the wall, and saying "Hut! Hut! Hut!" under his breath.

He was absolutely crestfallen when the other heaps turned out to be still where Modo had built them. The gardener, who had tagged along behind and had twice nearly been flattened by the Dean, fussed around them for a while.

"They're just lying low," said the Dean. "I say we blow up the godsdamn – "

"They're not even warm yet," said Modo. "That one must have been the oldest."

"You mean we haven't got anything to fight?" said the Archchancellor.

The ground shook underfoot. And then there was a faint jangling noise, from the direction of the cloisters.

Ridcully frowned.

"Someone's pushing those damn wire baskety things around again," he said. "There was one in my study tonight."

"Huh," said the Senior Wrangler. "There was one in my *bedroom*. I opened the wardrobe and there it was."

"In your wardrobe? What'd you put it in there for?" said Ridcully.

"*I* didn't. I told you. It was probably the students. It's their kind of humour. One of them put a hairbrush in my bed once."

"I fell over one earlier," said the Archchancellor, "and then when I looked round for it, someone had taken it away."

The jingling noise got closer.

"Right, Mr So-called Clever Dick Young-fella-me-lad," said Ridcully, tapping his staff once or twice on his palm in a meaningful way.

The wizards backed up against the wall.

The phantom trolley pusher was almost on them.

Ridcully snarled, and leapt out of hiding.

"Aha, my fine young – *bloody hellfire!*"

"Don't be pullin' moi leg," said Mrs Cake. "Cities ain't alive. I know people says they are, but they don't mean *really*."

158

Windle Poons turned one of the snowballs around in his hand.

"It must be laying thousands of them," he said. "But they wouldn't all survive, of course. Otherwise we'd be up to here in cities, yes?"

"You telling us that these little balls hatch out into huge *places*?" said Ludmilla.

not straight away. there's the mobile stage first.

"Something with wheels on," said Windle.

that's right. I can see you know already.

"I think I knew," said Windle Poons, "but I didn't understand. And what happens after the mobile stage?"

don't know.

Windle stood up.

"Then it's time to find out," he said.

He glanced at Ludmilla and Lupine. Ah. Yes. And why not? If you can help somebody as you pass this way, Windle thought, then your living, or whatever, shall not be in vain.

He let himself fall into a stoop and let a little crackle enter his voice.

"But I'm rather unsteady on my legs these days," he quavered. "It would really be a great favour if someone could help me along. Could you see me as far as the University, young lady?"

"Ludmilla doesn't go out much these days because her health – " Mrs Cake began briskly.

"Is absolutely fine," said Ludmilla. "Mother, you know it's been a whole day since full moo– "

"Ludmilla!"

"Well, it has."

"It's not safe for a young woman to walk the streets these days," said Mrs Cake.

"But Mr Poons' wonderful dog would frighten away the most *dangerous* criminal," said Ludmilla.

On cue, Lupine barked helpfully and begged. Mrs Cake regarded him critically.

"He's certainly a very obedient animal," she said, reluctantly.

"That's settled, then," said Ludmilla. "I'll fetch my shawl."

Lupine rolled over. Windle nudged him with a foot.

"Be good," he said.

There was a meaningful cough from One-Man-Bucket.

"All right, all right," said Mrs Cake. She took a bundle of matches from the dresser, lit one absent-mindedly with her fingernail, and dropped it into the whisky glass. It burned with a blue flame, and somewhere in the spirit world the spectre of a stiff double lasted just long enough.

As Windle Poons left the house, he thought he could hear a ghostly voice raised in song.

The trolley stopped. It swivelled from side to side, as if observing the wizards. Then it did a fast three-point turn and trundled off at high speed.

"Get it!" bellowed the Archchancellor.

He aimed his staff and got off a fireball which turned a small area of cobblestones into something yellow and bubbly. The speeding trolley rocked wildly but kept going, with one wheel rattling and squeaking.

"It's from the Dungeon Dimensions!" said the Dean. "Cream the basket!"

The Archchancellor laid a steadying hand on his shoulder. "Don't be daft. Dungeon Things have a lot more tentacles and things. They don't look *made*."

They turned at the sound of another trolley. It rattled unconcernedly down a side passage, stopped when it saw or otherwise perceived the wizards, and did a creditable impression of a trolley that had just been left there by someone.

The Bursar crept up to it.

"It's no use you looking like that," he said. "We know you can move."

"We all *seed* you," said the Dean.

The trolley maintained a low profile.

"It can't be thinking," said the Lecturer in Recent Runes. "There's no room for a brain."

"Who says it's thinking?" said the Archchancellor. "All it does is move. Who needs brains for that? *Prawns* move."

He ran his fingers over the metalwork.

"Actually, prawns are quite intell– " the Senior Wrangler began.

160

"Shut up," said Ridcully. "Hmm. *Is* this made, though?"

"It's wire," said the Senior Wrangler. "Wire's something that you have to make. And there's wheels. Hardly anything natural's got wheels."

"It's just that up close, it looks – "

" – all one thing," said the Lecturer in Recent Runes, who had knelt down painfully to inspect it the better. "Like one unit. Made all in one lump. Like a machine that's been grown. But that's ridiculous."

"Maybe. Isn't there a sort of cuckoo in the Ramtops that builds clocks to nest in?" said the Bursar.

"Yes, but that's just courtship ritual," said the Lecturer in Recent Runes airily. "Besides, they keep lousy time."

The trolley leapt for a gap in the wizards and would have made it except that the gap was occupied by the Bursar, who gave a scream and pitched forward into the basket. The trolley didn't stop but rattled onwards, towards the gates.

The Dean raised his staff. The Archchancellor grabbed it.

"You might hit the Bursar," he said.

"Just one small fireball?"

"It's tempting, but no. Come on. After it."

"Yo!"

"If you like."

The wizards lumbered in pursuit. Behind them, as yet unnoticed, a whole flock of the Archchancellor's swearwords fluttered and buzzed. And Windle Poons was leading a small deputation to the Library.

The Librarian of Unseen University knuckled his way hurriedly across the floor as the door shook to a thunderous knocking.

"I know you're in there," came the voice of Windle Poons. "You must let us in. It's *vitally* important."

"Oook."

"You won't open the doors?"

"Oook!"

"Then you leave me no choice . . ."

Ancient blocks of masonry moved aside slowly. Mortar crumbled.

Then part of the wall fell in, leaving Windle Poons standing in a Windle Poons-shaped hole. He coughed on the dust.

"I hate having to do that," he said. "I can't help feeling it's pandering to popular prejudice."

The Librarian landed on his shoulders. To the orangutan's surprise, this made very little difference. A 300-pound orangutan usually had a noticeable effect on a person's rate of progress, but Windle wore him like a collar.

"I think we need Ancient History," he said. "I wonder, could you stop trying to twist my head off?"

The Librarian looked around wildly. It was a technique that normally never failed.

Then his nostrils flared.

The Librarian hadn't always been an ape. A magical library is a dangerous place to work, and he'd been turned into an orangutan as a result of a magical explosion. He'd been a quite inoffensive human, although by now so many people had come to terms with his new shape that few people remembered it. But with the change had come the key to a whole bundle of senses and racial memories. And one of the deepest, most fundamental, most borne-in-the-bone of all of them was to do with shapes. It went back to the dawn of sapience. Shapes with muzzles, teeth and four legs were, in the evolving simian mind, definitely filed under Bad News.

A very large wolf had padded through the hole in the wall, followed by an attractive young woman. The Librarian's signal input was temporarily fused.

"Also," said Windle, "it is just possible that I could knot your arms behind you."

"Eeek!"

"He's not an ordinary wolf. You'd better believe it."

"Oook?"

Windle lowered his voice. "And she might not technically be a woman," he added.

The Librarian looked at Ludmilla. His nostrils flared again. His brow wrinkled.

"Oook?"

"All right, I may have put that rather clumsily. Do let go, there's a good fellow."

162

The Librarian released his grip very cautiously and sank to the floor, keeping Windle between himself and Lupine.

Windle brushed mortar fragments off the remains of his robe.

"We need to find out," he said, "about the lives of cities. Specifically, I need to know – "

There was a faint jangling noise.

A wire basket rolled nonchalantly around the massive stack of the nearest bookcase. It was full of books. It stopped as soon as it realised that it had been seen and contrived to look as though it had never moved at all.

"The mobile stage," breathed Windle Poons.

The wire basket tried to inch backwards without appearing to move. Lupine growled.

"Is that what One-Man-Bucket was talking about?" said Ludmilla. The trolley vanished. The Librarian grunted, and went after it.

"Oh, yes. Something that would make itself useful," said Windle, suddenly almost manically cheerful. "That's how it'd work. First, something that you'd want to keep, and put away somewhere. Thousands wouldn't get the right conditions, but that wouldn't matter, because there would *be* thousands. And then the next stage would be something that would be handy, and get everywhere, and no one would ever think it had got there by itself. But it's all happening at the wrong time!"

"But how can a city be alive? It's only made up of dead parts!" said Ludmilla.

"So're people. Take it from me. I *know*. But you are right, I think. This shouldn't be happening. It's all this extra life force. It's . . . it's tipping the balance. It's turning something that isn't really real into a reality. And it's happening too early, and it's happening too fast . . ."

There was a squeal from the Librarian. The trolley erupted from another row of shelves, wheels a blur, heading for the hole in the wall, with the orangutan hanging on grimly with one hand and flapping behind it like a very fat flag.

The wolf leapt.

"Lupine!" shouted Windle.

But from the days when the first caveman rolled a slice of log down a hill, canines have also had a deep racial urge to chase anything on wheels. Lupine was already snapping at the trolley.

His jaws met on a wheel. There was a howl, a scream from the Librarian, and ape, wolf and wire basket ended up in a heap against the wall.

"Oh, the poor thing! Look at him!"

Ludmilla rushed across the floor and knelt down by the stricken wolf.

"It went right over his paws, look!"

"And he's probably lost a couple of teeth," said Windle. He helped the Librarian up. There was a red glow in the ape's eyes. It had tried to steal his books. This was probably the best proof any wizard could require that the trolleys were brainless.

He reached down and wrenched the wheels off the trolley.

"Olé," said Windle.

"Oook?"

"No, Not 'with milk'," said Windle.

Lupine was having his head cradled in Ludmilla's lap. He had lost a tooth, and his fur was a mess. He opened one eye and fixed Windle with a conspiratorial yellow stare while his ears were stroked. There's a lucky dog, thought Windle, who's going to push his luck and hold up a paw and whine.

"Right," said Windle. "Now, Librarian . . . . you were about to help us, I think."

"Poor brave dog," said Ludmilla.

Lupine raised a paw pathetically, and whined.

Burdened by the screaming form of the Bursar, the other wire basket couldn't get up to the speed of its departed comrade. One wheel also trailed uselessly. It canted recklessly from side to side and nearly fell over as it shot through the gates, moving sideways.

"I can see it clear! I can see it clear!" screamed the Dean.

"Don't! You might hit the Bursar!" bellowed Ridcully. "You might damage University property!"

But the Dean couldn't hear for the roar of unaccustomed testosterone. A searing green fireball struck the skewing trolley. The air was filled with flying wheels.

164

Ridcully took a deep breath.

"You stupid – !" he screamed.

The word he uttered was unfamiliar to those wizards who had not had his robust country upbringing and knew nothing of the finer points of animal husbandry. But it plopped into existence a few inches from his face; it was fat, round, black and glossy, with horrible eyebrows. It blew him an insectile raspberry and flew up to join the little swarm of curses.

"What the hell was that?"

A smaller thing flashed into existence by his ear.

Ridcully snatched at his hat.

"Damn!" – the swarm increased by one – "Something just bit me!"

A squadron of newly-hatched Blasteds made a valiant bid for freedom. He swatted at them ineffectually.

"Get away, you b– " he began.

"Don't say it!" said the Senior Wrangler. "Shut up!"

People never told the Archchancellor to shut up. Shutting up was something that happened to other people. He shut up out of shock.

"I mean, every time you swear it comes alive," said the Senior Wrangler hurriedly. "Ghastly little winged things pop out of the air."

"Bloody hellfire!" said the Archchancellor.

Pop. Pop.

The Bursar crawled dazed out of the tangled wreckage of the wire trolley. He found his pointy hat, dusted it off, tried it on, frowned, and took a wheel out of it. His colleagues didn't seem to be paying him much attention.

He heard the Archchancellor say, "But I've always done it! Nothing wrong with a good swear, it keeps the blood flowing. Watch out, Dean, one of the bug– "

"Can't you say something else?" shouted the Senior Wrangler, above the buzz and whine of the swarm.

"Like what?"

"Like . . . oh . . . like . . . darn."

"*Darn?*"

"Yes, or maybe poot."

"*Poot*? You want me to say *poot*?"

165

The Bursar crept up to the group. Arguing over petty details at times of dimensional emergency was a familiar wizardly trait.

"Mrs Whitlow the housekeeper always says 'Sugar!' when she drops something," he volunteered.

The Archchancellor turned on him.

"She may *say* sugar," he growled, "but what she *means*, is shi– "

The wizards ducked. Ridcully managed to stop himself.

"Oh, darn," he said miserably. The swearwords settled amiably on his hat.

"They like you," said the Dean.

"You're their daddy," said the Lecturer in Recent Runes.

Ridcully scowled. "You b– boys can stop being silly at your Archchancellor's expense and da– jolly well find out what's going on," he said.

The wizards looked expectantly at the air. Nothing appeared.

"You're doing fine," said the Lecturer in Recent Runes. "Keep it up."

"Darn darn darn," said the Archchancellor. "Sugar sugar sugar. Pooty pootity poot." He shook his head. "It's no good, it doesn't relieve my feelings one bit."

"It's cleared the air, at any rate," said the Bursar.

They noticed his presence for the first time.

They looked at the remains of the trolley.

"Things zooming around," said Ridcully. "Things coming alive."

They looked up at a suddenly familiar squeaking noise. Two more wheeled baskets rattled across the square outside the gates. One was full of fruit. The other was half full of fruit and half full of small screaming child.

The wizards watched open-mouthed. A stream of people were galloping after the trolleys. Slightly in the lead, elbows scything through the air, a desperate and determined woman pounded past the University gates.

The Archchancellor grabbed a heavy-set man who was lumbering along gamely at the back of the crowd.

"What happened?"

"I was just loading some peaches into that basket thing when it upped and ran away on me!"

"What about the child?"

"Search me. This woman had one of the baskets and she bought some peaches off of me an' then – "

They all turned. A basket rattled out of the mouth of an alleyway, saw them, turned smartly and shot off across the square.

"But why?" said Ridcully.

"They're so handy to put things in, right?" said the man. "I got to get them peaches. You know how they bruise."

"And they're all going in the same direction," said the Lecturer in Recent Runes. "Anyone else notice that?"

"After them!" screamed the Dean. The other wizards, too bewildered to argue, lumbered after him.

"No – " Ridcully began, and realised that it was hopeless. And he was losing the initiative. He carefully formulated the most genteel battle cry in the history of bowdlerism.

"Darn them to Heck!" he yelled, and ran after the Dean.

Bill Door worked through the long heavy afternoon, at the head of a trail of binders and stackers.

Until there was a shout, and the men ran towards the hedge.

Iago Peedbury's big field was right on the other side. His farmhands were wheeling the Combination Harvester through the gate.

Bill joined the others leaning over the hedge. The distant figure of Simnel could be seen, giving instructions. A frightened horse was backed into the shafts. The blacksmith climbed into the little metal seat in the middle of the machinery and took up the reins.

The horse walked forward. The sparge arms unfolded. The canvas sheets started to revolve, and probably the riffling screw was turning, but that didn't matter because something somewhere went "clonk" and everything stopped.

From the crowd at the hedge there were shouts of "Get out and milk it!", "We had one but the end fell off!", "Tuppence more and up goes the donkey!" and other time-honoured witticisms.

Simnel got down, held a whispered conversation with Peedbury and his men, and then disappeared into the machinery for a moment.

"It'll never fly!"

"Veal will be cheap tomorrow!"

This time the Combination Harvester got several feet before one of the rotating sheets split and folded up.

By now some of the older men at the hedge were doubled up with laughter.

"Any old iron, sixpence a load!"

"Fetch the other one, this one's broke!"

Simnel got down again. Distant catcalls drifted towards him as he untied the sheet and replaced it with a new one; he ignored them.

Without moving his gaze from the scene in the opposite field, Bill Door pulled a sharpening stone out of his pocket and began to hone his scythe, slowly and deliberately.

Apart from the distant clink of the blacksmith's tools, the *schip-schip* of stone on metal was the only sound in the heavy air.

Simnel climbed back into the Harvester and nodded to the man leading the horse.

"Here we go again!"

"Any more for the Skylark?"

"Put a sock in it . . ."

The cries trailed off.

Half a dozen pairs of eyes followed the Combination Harvester up the field, stared while it was turned around on the headland, watched it come back again.

It clicked past, reciprocating and oscillating.

At the bottom of the field it turned around neatly.

It whirred by again.

After a while one of the watchers said, gloomily, "It'll never catch on, you mark my words."

"Right enough. Who's going to want a gadget like that?" said another.

"Sure and it's only like a big clock. Can't do anything more than go up and down a field –"

" – very fast – "

" – cutting the corn like that and stripping the grain off – "

"It's done three rows already."

"Bugger me!"

"You can't hardly see the bits move! What do you think of that, Bill? Bill?"

They looked around.

He was halfway up his second row, but accelerating.

*

168

Miss Flitworth opened the door a fraction.

"Yes?" she said, suspiciously.

"It's Bill Door, Miss Flitworth. We've brought him home."

She opened the door wider.

"What happened to him?"

The two men shuffled in awkwardly, trying to support a figure a foot taller than they were. It raised its head and squinted muzzily at Miss Flitworth.

"Don't know what come over him," said Duke Bottomley.

"He's a devil for working," said William Spigot. "You're getting your money's worth out of him all right, Miss Flitworth."

"It'll be the first time, then, in these parts," she said sourly.

"Up and down the field like a madman, trying to better that contraption of Ned Simnel's. Took four of us to do the binding. He nearly beat it, too."

"Put him down on the sofa."

"We *tole* him he was doing too much in all that sun – " Duke craned his neck to see around the kitchen, just in case jewels and treasure were hanging out of the dresser drawers.

Miss Flitworth eclipsed his view.

"I'm sure you did. Thank you. Now I expect you'll be wanting to be off home."

"If there's anything we can do – "

"I know where you live. And you ain't paid no rent there for five years, too. Goodbye, Mr Spigot."

She ushered them to the door and shut it in their faces. Then she turned around.

"What the hell have you been doing, Mr So-Called Bill Door?"

I AM TIRED AND IT WON'T STOP.

Bill Door clutched at his skull.

ALSO SPIGOT GAVE ME A HUMOROUS APPLE JUICE FERMENTED DRINK BECAUSE OF THE HEAT AND NOW I FEEL ILL.

"I ain't surprised. He makes it up in the woods. Apples isn't the half of it."

I HAVE NEVER FELT ILL BEFORE. OR TIRED.

"It's all part of being alive."

HOW DO HUMANS STAND IT?

"Well, fermented apple juice can help."

169

Bill Door sat staring gloomily at the floor.

BUT WE FINISHED THE FIELD, he said, with a hint of triumph. ALL STACKED IN STOOKS, OR POSSIBLY THE OTHER WAY AROUND.

He clutched at his skull again.

AARGH.

Miss Flitworth disappeared into the scullery. There was the creaking of a pump. She returned with a damp flannel and a glass of water.

THERE'S A NEWT IN IT!

"Shows it's fresh," said Miss Flitworth,* fishing the amphibian out and releasing it on the flagstones, where it scuttled away into a crack.

Bill Door tried to stand up.

NOW I ALMOST KNOW WHY SOME PEOPLE WISH TO DIE, he said. I HAD HEARD OF PAIN AND MISERY BUT I HAD NOT HITHERTO FULLY UNDERSTOOD WHAT THEY MEANT.

Miss Flitworth peered through the dusty window. The clouds that had been piling up all afternoon towered over the hills, grey with a menacing hint of yellow. The heat pressed down like a vice.

"There's a big storm coming."

WILL IT SPOIL MY HARVEST?

"No. It'll dry out after."

HOW IS THE CHILD?

Bill Door unfolded his palm. Miss Flitworth raised her eyebrows. The golden glass was there, the top bulb almost empty. But it shimmered in and out of vision.

"How come you've got it? It's upstairs! She was holding it like," – she floundered – "like someone holds something very tightly."

SHE STILL IS. BUT IT IS ALSO HERE. OR ANYWHERE. IT IS ONLY A METAPHOR, AFTER ALL.

"What she's holding looks real enough."

JUST BECAUSE SOMETHING IS A METAPHOR DOESN'T MEAN IT CAN'T BE REAL.

Miss Flitworth was aware of a faint echo in the voice, as though the words were being spoken by two people almost, but not quite, in sync.

"How long have you got?"

A MATTER OF HOURS.

---

* People have believed for hundreds of years that newts in a well mean that the water's fresh and drinkable, and *in all that time* never asked themselves whether the newts got out to go to the lavatory.

"And the scythe?"

I GAVE THE BLACKSMITH STRICT INSTRUCTIONS.

She frowned. "I'm not saying young Simnel's a bad lad, but are you sure he'll do it? It's asking a lot of a man like him to destroy something like that."

I HAD NO CHOICE. THE LITTLE FURNACE HERE ISN'T GOOD ENOUGH.

"It's a wicked sharp scythe."

I FEAR IT MAY NOT BE SHARP ENOUGH.

"And no one ever tried this on *you*?"

THERE IS A SAYING: YOU CAN'T TAKE IT WITH YOU?

"Yes."

HOW MANY PEOPLE HAVE SERIOUSLY BELIEVED IT?

"I remember reading once," said Miss Flitworth, "about these heathen kings in the desert somewhere who build huge pyramids and put all sorts of stuff in them. Even boats. Even gels in transparent trousers and a couple of saucepan lids. You can't tell me that's right."

I'VE NEVER BEEN VERY SURE ABOUT WHAT IS RIGHT, said Bill Door. I AM NOT SURE THERE IS SUCH A THING AS RIGHT. OR WRONG. JUST PLACES TO STAND.

"No, right's right and wrong's wrong," said Miss Flitworth. "I was brought up to tell the difference."

BY A CONTRABANDISTOR.

"A what?"

A MOVER OF CONTRABAND.

"There's nothing wrong with smuggling!"

I MERELY POINT OUT THAT SOME PEOPLE THINK OTHERWISE.

"They don't count!"

BUT –

Lightning struck, somewhere on the hill. The thunderclap rocked the house; a few bricks from the chimney rattled into the grate. Then the windows shook to a fierce pounding.

Bill Door strode across the room and threw open the door.

Hailstones the size of hens' eggs bounced off the doorstep and into the kitchen.

OH. DRAMA.

"Oh, hell!"

Miss Flitworth ducked under his arm.

171

"And where's the wind come from?"

THE SKY? said Bill Door, surprised at the sudden excitement.

"Come on!" She whirled back into the kitchen and scrabbled on the dresser for a candle lantern and some matches.

BUT YOU SAID IT WOULD DRY.

"In a normal storm, yes. In this lot? It's going to be ruined! We'll find it spread all over the hill in the morning!"

She fumbled the candle alight and ran back again.

Bill Door looked out into the storm. Straws whirred past, tumbling on the gale.

RUINED? MY HARVEST? He straightened up. BUGGER *THAT*.

The hail rumbled on the roof of the smithy.

Ned Simnel pumped the furnace bellows until the heart of the coals was white with the merest hint of yellow.

It had been a good day. The Combination Harvester had worked better than he'd dared to hope; old Peedbury had insisted on keeping it to do another field tomorrow, so it had been left out with a tarpaulin over it, securely tied down. Tomorrow he could teach one of the men to use it, and start work on a new improved model. Success was assured. The future definitely lay ahead.

Then there was the matter of the scythe. He went to the wall where it had been hung. A bit of a mystery, that. Here was the most superb instrument of its kind he'd ever seen. You couldn't even blunt it. Its sharpness extended well beyond its actual edge. And yet he was supposed to destroy it. Where was the sense in that? Ned Simnel was a great believer in sense, of a certain specialised kind.

Maybe Bill Door just wanted to be rid of it, and that was understandable, because even now when it hung innocuously enough from the wall it seemed to radiate sharpness. There was a faint violet corona around the blade, caused by the draughts in the room driving luckless air molecules to their severed death.

Ned Simnel picked it up with great care.

Weird fellow, Bill Door. He'd said he wanted to be sure it was absolutely dead. As if you could kill a *thing*.

Anyway, how could anyone destroy it? Oh, the handle would burn and the metal would calcine and, if he worked hard enough, eventually there'd be nothing more than a little heap of dust and ashes. That was what the customer wanted.

On the other hand, *presumably* you could destroy it just by taking the blade off the handle . . . After all, it wouldn't be a scythe if you did that. It'd just be, well . . . bits. Certainly, you could make a scythe out of them, but you could probably do that with the dust and ashes if you knew how to do it.

Ned Simnel was quite pleased with this line of argument. And, after all, Bill Door hadn't even asked for proof that the thing had been, er, killed.

He took sight carefully and then used the scythe to chop the end off the anvil. Uncanny.

Total sharpness.

He gave in. It was unfair. You couldn't ask someone like him to destroy something like this. It was a work of art.

It was better than that. It was a work of craft.

He walked across the room to a stack of timber and thrust the scythe well out of the way behind the heap. There was a brief, punctured squeak.

Anyway, it would be all right. He'd give Bill his farthing back in the morning.

The Death of Rats materialised behind the heap in the forge, and trudged to the sad little heap of fur that had been a rat that got in the way of the scythe.

Its ghost was standing beside it, looking apprehensive. It didn't seem very pleased to see him.

"Squeak? Squeak?"

SQUEAK, the Death of Rats explained.

"*Squeak?*"

SQUEAK, the Death of Rats confirmed.

"[Preen whiskers] [twitch nose]?"

The Death of Rats shook its head.

SQUEAK.

The rat was crestfallen. The Death of Rats laid a bony but not entirely unkind paw on its shoulder.

SQUEAK.

The rat nodded sadly. It had been a good life in the forge. Ned's

173

housekeeping was almost non-existent, and he was probably the world champion absent-minded-leaver of unfinished sandwiches. It shrugged, and trooped after the small robed figure. It wasn't as if it had any choice.

People were streaming through the streets. Most of them were chasing trolleys. Most of the trolleys were full of whatever people had found a trolley useful to carry – firewood, children, shopping.

And they were no longer dodging, but moving blindly, all in the same direction.

You could stop a trolley by turning it over, when its wheels spun madly and uselessly. The wizards saw a number of enthusiastic individuals trying to smash them, but the trolleys were practically indestructible – they bent but didn't break, and if they had even one wheel left they'd make a valiant attempt to keep going.

"Look at that one!" said the Archchancellor. "It's got my laundry in it! My actual laundry! Darn that for a lark!"

He pushed his way through the crowds and rammed his staff into the trolley's wheels, toppling it over.

"We can't get a clear shot at anything with all these civilians around," complained the Dean.

"There's hundreds of trolleys!" said the Lecturer in Recent Runes. "It's just like vermine!* Get away from me, you – you *basket!*"

He flailed at an importunate trolley with his staff.

The tide of wheeled baskets was flowing out of the city. The struggling humans gradually dropped out or fell under the wobbling wheels. Only the wizards stayed in the flowing tide, shouting at one another and attacking the silvery swarm with their staves. It wasn't that magic didn't work. It worked quite well. A good zap

---

* Vermine are small black-and-white rodents found in the Ramtop Mountains. They are ancestors of the lemming, which as is well known throws itself over cliffs and drowns in lakes on a regular basis. Vermine used to do that, too. The point is, though, that dead animals don't breed, and over the millennia more and more vermine were descendants of those vermine who, when faced with a cliff edge, squeaked the rodent equivalent of Blow that for a Game of Soldiers. Vermine now abseil down cliffs, and build small boats to cross lakes. When their rush leads them to the seashore they sit around avoiding one another's gaze for a while, and then leave early to get home before the rush.

could turn a trolley into a thousand intricate little wire puzzles. But what good did that do? A moment later two others would trundle over their stricken sibling.

Around the Dean trolleys were being splashed into metal droplets.

"He's really getting the hang of it, isn't he?" said the Senior Wrangler, as he and the Bursar levered yet another basket onto its back.

"He's certainly saying Yo a lot," said the Bursar.

The Dean himself didn't know when he'd been happier. For sixty years he'd been obeying all the self-regulating rules of wizardry, and suddenly he was having the time of his life. He'd never realised that, deep down inside, what he really wanted to do was make things go splat.

Fire leapt from the tip of his staff. Handles and bits of wire and pathetically spinning wheels tinkled down around him. And what made it even better was that there was no end to the targets. A second wave of trolleys, crammed into a tighter space, was trying to advance over the tops of those still in actual contact with the ground. It wasn't working, but they were trying anyway. And trying desperately, because a third wave was already crunching and smashing its way over the top of them. Except that you couldn't use the word "trying". It suggested some sort of conscious effort, some sort of possibility that there might also be a state of "not trying". Something about the relentless movement, the way they crushed one another in their surge, suggested that the wire baskets had as much choice in the matter as water has about flowing downhill.

"Yo!" shouted the Dean. Raw magic smacked into the grinding tangle of metal. It rained wheels.

"Eat hot thaumaturgy, you m– ", the Dean began.

"Don't swear! Don't swear!" shouted Ridcully above the noise. He tried to swat a Silly Bugger that was orbiting his hat. "There's no telling what it might turn into!"

"Bother!" screamed the Dean.

"It's no good. We might as well be trying to hold back the sea," said the Senior Wrangler. "I vote we head back to the University and pick up some really *tough* spells."

175

"Good idea," said Ridcully. He looked up at the advancing wall of twisted wire. "Any idea how?" he said.

"Yo! Scallywags!" said the Dean. He aimed his staff again. It made a sad little noise that, if it was written down, could only be spelled *pfffft*. A feeble spark fell off the end and onto the cobbles.

Windle Poons slammed another book shut. The Librarian winced.

"Nothing! Volcanoes, tidal waves, wrath of gods, meddling wizards . . . I don't want to know how other cities have been *killed*, I want to know how they ended . . ."

The Librarian stacked another pile of books on the reading desk. Another plus about being dead, Windle was finding, was an ability with languages. He could see the *sense* in the words without knowing the actual meaning. Being dead wasn't like falling asleep after all. It was like waking up.

He glanced across the Library to where Lupine was having his paw bandaged.

"Librarian?" he said softly.

"Oook?"

"You've changed species in your time . . . what would you do if, for the sake of argument, you found a couple of people who . . . well, suppose there was a wolf that changed into a wolfman at the full moon, and a woman that changed into a wolfwoman at the full moon . . . you know, approaching the same shape but from opposite directions? And they'd met. What do you tell them? Do you let them sort it out for themselves?"

"Oook," said the Librarian, instantly.

"It's tempting."

"Oook."

"Mrs Cake wouldn't like it, though."

"Eeek oook."

"You're right. You could have put it a little less coarsely, but you're right. Everyone has to sort things out for themselves."

He sighed, and turned the page. His eyes widened.

"The city of Kahn Li," he said. "Ever heard of it? What's this book? 'Stripfettle's Believe-It-Or-Not Grimoire.' Says here . . . 'little carts . . . none knew from where they came . . . of such great

176

use, men were employed to herd them and bring them into the city . . . of a sudden, like unto a rush of creatures . . . men followed them and behold, there was a new city outside the walls, a city as of merchants' booths wherein the carts ran' . . ."

He turned the page.

"It seems to say . . ."

I still haven't understood it properly, he told himself. One-Man-Bucket thinks we're talking about the breeding of cities. But that doesn't feel right.

A city is alive. Supposing you were a great slow giant, like a Counting Pine, and looked down at a city? You'd see buildings grow; you'd see attackers driven off; you'd see fires put out. You'd see the city was alive but you wouldn't see people, because they'd move too fast. The life of a city, the thing that drives it, isn't some sort of mysterious force. The life of a city is people.

He turned the pages absently, not really looking . . .

So we have the cities – big, sedentary creatures, growing from one spot and hardly moving at all for thousands of years. They breed by sending out people to colonise new land. They themselves just lie there. They're alive, but only in the same way that a jellyfish is alive. Or a fairly bright vegetable. After all, we call Ankh-Morpork the Big Wahooni . . .

And where you get big slow living things, you get small fast things that eat them . . .

Windle Poons felt the brain cells firing. Connections were made. Thought gushed along new channels. Had he ever really thought properly when he was alive? He doubted it. He'd just been a lot of complicated reactions attached to a lot of nerve endings, with everything from idle rumination about the next meal to random, distracting memories getting between him and real thought.

It'd grow inside the city, where it's warm and protected. And then it'd break out, outside the city, and build . . . something, not a real city, a false city . . . that pulls the people, the life, out of the host . . .

The word we're looking for here is *predator*.

The Dean stared at his staff in disbelief. He gave it a shake, and aimed it again.

This time the sound would be spelled *pfwt*.

He looked up. A curling wave of trolleys, rooftop high, was poised to fall on him.

"Oh . . . *shucks*," he said, and folded his arms over his head.

Someone grabbed the back of his robe and pulled him away as the trolleys crashed down.

"Come *on*," said Ridcully. "If we run we can keep ahead of 'em."

"I'm out of magic! I'm out of magic!" moaned the Dean.

"You'll be out of a lot more if you don't hurry," said the Archchancellor.

Trying to keep together, bumping into one another, the wizards staggered ahead of the trolleys. Streams of them were surging out of the city and across the fields.

"Know what this reminds me of?" said Ridcully, as they fought their way through.

"Do tell," muttered the Senior Wrangler.

"Salmon run," said the Archchancellor.

"What?"

"Not in the Ankh, of course," said Ridcully. "I don't reckon a salmon could get upstream in *our* river – "

"Unless it walked," said the Senior Wrangler.

" – but I've seen 'em thick as milk in some rivers," said Ridcully. "Fightin' to get ahead. The whole river just a mass of silver."

"Fine, fine," said the Senior Wrangler. "What'd they do that for?"

"Well . . . it's all to do with breeding."

"Disgusting. And to think we *have* to drink water," said the Senior Wrangler.

"Right, we're in the open now, this is where we outflank 'em," said Ridcully. "We'll just aim for a clear space and – "

"I don't think so," said the Lecturer in Recent Runes.

Every direction was filled with an advancing, grinding, fighting wall of trolleys.

"They're coming to *get* us! They're coming to *get* us!" wailed the Bursar. The Dean snatched his staff.

"Hey, that's mine!"

The Dean pushed him away and blew off the wheels of a leading trolley.

"That's my staff!"

178

The wizards stood back to back in a narrowing ring of metal.

"They're not right for this city," said the Lecturer in Recent Runes.

"I know what you mean," said Ridcully. "Alien."

"I suppose no one's got a flying spell on them today?" the Senior Wrangler enquired.

The Dean took aim again and melted a basket.

"That's my staff you're using, you know."

"Shut up, Bursar," said the Archchancellor. "And, Dean, you're getting nowhere picking them off one by one like that. Okay, lads? We want to do them all as much damage as possible. Remember – wild, uncontrolled bursts . . ."

The trolleys advanced.

Ow. Ow.

Miss Flitworth staggered through the wet, rattling gloom. Hailstones crunched underfoot. Thunder cannonaded around the sky.

"They sting, don't they," she said.

THEY ECHO.

Bill Door fielded a stook as it was blown past, and stacked it with the others. Miss Flitworth scuttled past him, bent double under a load of corn.* The two of them worked steadily, crisscrossing the field in the teeth of the storm to snatch up the harvest before the wind and hail stole it away. Lightning flickered around the sky. It wasn't a normal storm. It was war.

"It's going to pour with rain in a minute," screamed Miss Flitworth, above the noise. "We'll never get it down to the barn! Go and fetch a tarpaulin or something! That'll do for tonight!"

Bill Door nodded, and ran through the squelching darkness towards the farm buildings. Lightning was striking so many times around the fields that the air itself was sizzling, and a corona danced along the top of the hedge.

And there was Death.

---

* The ability of skinny old ladies to carry huge loads is phenomenal. Studies have shown that an ant can carry one hundred times its own weight, but there is no known limit to the lifting power of the average tiny eighty-year-old Spanish peasant grandmother.

179

He saw it looming ahead of him, a crouched skeletal shape poised to spring, its robe flapping and rattling behind it in the wind.

Tightness gripped him, trying to force him to run while at the same time rooting him to the spot. It invaded his mind and froze there, blocking all thought save for the innermost, tiny voice which said, quite calmly: SO *THIS* IS TERROR.

Then Death vanished as the lightning glow faded, reappeared as a fresh arc was struck on the next hill.

Then the quiet, internal voice added: BUT WHY DOESN'T IT MOVE?

Bill Door let himself inch forward slightly. There was no response from the hunched thing.

Then it dawned on him that the thing on the other side of the hedge was only a robed assemblage of ribs and femurs and vertebrae if viewed from one point of view but, if looked at slightly differently, was equally just a complexity of sparging arms and reciprocating levers that had been covered by a tarpaulin which was now blowing off.

The Combination Harvester was in front of him.

Bill Door grinned horribly. Un-Bill Door thoughts rose up in his mind. He stepped forward.

The wall of trolleys surrounded the wizards.

The last flare from a staff melted a hole, which was instantly filled up by more trolleys.

Ridcully turned to his fellow wizards. They were red in the face, their robes were torn, and several over-enthusiastic shots had resulted in singed beards and burnt hats.

"Hasn't anyone got *any* more spells on them?" he said.

They thought feverishly.

"I think I can remember one," said the Bursar hesitantly.

"Go on, man. Anything's worth trying at a time like this."

The Bursar stretched out a hand. He shut his eyes. He muttered a few syllables under his breath.

There was a brief flicker of octarine light and —

"Oh," said the Archchancellor. "And that's all of it?"

"'Eringyas' Surprising Bouquet'," said the Bursar, bright eyed and twitching. "I don't know why, but it's one I've always been able to do. Just a knack, I suppose."

Ridcully eyed the huge bunch of flowers now gripped in the Bursar's fist.

"But not, I venture to point out, entirely useful at this time," he added.

The Bursar looked at the approaching walls and his smile faded. "I suppose not," he said.

"Anyone else got any ideas?" said Ridcully.

There was no reply.

"Nice roses, though," said the Dean.

"That was quick," said Miss Flitworth, when Bill Door arrived at the pile of stooks dragging a tarpaulin behind him.

YES, WASN'T IT, he mumbled non-committally, as she helped him drag it over the stack and weigh it down with stones. The wind caught at it and tried to drag it out of his hands; it might as well have tried to blow a mountain over.

Rain swept over the fields, among shreds of mist that shimmered with blue electric energies.

"Never known a night like it," Miss Flitworth said.

There was another crack of thunder. Sheet lightning fluttered around the horizon.

Miss Flitworth clutched Bill Door's arm.

"Isn't that . . . a figure on the hill?" she said. "Thought I saw a . . . shape."

NO, IT'S MERELY A MECHANICAL CONTRIVANCE.

There was another flash.

"On a horse?" said Miss Flitworth.

A third sheet seared across the sky. And this time there was no doubt about it. There was a mounted figure on the nearest hilltop. Hooded. Holding a scythe as proudly as a lance.

POSING. Bill Door turned towards Miss Flitworth. POSING. I NEVER DID ANYTHING LIKE THAT. WHY DO ANYTHING LIKE THAT? WHAT PURPOSE DOES IT SERVE?

He opened his palm. The gold timer appeared.

"How much longer have you got?"

PERHAPS AN HOUR. PERHAPS MINUTES.

"Come on, then!"

181

Bill Door remained where he was, looking at the timer.

"I said, come on!"

IT WON'T WORK. I WAS WRONG TO THINK THAT IT WOULD. BUT IT WON'T. THERE ARE SOME THINGS THAT YOU CANNOT ESCAPE. YOU CANNOT LIVE FOR EVER.

"Why not?"

Bill Door looked shocked. WHAT DO YOU MEAN?

"Why can't you live for ever?"

I DON'T KNOW. COSMIC WISDOM?

"What does cosmic wisdom know about it? Now, will you come on?"

The figure on the hill hadn't moved.

The rain had turned the dust into a fine mud. They slithered down the slope and hurried across the yard and into the house.

I SHOULD HAVE PREPARED MORE. I HAD PLANS —

"But there was the harvest."

YES.

"Is there any way we can barricade the doors or something?"

DO YOU KNOW WHAT YOU'RE SAYING?

"Well, think of something! Didn't anything ever work against you?"

No, said Bill Door, with a tiny touch of pride.

Miss Flitworth peered out of the window, and then flung herself dramatically against the wall on one side of it.

"He's gone!"

IT, said Bill Door. IT WON'T BE A HE YET.

"It's gone. It could be anywhere."

IT CAN COME THROUGH THE WALL.

She darted forward, and then glared at him.

VERY WELL. FETCH THE CHILD. I THINK WE SHOULD LEAVE HERE. A thought struck him. He brightened up a little bit. WE DO HAVE SOME TIME. WHAT IS THE HOUR?

"I don't know. You go around stopping the clocks the whole time."

BUT IT IS NOT YET MIDNIGHT?

"I shouldn't think it's more than a quarter past eleven."

THEN WE HAVE THREE-QUARTERS OF AN HOUR.

"How can you be sure?"

BECAUSE OF DRAMA, MISS FLITWORTH. THE KIND OF DEATH WHO POSES AGAINST THE SKYLINE AND GETS LIT UP BY LIGHTNING FLASHES, said Bill Door, disapprovingly, DOESN'T TURN UP AT

FIVE-AND-TWENTY PAST ELEVEN IF HE CAN POSSIBLY TURN UP AT MIDNIGHT.

She nodded, white-faced, and disappeared upstairs. After a minute or two she returned, with Sal wrapped up in a blanket.

"Still fast asleep," she said.

THAT'S NOT SLEEP.

The rain had stopped, but the storm still marched around the hills. The air sizzled, still seemed oven-hot.

Bill Door led the way past the henhouse, where Cyril and his elderly harem were crouched back in the darkness, all trying to occupy the same few inches of perch.

There was a pale green glow hovering around the farmhouse chimney.

"We call that Mother Carey's Fire," said Miss Flitworth. "It's an omen."

AN OMEN OF WHAT?

"What? Oh, don't ask me. Just an omen, I suppose. Just basic omenery. Where are we going?"

INTO THE TOWN.

"To be near the scythe?"

YES.

He disappeared into the barn. After a while he came out leading Binky, saddled and harnessed. He mounted up, then leaned down and pulled both her and the sleeping child onto the horse in front of him.

IF I'M WRONG, he added, THIS HORSE WILL TAKE YOU WHEREVER YOU WANT TO GO.

"I shan't want to go anywhere except back home!"

WHEREVER.

Binky broke into a trot as they turned onto the road to the town. Wind blew the leaves off the trees, which tumbled past them and on up the road. The occasional flash of lightning still hissed across the sky.

Miss Flitworth looked at the hill beyond the farm.

"Bill – "

I KNOW.

" – it's there again – "

I KNOW.

"Why isn't it chasing us?"

WE'RE SAFE UNTIL THE SAND RUNS OUT.

"And you die when the sand runs out?"

NO. WHEN THE SAND RUNS OUT IS WHEN I *SHOULD* DIE. I WILL BE IN THE SPACE BETWEEN LIFE AND AFTERLIFE.

"Bill, it looked as though the thing it was riding . . . I thought it was a proper horse, just very skinny, but . . ."

IT'S A SKELETAL STEED. IMPRESSIVE BUT IMPRACTICAL. I HAD ONE ONCE BUT THE HEAD FELL OFF.

"A bit like flogging a dead horse, I should think."

HA. HA. MOST AMUSING, MISS FLITWORTH.

"I think that at a time like this you can stop calling me Miss Flitworth," said Miss Flitworth.

RENATA?

She looked startled. "How did you know my name? Oh. You've probably seen it written down, right?"

ENGRAVED.

"On one of them hourglasses?"

YES.

"With all them sands of time pouring through?"

YES.

"Everyone's got one?"

YES.

"So you know how long I've –"

YES.

"It must be very odd, knowing . . . the kind of things you know . . ."

DO NOT ASK ME.

"That's not fair, you know. If we knew when we were going to die, people would live better lives."

IF PEOPLE KNEW WHEN THEY WERE GOING TO DIE, I THINK THEY PROBABLY WOULDN'T LIVE AT ALL.

"Oh, very gnomic. And what do you know about it, Bill Door?"

EVERYTHING.

Binky trotted up one of the town's meagre handful of streets and over the cobbles of the square. There was no one else around. In cities like Ankh-Morpork midnight was just late evening, because there was no civic night at all, just evenings fading into dawns. But here people regulated their lives by things like sunsets and mispronounced cock-crows. Midnight meant what it said.

Even with the storm stalking the hills, the square itself was hushed.

The ticking of the clock in its tower, unnoticeable at midday, now seemed to echo off the buildings.

As they approached, something whirred deep in its cogwheeled innards. The minute hand moved with a clonk, and shuddered to a halt on the 9. A trapdoor opened in the clock face and two little mechanical figures whirred out self-importantly and tapped a small bell with great apparent effort.

Ting-ting-ting.

The figures lined up and wobbled back into the clock.

"They've been there ever since I was a girl. Mr Simnel's great-great-grandad made them," said Miss Flitworth. "I always wondered what they did between chimes, you know. I thought they had a little house in there, or something."

I DON'T THINK SO. THEY'RE JUST A THING. THEY'RE NOT ALIVE.

"Hmm. Well, they've been there for hundreds of years. Maybe life is something you sort of acquire?"

YES.

They waited in silence, except for the occasional thud as the minute hand climbed the night.

"It's – been quite nice having you around the place, Bill Door."

He didn't reply.

"Helping me with the harvest and everything."

IT WAS . . . INTERESTING.

"It was wrong of me to delay you, just for a lot of corn."

NO. THE HARVEST IS IMPORTANT.

Bill Door unfolded his palm. The timer appeared.

"I still can't work out how you do that."

IT IS NOT DIFFICULT.

The hiss of the sand grew until it filled the square.

"Have you got any last words?"

YES. I DON'T WANT TO GO.

"Well. Succinct, anyway."

Bill Door was amazed to find she was trying to hold his hand.

Above him, the hands of midnight came together. There was a whirring from the clock. The door opened. The automata marched out. They clicked to a halt on either side of the hour bell, bowed to one another, and raised their hammers.

Dong.

185

And then there was the sound of a horse trotting.

Miss Flitworth found the edge of her vision filling with purple and blue blotches, like the flashes of after-image with no image to come after.

If she jerked her head quickly and peered out of the tail of her eye, she could see small grey-clad shapes hovering around the walls.

The Revenooers, she thought. They've come to make sure it all happens.

"Bill?" she said.

He closed his palm over the gold timer.

NOW IT STARTS.

The hoofbeats grew louder, and echoed off the buildings behind them.

REMEMBER: YOU ARE IN NO DANGER.

Bill Door stepped back into the gloom.

Then he reappeared momentarily.

PROBABLY, he added, and retreated into the darkness.

Miss Flitworth sat down on the steps of the clock, cradling the body of the girl across her knees.

"Bill?" she ventured.

A mounted figure rode into the square.

It was, indeed, on a skeletal horse. Blue flame crackled over the creature's bones as it trotted forward; Miss Flitworth found herself wondering whether it was a real skeleton, animated in some way, something that had once been the inside of a horse, or a skeletal *creature* in its own right. It was a ridiculous chain of thought to follow, but it was better than dwelling on the ghastly reality that was approaching.

Did it get rubbed down, or just given a good polish?

Its rider dismounted. It was much taller than Bill Door had been, but the darkness of its robe hid any details. It held something that wasn't exactly a scythe but which might have had a scythe in its ancestry, in the same way that even the most cunningly-fashioned surgical implement has a stick somewhere in its past. It was a long way from any implement that ever touched a straw.

The figure stalked towards Miss Flitworth, scythe over its shoulder, and stopped.

Where is He?

"Don't know who you're talking about," said Miss Flitworth. "And if I was you, young man, I'd feed my horse."

The figure appeared to have trouble digesting this information, but

186

finally it seemed to reach a conclusion. It unshipped the scythe and looked down at the child.

I will find Him, it said. *But first —*

It stiffened.

A voice behind it said:

DROP THE SCYTHE, AND TURN AROUND SLOWLY.

Something within the city, Windle thought. Cities grow up full of people, but they're also full of commerce and shops and religions and . . .

This is stupid, he told himself. They're just *things*. They're not alive.

Maybe life is something you acquire.

Parasites and predators, but not like the sort affecting animals and vegetables. They were some kind of big, slower, metaphorical lifeform, living off cities. But they incubate in the cities, like those, what are they? those icky newman wasp things. He could remember now, just as he could remember everything, reading as a student about creatures that laid their eggs inside other creatures. For months after he'd refused omelettes and caviar, just in case.

And the eggs would . . . look like the city, in a way, so that citizens would carry them home. Like cuckoo eggs.

I wonder how many cities died in the past? Ringed by parasites, like a coral reef surrounded by starfish. They'd just become empty, they'd lose whatever spirit they had.

He stood up.

"Where's everyone gone, Librarian?"

"Oook oook."

"Just like them. I'd have done that. Rush off without thinking. May the gods bless them and help them, if they can find the time from their eternal family squabbles."

And then he thought: well, what now? I've thought, and what am I going to do?

Rush off, of course. But slowly.

The centre of the heap of trolleys was no longer visible. Something was going on. A pale blue glow hung over the huge pyramid of twisted metal, and there were occasional flashes of lightning deep within the pile. Trolleys slammed into it like asteroids accreting around the core of a new planet, but a few arrivals did something else. They headed for tunnels that had opened within the structure, and disappeared into the glittering core.

Then there was a movement at the tip of the mountain and something thrust its way up through the broken metal. It was a glistening spike, supporting a globe about two metres across. It did nothing very much for a minute or two and then, as the breeze dried it out, it split and crumbled.

White objects cascaded out, were caught by the wind, and fountained over Ankh-Morpork and the watching crowds.

One of them zig-zagged gently down across the rooftops and landed at the feet of Windle Poons as he lurched outside the Library.

It was still damp, and there was writing on it. At least, an attempt at writing. It looked like the strange organic inscription of the snowflake balls – words created by something that was not at all at home with words:

sale ! sale !! sale !!!

starts tomorrow !!!

Windle reached the University gateway. People were streaming past.

Windle knew his fellow citizens. They'd go to look at anything. They were suckers for anything written down with more than one exclamation mark after it.

He felt someone looking at him, and turned. A trolley was watching from an alleyway; it backed up and whizzed away.

"What's happening, Mr Poons?" said Ludmilla.

There was something unreal about the expression of the passers-by. They wore an expression of unbudgeable anticipation.

You didn't have to be a wizard to know that something was wrong. And Windle's senses were whining like a dynamo.

Lupine leapt at a drifting sheet of paper and brought it to him.

amazing reductions !!!!!

Windle shook his head sadly. Five exclamation marks, the sure sign of an insane mind.

And then he heard the music.

Lupine sat back on his haunches and howled.

In the cellar under Mrs Cake's house, Schleppel the bogeyman paused halfway through his third rat and listened.

Then he finished his meal and reached for his door.

Count Arthur Winkings Notfaroutoe was working on the crypt.

Personally, he could have lived, or re-lived, or un-lived, or whatever it was he was supposed to be doing, without a crypt. But you had to have a crypt. Doreen had been very definite about the crypt. It gave the place *ton*, she said. You had to have a crypt *and* a vault, otherwise the rest of vampire society would look down their teeth at you.

They never told you about that sort of thing when you started vampiring. They never told you to build your own crypt out of some cheap two-by-four from Chalky the Troll's Wholesale Building Supplies. It wasn't something that happened to most vampires, Arthur reflected. Not your *proper* vampires. Your actual Count Jugular, for example. No, a toff like him'd have someone for it. When the villagers came to burn the place down, you wouldn't catch the Count his own self whipping down to the gate to drop the drawbridge. Oh, no. He'd just say, "Igor" – as it might be – "Igor, just svort it out, chop chop".

Huh. Well, they'd had an advert in Mr Keeble's job shop for months now. Bed, three meals a day, and hump provided if necessary. Not so much as an enquiry. And people said there was all this unemployment around. It made you livid.

He picked up another piece of wood and measured it, grimacing as he unfolded the ruler.

Arthur's back ached from digging the moat. And that was

189

another thing your posh vampire didn't have to worry about. The moat came with the job, style of thing. And it went all the way round, because other vampires didn't have the street out in front of them and old Mrs Pivey complaining on one side and a family of trolls Doreen wasn't speaking to on the other and therefore they didn't end up with a moat that just went across the back yard. Arthur kept falling in it.

And then there was the biting the necks of young women. Or rather, there wasn't. Arthur was always prepared to see the other person's point of view, but he felt certain that young women came into the vampiring somewhere, whatever Doreen said. In diaphanous pegnoyers. Arthur wasn't quite certain what a diaphanous pegnoyer was, but he'd read about them and he definitely felt that he'd like to see one before he died . . . or whatever . . .

And other vampires didn't suddenly find their wives talking with Vs instead of Ws. The reason being, your natural vampire talked like that anyway.

Arthur sighed.

It was no life, or half-life or after-life or whatever it was, being a lower-middle-class wholesale fruit and vegetable merchant with an upper-class condition.

And then the music filtered in through the hole in the wall that he'd knocked out to put in the barred window.

"Ow," he said, and clutched at his jaw. "Doreen?"

Reg Shoe thumped his portable podium.

" – and, let me say, we shall not lie back and let the grass grow over our heads," he bellowed. "So what is your seven-point plan for Equal Opportunities with the living, I hear you cry?"

The wind blew the dried grasses in the cemetery. The only creature apparently paying any attention to Reg was a solitary raven.

Reg Shoe shrugged and lowered his voice. "You might at least make some effort," he said, to the next world at large. "Here's me wearing my fingers to the bone" – he flexed his hands to demonstrate – "and do I hear a word of thanks?"

190

He paused, just in case.

The raven, which was one of the extra large, fat ones that infested the rooftops of the University, put its head on one side and gave Reg Shoe a thoughtful look.

"You know," said Reg, "sometimes I just feel like giving up – "

The raven cleared its throat.

Reg Shoe spun around.

"You say one word," he said, "just one bloody *word* . . ."

And then he heard the music.

Ludmilla risked removing her hands from her ears.

"It's horrible! What is it, Mr Poons?"

Windle tried to pull the remains of his hat over his ears.

"Don't know," he said. "It *could* be music. If you'd never heard music before."

There weren't notes. There were strung-together noises that might have been intended to be notes, put together as one might draw a map of a country that one had never seen.

Hnyip. Ynyip. Hwyomp.

"It's coming from outside the city," said Ludmilla. "Where all the people . . . are . . . going . . . They can't *like* it, can they?"

"I can't imagine why they should," said Windle.

"It's just that . . . you remember the trouble with the rats last year? That man who said he had a pipe that played music only rats could hear?"

"Yes, but that wasn't really true, it was all a fraud, it was just the Amazing Maurice and his Educated Rodents – "

"But supposing it *could* have been true?"

Windle shook his head.

"Music to attract humans? Is that what you're getting at? But that can't be true. It's not attracting *us*. Quite the reverse, I assure you."

"Yes, but you're not human . . . exactly," said Ludmilla. "And – " She stopped, and went red in the face.

Windle patted her on the shoulder.

"Good point. Good point," was all he could think of to say.

"You know, don't you," she said, without looking up.

"Yes. I don't think it's anything to be ashamed of, if that's any help."

"Mother said it would be dreadful if anyone ever found out!"

"That probably depends on who it is," said Windle, glancing at Lupine.

"Why is your dog staring at me like that?" said Ludmilla.

"He's very intelligent," said Windle.

Windle felt in his pocket, tipped out a couple of handfuls of soil, and unearthed his diary. Twenty days to next full moon. Still, it'd be something to look forward to.

The metal debris of the heap started to collapse. Trolleys whirred around it, and a large crowd of Ankh-Morpork's citizens were standing in a big circle, trying to peer inside. The unmusical music filled the air.

"There's Mr Dibbler," said Ludmilla, as they pushed their way through the unresisting people.

"What's he selling this time?"

"I don't think he's trying to sell anything, Mr Poons."

"It's that bad? Then we're probably in lots of trouble."

Blue light shone out from one of the holes in the heap. Bits of broken trolley tinkled to the ground like metal leaves.

Windle bent down stiffly and picked up a pointy hat. It was battered and had been run over by a lot of trolleys, but it was still recognisable as something that by rights should be on someone's head.

"There's wizards in there," he said.

Silver light glittered off the metal. It moved like oil. Windle reached out and a fat spark jumped across and grounded itself on his fingers.

"Hmm," he said. "Lot of potential, too – "

Then he heard the cry of the vampires.

"Coo-ee, Mr Poons!"

He turned. The Notfaroutoes were bearing down on him.

"We – I mean, Ve vould have been here sooner, only – "

" – I couldn't find the blasted collar stud," muttered Arthur, looking hot and flustered. He was wearing a collapsible opera hat,

192

which was fine on the collapsible part but regrettably lacking in hatness, so that Arthur appeared to be looking at the world from under a concertina.

"Oh, hallo," said Windle. There was something dreadfully fascinating about the Winkings' dedication to accurate vampirism.

"Unt who iss the yunk laty?" said Doreen, beaming at Ludmilla.

"Pardon?" said Windle.

"Vot?"

"Doreen – I mean, the *Countess* asked who she is," Arthur supplied, wearily.

"*I* understood what I said," snapped Doreen, in the more normal tones of one born and brought up in Ankh-Morpork rather than some tran-sylvanian fastness. "Honestly, if I left it to you, we'd have no standards at all – "

"My name's Ludmilla," said Ludmilla.

"Charmed," said the Countess Notfaroutoe graciously, extending a hand that would have been thin and pale if it had not been pink and stubby. "Alvays nice to meet fresh blood. If you ever fancy a dog biscuit when you're out and about, our door iss alwace open."

Ludmilla turned to Windle Poons.

"It's not written on my forehead, is it?" she said.

"These are a special kind of people," said Windle gently.

"I should think so," said Ludmilla, levelly. "I hardly know anyone who wears an opera cloak the whole time."

"You've got to have the cloak," said Count Arthur. "For the wings, you see. Like – "

He spread the cloak dramatically. There was a brief, implosive noise, and a small fat bat hung in the air. It looked down, gave an angry squeak, and nosedived onto the soil. Doreen picked it up by its feet and dusted it off.

"It's having to sleep with the window open all night that I object to," she said vaguely. "I wish they'd stop that music! I'm getting a headache."

There was another *whoomph*. Arthur reappeared upside down and landed on his head.

"It's the drop, you see," said Doreen. "It's like a run-up, sort of thing. If he doesn't get at least a one-storey start he can't get up a proper airspeed."

"I can't get a proper airspeed," said Arthur, struggling to his feet.

"Excuse me," said Windle, "The music doesn't affect you?"

"It puts my teeth on edge is what it does," said Arthur. "Which is not a good thing for a vampire, I prob'ly don't have to tell you."

"Mr Poons thinks it does something to people," said Ludmilla.

"Sets everyone's teeth on edge?" said Arthur.

Windle looked at the crowd. No one was taking any notice of the Fresh Starters.

"They look as though they're waiting for something," said Doreen. "Vaiting, I mean."

"It's scary," said Ludmilla.

"Nothing wrong with scary," said Doreen. "*We're* scary."

"Mr Poons wants to go inside the heap," said Ludmilla.

"Good idea. Get them to turn that damn music off," said Arthur.

"But you could get killed!" said Ludmilla.

Windle clapped his hands together, and rubbed them thoughtfully.

"Ah," he said, "that's where we're ahead of the game."

He walked into the glow.

He'd never seen such bright light. It seemed to emanate from everywhere, hunting down every last shadow and eradicating it ruthlessly. It was much brighter than daylight without being anything like it – there was a blue edge to it that cut vision like a knife.

"You all right, Count?" he said.

"Fine, fine," said Arthur.

Lupine growled.

Ludmilla pulled at a tangle of metal.

"There's something under this, you know. It looks like . . . marble. Orange-coloured marble." She ran her hand over it. "But warm. Marble shouldn't be warm, should it?"

"It can't be marble. There can't be this much marble in the whole world . . . vorld," said Doreen. "We tried to get marble for the vault," she tasted the sound of the word and nodded to herself, "the vault, yes. Those dwarfs should be shot, the prices they charge. It's a disgrace."

"I don't think dwarfs built this," said Windle. He knelt down awkwardly to examine the floor.

194

"I shouldn't think so, the lazy little buggers. They wanted nearly seventy dollars to do our vault. Didn't they, Arthur?"

"Nearly seventy dollars," said Arthur.

"I don't think anyone built it," said Windle quietly. Cracks. There should be cracks, he thought. Edges and things, where one slab joins another. It shouldn't be all one piece. And slightly sticky.

"So Arthur did it himself."

"I did it myself."

Ah. Here was an edge. Well, not exactly an edge. The marble became clear, like a window, looking into another brightly lit space. There were things in there, indistinct and melted-looking, but no way in to them.

The chatter of the Winkings flowed over him as he crept forward.

" – more of a vaultette, really. But he got a dungeon in, even if you have to go out into the hall to shut the door properly – "

Gentility meant all sorts of things, Windle thought. To some people it was *not* being a vampire. To others it was a matched set of flying plaster bats on the wall.

He ran his fingers over the clear substance. The world here was all rectangles. There were corners, and the corridor was lined on both sides with the clear panels. And the non-music played all the time.

It *couldn't* be alive, could it? Life was . . . more rounded.

"What do you think, Lupine?" he said.

Lupine barked.

"Hmm. Not a lot of help."

Ludmilla knelt down and put her hand on Windle's shoulder.

"What did you mean, no one built it?" she said.

Windle scratched his head.

"I'm not sure . . . but I think maybe it was . . . secreted."

"Secreted? From what? *By* what?"

They looked up. A trolley whirred out of the mouth of a side corridor and skidded away down another on the opposite side of the passage.

"*Them?*" said Ludmilla.

"I shouldn't think so. I think they're more like servants. Like ants. Bees in a hive, maybe."

"What's the honey?"

195

"Not sure. But it's not ripe yet. I don't think things are quite finished. No one touch *anything*."

They walked onward. The passage opened up into a wide, bright, domed area. Stairways led up and down to different floors, and there was a fountain and a grove of potted plants that looked too healthy to be real.

"Isn't it nice?" said Doreen.

"You keep thinking there should be people," said Ludmilla. "Lots of people."

"There should at least be wizards," muttered Windle Poons. "Half a dozen wizards don't just disappear."

The five of them moved closer. Passages the size of the one they'd just walked down could have accommodated a couple of elephants walking abreast.

"Do you think it might be a good idea to go back outside?" said Doreen.

"What good would that do?" said Windle.

"Well, it'd get us out of here."

Windle turned, counting. Five of the passages radiated equidistantly out of the domed area.

"And presumably it's the same above and below," he said aloud.

"It's very clean here," Doreen said nervously. "Isn't it clean, Arthur?"

"It's very clean."

"What's that noise?" said Ludmilla.

"What noise?"

"That noise. Like someone sucking something."

Arthur looked around with a certain amount of interest.

"It's not me."

"It's the stairs," said Windle.

"Don't be silly, Mr Poons. Stairs don't suck."

Windle looked down.

"These do."

They were black, like a sloping river. As the dark substance flowed out from under the floor it humped itself into something resembling steps, which travelled up the slope until they disappeared under the floor again, somewhere above. When the steps emerged they made a slow, rhythmic shlup-shlup noise, like some-one investigating a particularly annoying dental cavity.

"Do you know," said Ludmilla, "that's quite possibly the most unpleasant thing I've ever seen?"

"I've seen worse," said Windle. "But it's pretty bad. Shall we go up or down?"

"You want to *stand* on them?"

"No. But the wizards aren't on this floor and it's that or slide down the handrail. Have you looked closely at the handrail?"

They looked at the handrail.

"I think," said Doreen nervously, "that *down* is more us."

They went down in silence. Arthur fell over at the point where the travelling stairs were sucked into the floor again.

"I had this horrible feeling it was going to drag me under," he said apologetically, and then looked around him.

"It's big," he concluded. "Roomy. I could do wonders down here with some stone-effect wallpaper."

Ludmilla wandered over to the nearest wall.

"You know," she said, "there's more glass than I've seen before, but these clear bits look a bit like shops. Does that make sense? A great big shop full of shops?"

"And not ripe yet," said Windle.

"Sorry?"

"Just thinking aloud. Can you see what the merchandise is?"

Ludmilla shaded her eyes.

"It just looks like a lot of colour and glitter."

"Let me know if you see a wizard."

Someone screamed.

"Or hear one, for example," Windle added. Lupine bounded off down a passageway. Windle lurched swiftly after him.

Someone was on their back, trying desperately to fight off a couple of the trolleys. They were bigger than the ones Windle had seen before, with a golden sheen to them.

"Hey!" he yelled.

They stopped trying to gore the prone figure and three-point-turned towards him.

"Oh," he said, as they got up speed.

The first one dodged Lupine's jaws and butted Windle full in the knees, knocking him over. As the second passed over him he reached up wildly, grabbed randomly at the metal, and pulled hard. A wheel spun off and the trolley cartwheeled into the wall.

He scrambled up in time to see Arthur hanging grimly onto the handle of the other trolley as the two of them whirred around in a mad centrifugal waltz.

"Let go! Let go!" Doreen screamed.

"I can't! I can't!"

"Well, do *something!*"

There was a pop of inrushing air. The trolley was suddenly not straining against the weight of a middle-aged wholesale fruit and vegetable entrepreneur but only against a small terrified bat. It rocketed into a marble pillar, bounced off, hit a wall and landed on its back, wheels spinning.

"The wheels!" shouted Ludmilla. "Pull the wheels off!"

"I'll do that," said Windle. "You help Reg."

"Is that *Reg* down there?" said Doreen.

Windle jerked his thumb towards the distant wall. The words "Better late than nev" ended in a desperate streak of paint.

"Show him a wall and a paint pot and he doesn't know what world he's in," said Doreen.

"He's only got a choice of two," said Windle, throwing the trolley wheels across the floor. "Lupine, keep a look-out in case there's any more."

The wheels had been sharp, like ice skates. He was definitely feeling tattered around the legs. Now, how did healing go?

Reg Shoe was helped into a sitting position.

"What's happening?" he said. "No one else was coming in, and I came down here to see where the music was coming from, and the next thing, there's these *wheels –* "

Count Arthur returned to his approximately human form, looked around proudly, realised that no one was paying him any attention, and sagged.

"They looked a lot tougher than the others," said Ludmilla. "Bigger and nastier and covered in sharp edges."

"Soldiers," said Windle. "We've seen the workers. And now there's soldiers. Just like ants."

"I had an ant farm when I was a lad," said Arthur, who had hit the

198

floor rather heavily and was having temporary trouble with the nature of reality.

"Hang on," said Ludmilla. "I know about ants. We have ants in the back yard. If you have workers and soldiers, then you must also have a – "

"I know. I know," said Windle.

" – mind you, they called it a *farm*, I never saw them doing any farming – "

Ludmilla leaned against the wall.

"It'll be somewhere close," she said.

"I think so," said Windle.

"What does it look like, do you think?"

" – what you do is, you get two bits of glass and some ants – "

"I don't know. How should I know? But the wizards will be somewhere near it."

"I don't see vy you're bothering about them," said Doreen. "They buried you alive just because you vere dead."

Windle looked up at the sound of wheels. A dozen warrior baskets turned the corner and pulled up in formation.

"They thought they were doing it for the best," said Windle. "People often do. It's amazing, the things that seem a good idea at the time."

The new Death straightened up.

Or?

AH.

ER.

Bill Door stepped back, turned round, and ran for it.

It was, as he was wonderfully well placed to know, merely putting off the inevitable. But wasn't that what living was all about?

No one had ever run away from him after they were dead. Many had tried it *before* they were dead, often with great ingenuity. But the normal reaction of a spirit, suddenly pitched from one world into the next, was to hang around hopefully. Why run, after all? It wasn't as if you knew where you were running to.

The ghost Bill Door knew where he was running to.

Ned Simnel's smithy was locked up for the night, although this did not

199

present a problem. Not alive and not dead, the spirit of Bill Door dived through the wall.

The fire was a barely-visible glow, settling in the forge. The smithy was full of warm darkness.

What it didn't contain was the ghost of a scythe.

Bill Door looked around desperately.

SQUEAK?

There was a small, dark-robed figure sitting on a beam above him. It gestured frantically towards the corner.

He saw a dark handle sticking out from the load of timber. He tried to pull at it with fingers now as substantial as a shadow.

HE SAID HE WOULD DESTROY IT FOR ME!

The Death of Rats shrugged sympathetically.

The new Death stepped through the wall, scythe held in both hands. It advanced on Bill Door.

There was a rustling. The grey robes were pouring into the smithy.

Bill Door grinned in terror.

The new Death stopped, posing dramatically in the glow from the forge.

It swung.

It almost lost its balance.

You're not supposed to duck!

Bill Door dived through the wall again and pounded across the square, skull down, spectral feet making no noise on the cobbles. He reached the little group by the clock.

ON THE HORSE! GO!

"What's happening? What's *happening!*"

IT HASN'T WORKED!

Miss Flitworth gave him a panicky look but put the unconscious child on Binky's back and climbed up after her. Then Bill Door brought his hand down hard on the horse's flank. There at least there was contact – Binky existed in all worlds.

GO!

He didn't look around but darted on up the road towards the farm.

A weapon!

Something he could hold!

The only weapon in the undead world was in the hands of the new Death.

As Bill Door ran he was aware of a faint, higher-pitched clicking noise. He looked down. The Death of Rats was keeping pace with him.

It gave him an encouraging squeak.

He skidded through the farm gate and flung himself against the wall. There was the distant rumble of the storm. Apart from that, silence.

He relaxed slightly, and crept cautiously along the wall towards the back of the farmhouse.

He caught a glimpse of something metallic. Leaning against the wall there, where the men from the village had left it when they brought him back, was his scythe; not the one he'd carefully prepared, but the one he'd used for the harvest. What edge it had had been achieved only by the whetstone and the caress of the stalks, but it was a familiar shape and he made a tentative grab at it. His hand passed right through.

The further you run, the closer you get.

The new Death stepped unhurriedly out of the shadows.

You should know that, it added.

Bill Door straightened up.

We will enjoy this.

ENJOY?

The new Death advanced. Bill Door backed away.

Yes. The taking of one Death is the same as achieving the end of a billion lesser lives.

LESSER LIVES? THIS IS NOT A GAME!

The new Death hesitated. *What is a game?*

Bill Door felt the tiny flicker of hope.

I COULD SHOW YOU –

The end of the scythe handle caught him under the chin and knocked him against the wall, where he slid to the ground.

We detect a trick. We do not listen. The reaper does not listen to the harvest.

Bill Door tried to get up.

The scythe handle struck him again.

We will not make the same mistakes.

Bill Door looked up. The new Death was holding the golden timer; the top bulb was empty. Around both of them the landscape shifted, reddened, began to take on the unreal appearance of reality seen from the other side . . .

You're out of Time, Mr Bill Door.

201

The new Death raised his cowl.

There was no face there. There was not even a skull. Smoke curled formlessly between the robe and a golden crown.

Bill Door raised himself on his elbows.

A *CROWN*? His voice shook with rage. I NEVER WORE A CROWN!

You never wanted to rule.

The Death swung the scythe back.

And then it dawned on the old Death and the new Death that the hissing of passing time had not, in fact, stopped.

The new Death hesitated, and took out the golden glass.

It shook it.

Bill Door looked into the empty face under the crown. There was an expression of puzzlement there, even with no features actually to wear it; the expression hung in the air all by itself.

He saw the crown turn.

Miss Flitworth stood with her hands held a foot apart and her eyes closed. Between her hands, in the air in front of her hovered the faint outline of a lifetimer, its sand pouring away in a torrent.

The Deaths could just make out, on the glass, the spidery name: Renata Flitworth.

The new Death's featureless expression became one of terminal puzzlement. It turned to Bill Door.

For YOU?

But Bill Door was already rising and unfolding like the wrath of kings. He reached behind him, growling, living on loaned time, and his hands closed around the harvest scythe.

The crowned Death saw it coming and raised its own weapon but there was very possibly nothing in the world that would stop the worn blade as it snarled through the air, rage and vengeance giving it an edge beyond any definition of sharpness. It passed through the metal without slowing.

NO CROWN, said Bill Door, looking directly into the smoke. NO CROWN. ONLY THE HARVEST.

The robe folded up around his blade. There was a thin wail, rising beyond the peak of hearing. A black column, like the negative of lightning, flashed up from the ground and disappeared into the clouds.

Death waited for a moment, and then gingerly gave the robe a prod with his foot. The crown, bent slightly out of shape, rolled out of it a little way before evaporating.

202

OH, he said, dismissively. DRAMA.

He walked over to Miss Flitworth and gently pressed her hands together. The image of the lifetimer disappeared. The blue-and-violet fog on the edge of sight faded as solid reality flowed back.

Down in the town, the clock finished striking midnight.

The old woman was shivering. Death snapped his fingers in front of her eyes.

MISS FLITWORTH? RENATA?

"I – I didn't know what to do and you said it wasn't difficult and – "

Death walked into the barn. When he came out, he was wearing his black robe.

She was still standing there.

"I didn't know what to do," she repeated, possibly not to him. "What happened? Is it all over?"

Death looked around. The grey shapes were pouring into the yard.

POSSIBLY NOT, he said.

More trolleys appeared behind the row of soldiers. They looked like the small silvery workers with the occasional pale golden gleam of a warrior.

"We should retreat back to the stairs," said Doreen.

"I think that's where they want us to go," said Windle.

"Then that's fine by me. Anyway, I vouldn't think those wheels could manage steps, could they?"

"And you can't exactly fight to the death," said Ludmilla. Lupine was keeping close to her, yellow eyes fixed on the slowly advancing wheels.

"Chance would be a fine thing," said Windle. They reached the moving stairs. He looked up. Trolleys clustered around the top of the upward stair, but the way to the floor below looked clear.

"Perhaps we could find another way up?" said Ludmilla hopefully.

They shuffled on to the moving stair. Behind them, the trolleys moved in to block their return.

The wizards were on the floor below. They were standing so still among the potted plants and fountains that Windle passed them at first, assuming that they were some sort of statue or piece of esoteric furniture.

The Archchancellor had a false red nose and was holding some balloons. Beside him, the Bursar was juggling coloured balls, but like a machine, his eyes staring blankly at nothing.

The Senior Wrangler was standing a little way off, wearing a pair of sandwich boards. The writing on them hadn't fully ripened yet, but Windle would have bet his afterlife that it would eventually say something like SALE!!!!

The other wizards were clustered together like dolls whose clockwork hadn't been wound up. Each one had a large oblong badge on his robe. The familiar organic-looking writing was growing into a word that looked like:

Security

although why it was doing so was a complete mystery. The wizards certainly didn't look very secure.

Windle snapped his fingers in front of the Dean's pale eyes. There was no response.

"He's not dead," said Reg.

"Just resting," said Windle. "Switched off."

Reg gave the Dean a push. The wizard tottered forward, and then staggered to a precarious, swaying halt.

"Well, we'll never get them out," said Arthur. "Not like that. Can't you wake them up?"

"Light a feather under their nose," Doreen volunteered.

"I don't think that will work," said Windle. He based the statement on the fact that Reg Shoe was very nearly under their noses, and anyone whose nasal equipment failed to register Mr Shoe would certainly not react to a mere burning feather. Or a heavy weight dropped from a great height, if it came to that.

"Mr Poons," said Ludmilla.

"I used to know a golem looked like him," said Reg Shoe. "Just like him. Great big chap, made out of clay. That's what your typical golem basically is. You just have to write a special holy word on 'em to start 'em up."

"What, like 'security'?"

"Could be."

Windle peered at the Dean. "No," he said at last, "no one's got *that* much clay." He looked around them. "We ought to find out where that blasted music's coming from."

"Where the musicians are hidden, you mean?"

"I don't think there are musicians."

"You've got to have musicians, brother," said Reg. "That's why it's called music."

"Firstly, this isn't like any music I've ever heard, and secondly I always thought you've got to have oil lamps or candles to make light and there aren't any and there's still light shining everywhere," said Windle.

"Mr Poons?" said Ludmilla again, prodding him.

"Yes?"

"Here come some trolleys again."

They were blocking all five passages leading off the central space.

"There's no stairs down," said Windle.

"Maybe it's – *she's* – in one of the glassy bits," said Ludmilla. "The shops?"

"I don't think so. They don't look finished. Anyway, that feels wrong – "

Lupine growled. Spikes glistened on the leading trolleys, but they weren't rushing to attack.

"They must have seen what we did to the others," said Arthur.

"Yes. But how could they? That was upstairs," said Windle.

"Well, maybe they talk to each other."

"How can they talk? How can they think? There can't be any brains in a lot of wire," said Ludmilla.

"Ants and bees don't think, if it comes to that," said Windle. "They're just controlled – "

He looked upwards.

They looked upwards.

"It's coming from somewhere in the ceiling," he said. "We've got to find it right now!"

"There's just panels of light," said Ludmilla.

"Something else! Look for something it could be coming from!"

"It's coming from *everywhere*!"

"Whatever you're thinking of doing," said Doreen, picking up a potted plant and holding it like a club, "I hope you do it fast."

"What's that round black thing up there?" said Arthur.

"Where?"

"There." Arthur pointed.

"Okay, Reg and me will help you up, come on – "

"Me? But I can't stand heights!"

"I thought you could turn into a bat?"

"Yeah, but a very nervous one!"

"Stop complaining. Right – one foot here, now your hand *here*, now put your foot on Reg's shoulder – "

"And don't go through," said Reg.

"I don't like this!" Arthur moaned, as they hoisted him up.

Doreen stopped glaring at the creeping trolleys.

"Artor! Nobblyesse obligay!"

"What? Is that some sort of vampire code?" Reg whispered.

"It means something like: a count's gotta do what a count's gotta do," said Windle.

"Count!" snarled Arthur, swaying dangerously. "I never should have listened to that lawyer! I should have known nothing good ever comes in a long brown envelope! And I can't reach the bloody thing anyway!"

"Can't you jump?" said Windle.

"Can't you drop dead?"

"No."

"And I'm not jumping!"

"Fly, then. Turn into a bat and fly."

"I can't get the airspeed!"

"You could throw him up," said Ludmilla. "You know, like a paper dart."

"Blow that! I'm a count!"

"You just said you didn't want to be," said Windle mildly.

"On the *ground* I don't want to be, but when it comes to being chucked around like a frisbee – "

"Arthur! Do what Mr Poons says!"

"I don't see why – "

"Arthur!"

Arthur as a bat was surprisingly heavy. Windle held him by the ears like a misshapen bowling ball and tried to take aim.

"Remember – I'm an endangered species!" the Count squeaked, as Windle brought his arm back.

It was an accurate throw. Arthur fluttered to the disc in the ceiling and gripped it in his claws.

"Can you move it?"

"No!"

"Then hang on tight and change back."

"No!"

"We'll catch you."

"No!"

"Arthur!" screamed Doreen, prodding an advancing trolley with her makeshift club.

"Oh, all right."

There was a momentary vision of Arthur Winkings clinging desperately to the ceiling, and then he dropped on Windle and Reg, the disc clasped to his chest.

The music stopped abruptly. Pink tubing poured out of the ravaged hole above them and coiled upon Arthur, making him look like a very cheap plate of spaghetti and meatballs. The fountains seemed to operate in reverse for a moment, and then dried up.

The trolleys halted. The ones at the back ran into the ones at the front, and there was a chorus of pathetic clanking noises.

Tubing still poured out of the hole. Windle picked up a bit. It was an unpleasant pink, and sticky.

"What do you think it is?" said Ludmilla.

"I think," said Windle, "that we'd better get out of here now."

The floor trembled. Steam gushed from the fountain.

"If not sooner," Windle added.

There was a groan from the Archchancellor. The Dean slumped forward. The other wizards remained upright, but only just.

"They're coming out of it," said Ludmilla. "But I don't think they'll manage the stairs."

"I don't think anyone should even think about trying to manage the stairs," said Windle. "Look at them."

The moving stairs weren't. The black steps glistened in the shadowless light.

"I see what you mean," said Ludmilla. "I'd rather try and walk on quicksand."

"It'd probably be safer," said Windle.

"Maybe there's a ramp? There must be some way for the trolleys to get around."

"Good idea."

Ludmilla eyed the trolleys. They were milling around aimlessly. "I think I might have an even better one . . ." she said, and grabbed a passing handle.

The trolley fought for a moment and then, lacking any contrary instructions, settled down docilely.

"The ones that can walk'll walk, and the ones that can't walk'll get pushed. Come on, grandad." This was to the Bursar, who was persuaded to flop across the trolley. He said "yo", faintly, and shut his eyes again.

The Dean was manhandled on top of him.*

"And now where?" said Doreen.

A couple of floor tiles buckled upwards. A heavy grey vapour started to pour out.

"It must be somewhere at the end of a passage," said Ludmilla. "Come on."

Arthur looked down at the mists coiling around his feet.

"I wonder how you can do that?" he said. "It's amazingly difficult to get stuff that does that. We tried it, you know, to make our crypt more . . . more cryptic, but it just smokes up the place and sets fire to the curtains – "

"Come *on*, Arthur. We are *going*."

"You don't think we've done too much damage, do you? Perhaps we should leave a note – "

"Yeah, I could write something on the wall if you like," said Reg.

He picked up a struggling worker trolley by its handle and, with some satisfaction, smashed it against a pillar until its wheels dropped off.

---

* It is traditional, when loading wire trolleys, to put the most fragile items at the bottom.

Windle watched the Fresh Start Club head up the nearest passage, pushing a bargain assortment of wizardry.

"Well, well, well," he said. "As simple as that. That's all we had to do. Hardly any drama at all."

He went to move forward, and stopped.

Pink tubes were forcing their way through the floor and were already coiled tightly around his legs.

More floor tiles leapt into the air. The stairways shattered, revealing the dark, serrated and above all *living* tissue that had powered them. The walls pulsed and caved inwards, the marble cracking to reveal purple and pinkness underneath.

Of course, thought a tiny calm part of Windle's mind, none of this is *really* real. Buildings aren't *really* alive. It's all just a metaphor, only at the moment metaphors are like candles in a firework factory.

That being said, what sort of creature *is* the Queen? Like a queen bee, except she's also the hive. Like a caddis fly, which builds, if I'm not mistaken, a shell out of bits of stone and things, to camouflage itself. Or like a nautilus, which adds onto its shell as it gets bigger. And very much, to judge by the way the floors are ripping up, like a very angry starfish.

I wonder how cities would defend themselves against this sort of thing? Creatures generally evolve some sort of defence against predators. Poisons and stings and spikes and things.

Here and now, that's probably me. Spiky old Windle Poons.

At least I can try to see to it that the others get out all right. Let's make my presence felt . . .

He reached down, grabbed a double handful of pulsating tubes, and heaved.

The Queen's screech of rage was heard all the way to the University.

The storm clouds sped towards the hill. They piled up in a towering mass, very fast. Lightning flashed, somewhere in the core.

THERE'S TOO MUCH LIFE AROUND, said Death. NOT THAT I'M ONE TO COMPLAIN. WHERE'S THE CHILD?

"I put her to bed. She's sleeping now. Just ordinary sleep."

Lightning struck on the hill, like a thunderbolt. It was followed by a clanking, grinding noise, somewhere in the middle distance.

Death sighed.

AH. MORE DRAMA.

He walked around the barn, so that he could command a good view of the dark fields. Miss Flitworth followed very closely on his heels, using him as a shield against whatever terrors were out there.

A blue glow crackled behind a distant hedge. It was moving.

"What is it?"

IT WAS THE COMBINATION HARVESTER.

"*Was?* What is it now?"

Death glanced at the clustering watchers.

A POOR LOSER.

The Harvester tore across the soaking fields, cloth arms whirring, levers moving inside an electric blue nimbus. The shafts for the horse waved uselessly in the air.

"How can it go without a horse? It had a horse yesterday!"

IT DOESN'T NEED ONE.

He looked around at the grey watchers. There were ranks of them now.

"Binky's still in the yard. Come on!"

NO.

The Combination Harvester accelerated towards them. The *schip-schip* of its blades became a whine.

"Is it angry because you stole its tarpaulin?"

THAT'S NOT ALL I STOLE.

Death grinned at the watchers. He picked up his scythe, turned it over in his hands and then, when he was sure their gaze was fixed upon it, let it fall to the ground.

Then he folded his arms.

Miss Flitworth dragged at him.

"What do you think you're doing?"

DRAMA.

The Harvester reached the gate into the yard and came through in a cloud of sawdust.

"Are you sure we'll be all right?"

Death nodded.

"Well. That's all right then."

The Harvester's wheels were a blur.

210

PROBABLY.

And then . . .

. . . something in the machinery went clonk.

Then the Harvester was still travelling, but in pieces. Sparks fountained up from its axles. A few spindles and arms managed to hold together, jerking madly as they spun away from the whirling, slowing confusion. The circle of blades tore free, smashed up through the machine, and skimmed away across the fields.

There was a jangle, a clatter, and then the last isolated *boing*, which is the audible equivalent of the famous pair of smoking boots.

And then there was silence.

Death reached down calmly and picked up a complicated-looking spindle as it pinwheeled towards his feet. It had been bent into a right-angle.

Miss Flitworth peered around him.

"What happened?"

I THINK THE ELLIPTICAL CAM HAS GRADUALLY SLID UP THE BEAM SHAFT AND CAUGHT ON THE FLANGE REBATE, WITH DISASTROUS RESULTS.

Death stared defiantly at the grey watchers. One by one, they began to disappear.

He picked up the scythe.

AND NOW I MUST GO, he said.

Miss Flitworth looked horrified. "What? Just like that?"

YES. EXACTLY LIKE THAT. I HAVE A LOT OF WORK TO DO.

"And I won't see you again? I mean – "

OH, YES. SOON. He sought for the right words, and gave up. THAT'S A PROMISE.

Death pulled up his robe and reached into the pocket of his Bill Door overall, which he was still wearing underneath.

WHEN MR SIMNEL COMES TO COLLECT THE BITS IN THE MORNING HE WILL PROBABLY BE LOOKING FOR THIS, he said, and dropped something small and bevelled into her hand.

"What is it?"

A THREE-EIGHTHS GRIPLEY.

Death walked over to his horse, and then remembered something.

AND HE OWES ME A FARTHING, TOO.

*

Ridcully opened one eye. People were milling around. There were lights and excitement. Lots of people were talking at once.

He seemed to be sitting in a very uncomfortable pram, with some strange insects buzzing around him.

He could hear the Dean complaining, and there were groans that could only be coming from the Bursar, and the voice of a young woman. People were being ministered to, but no one was paying *him* any attention. Well, if there was ministering going on, he was damn well going to get ministered to as well.

He coughed loudly.

"You could try," he said, to the cruel world in general, "forcing some brandy between m'lips."

An apparition appeared above him holding a lamp over its head. It was a size five face in a size thirteen skin; it said "Oook?" in a concerned way.

"Oh, it's you," said Ridcully. He tried to sit up quickly, just in case the Librarian tried the kiss of life.

Confused memories wobbled across his brain. He could remember a wall of clanking metal, and then pinkness, and then . . . music. Endless music, designed to turn the living brain to cream cheese.

He turned around. There was a building behind him, surrounded by crowds of people. It was squat and clung to the ground in a strangely animal way, as if it might be possible to lift up a wing of the building and hear the pop-pop-pop of suckers letting go. Light streamed out of it, and steam curled out of its doors.

"Ridcully's woken up!"

More faces appeared. Ridcully thought: it's not Soul Cake Night, so they're not wearing masks. Oh, blast.

Behind them he heard the Dean say, "I vote we work up Herpetty's Seismic Reorganiser and lob it through the door. No more problem."

"No! We're too close to the city walls! We just need to drop Quondum's Attractive Point in the right place – "

"Or Sumpjumper's Incendiary Surprise, perhaps?" This was the Bursar's voice. "Burn it out, it's the best way – "

"Yeah? Yeah? And what do *you* know about military tactics? *You* can't even say 'yo' properly!"

212

Ridcully gripped the sides of the trolley.

"Would anyone mind tellin' me," he said, "what the – what the heck is goin' on?"

Ludmilla pushed her way through the members of the Fresh Start Club.

"You've got to stop them, Archchancellor!" she said. "They're talking about destroying the big shop!"

More nasty recollections settled on Ridcully's mind.

"Good idea," he said.

"But Mr Poons is still in there!"

Ridcully tried to focus on the glowing building.

"What, *dead* Windle Poons?"

"Arthur flew back when we realised he wasn't with us and he said Windle was fighting something that'd come out of the walls! We saw lots of trolleys but they weren't bothered about us! He let us get out!"

"What, dead Windle *Poons*?"

"You can't magic the place to bits with one of your wizards in there!"

"What, dead *Windle* Poons?"

"Yes!"

"But he's dead," said Ridcully. "Isn't he? He *said* he was."

"Ha!" said someone who had much less skin than Ridcully would have liked him to have. "That's typical. That's naked vitalism, that is. I bet they'd rescue someone in there if they happened to be *alive*."

"But he wanted . . . he wasn't keen on . . . he . . ." Ridcully hazarded. A lot of this was beyond him, but to people like Ridcully this didn't matter for very long. Ridcully was simple-minded. This doesn't mean stupid. It just meant that he could only think properly about things if he cut away all the complicated bits around the edges.

He concentrated on the single main fact. Someone who was technically a wizard was in trouble. He could relate to that. It struck a chord. The whole dead-or-alive business could wait.

There was another minor point that nagged at him, though.

". . . Arthur? . . . flew? . . ."

"Hallo."

Ridcully turned his head. He blinked slowly.

"Nice teeth you got there," he said.

"Thank you," said Arthur Winkings.

"All your own, are they?"

"Oh, yes."

"Amazing. Of course, I expect you brush regularly."

"Yes?"

"Hygienic. That's the important thing."

"So what are you going to *do*?" said Ludmilla.

"Well, we'll just go and fetch him out," said Ridcully. What was it about the girl? He felt a strange urge to pat her on the head. "We'll get some magic and get him out. Yes. Dean!"

"Yo!"

"We're just going to go in there to get Windle out."

"Yo!"

"*What*?" said the Senior Wrangler. "You must be out of your mind!"

Ridcully tried to look as dignified as possible, given his situation.

"Remember that I am your Archchancellor," he snapped.

"Then you must be out of your mind, Archchancellor!" said the Senior Wrangler. He lowered his voice. "Anyway, he's an undead. I don't see how you can save undeads. It's a sort of contradiction in terms."

"A dichotomy," said the Bursar helpfully.

"Oh, I don't think surgery is involved."

"Anyway, didn't we bury him?" said the Lecturer in Recent Runes.

"And now we dig him up again," said the Archchancellor. "It's probably a miracle of existence."

"Like pickles," said the Bursar, happily.

Even the Fresh Starters went blank.

"They do that in parts of Howondaland," said the Bursar. "They make these big, big jars of special pickles and then they bury them in the ground for months to ferment and they get this lovely piquant – "

"Tell me," Ludmilla whispered to Ridcully, "is this how wizards usually behave?"

"The Senior Wrangler is an amazingly fine example," said Ridcully. "Got the same urgent grasp of reality as a cardboard cut-out. Proud to have him on the team." He rubbed his hands together. "Okay, lads. Volunteers?"

"Yo! Hut!" said the Dean, who was in an entirely different world now.

"I would be remiss in my duty if I failed to help a brother," said Reg Shoe.

"Oook."

"You? We can't take *you*," said the Dean, glaring at the Librarian. "You don't know a thing about guerrilla warfare."

"Oook!" said the Librarian, and made a surprisingly comprehensive gesture to indicate that, on the other hand, what he didn't know about orangutan warfare could be written on the very small pounded-up remains of, for example, the Dean.

"Four of us should be enough," said the Archchancellor.

"I've never even heard him say 'Yo'," muttered the Dean.

He removed his hat, something a wizard doesn't ordinarily do unless he's about to pull something out of it, and handed it to the Bursar. Then he tore a thin strip off the bottom of his robe, held it dramatically in both hands, and tied it around his forehead.

"It's part of the ethos," he said, in answer to their penetratingly unspoken question. "That's what the warriors on the Counterweight Continent do before they go into battle. And you have to shout – " He tried to remember some far-off reading. "– er, bonsai. Yes. Bonsai!"

"*I* thought that meant chopping bits off trees to make them small," said the Senior Wrangler.

The Dean hesitated. He wasn't too sure himself, if it came to it. But a good wizard never let uncertainty stand in his way.

"No, it's definitely got to be bonsai," he said. He considered it some more and then brightened up. "On account of it all being part of bushido. Like . . . small trees. Bush-i-do. Yeah. Makes sense, when you think about it."

"But you can't shout 'bonsai!' *here*," said the Lecturer in Recent Runes. "We've got a totally different cultural background. It'd be useless. No one will know what you mean."

"I'll work on it," said the Dean.

He noticed Ludmilla standing with her mouth open.

"This is wizard talk," he said.

"It is, isn't it," said Ludmilla. "I never would have guessed."

The Archchancellor had got out of the trolley and was wheeling it experimentally back and forth. It usually took quite a long time for a fresh idea to fully lodge in Ridcully's mind, but he felt instinctively that there were all sorts of uses for a wire basket on four wheels.

"Are we going or are we standin' around all night bandagin' our heads?" he said.

"Yo!" snapped the Dean.

"Yo?" said Reg Shoe.

"Oook!"

"Was that a yo?" said the Dean, suspiciously.

"Oook."

"Well . . . all right, then."

Death sat on a mountaintop. It wasn't particularly high, or bare, or sinister. No witches held naked sabbats on it; Discworld witches, on the whole, didn't hold with taking off any more clothes than was absolutely necessary for the business in hand. No spectres haunted it. No naked little men sat on the summit dispensing wisdom, because the first thing the truly wise man works out is that sitting around on mountaintops gives you not only haemorrhoids but *frostbitten* haemorrhoids.

Occasionally people would climb the mountain and add a stone or two to the cairn at the top, if only to prove that there is nothing really damn stupid that humans won't do.

Death sat on the cairn and ran a stone down the blade of his scythe in long, deliberate strokes.

There was a movement of air. Three grey servants popped into existence.

One said, You think you have won?

One said, You think you have triumphed?

Death turned the stone in his hand, to get a fresh surface, and brought it slowly down the length of the blade.

One said, We will inform Azrael.

One said, You are only, after all, a *little* Death.

Death held the blade up to the moonlight, twisting it this way and that, noting the play of light on the tiny flecks of metal on its edge.

Then he stood up, in one quick movement. The servants backed away hurriedly.

He reached out with the speed of a snake and grasped a robe, pulling its empty hood level with his eye sockets.

DO YOU KNOW WHY THE PRISONER IN THE TOWER WATCHES THE FLIGHT OF BIRDS? he said.

It said, Take your hands off me . . . oops . . .

Blue flame flared for a moment.

Death lowered his hand and looked around at the other two.

One said, You haven't heard the last of this.

They vanished.

Death brushed a speck of ash off his robe, and then planted his feet squarely on the mountaintop. He raised the scythe over his head in both hands, and summoned all the lesser Deaths that had arisen in his absence.

After a while they streamed up the mountain in a faint black wave.

They flowed together like dark mercury.

It went on for a long time and then stopped.

Death lowered the scythe, and examined himself. Yes, all there. Once again, he was *the* Death, containing all the deaths of the world. Except for –

For a moment he hesitated. There was one tiny area of emptiness somewhere, some fragment of his soul, something unaccounted for . . .

He couldn't be quite certain what it was.

He shrugged. Doubtless he'd find out. In the meantime, there was a lot of work to be done . . .

He rode away.

Far off, in his den under the barn, the Death of Rats relaxed his determined grip on a beam.

Windle Poons brought both feet down heavily on a tentacle snaking out from under the tiles, and lurched off through the steam. A slab of marble smashed down, showering him with fragments. Then he kicked the wall, savagely.

There was very probably no way out now, he realised, and even if there was he couldn't find it. Anyway, he was already *inside* the thing. It was shaking its own walls down in an effort to get at him. At least he could give it a really bad case of indigestion.

217

He headed towards an orifice that had once been the entrance to a wide passage, and dived awkwardly through it just before it snapped shut. Silver fire crackled over the walls. There was so much life here it couldn't be contained.

There were a few trolleys still here, skittering madly across the shaking floor, as lost as Windle.

He set off along another likely-looking corridor, although most corridors he'd been down in the last one hundred and thirty years hadn't pulsated and dripped so much.

Another tentacle thrust through the wall and tripped him up.

Of course, it couldn't kill him. But it could make him bodiless. Like old One-Man-Bucket. A fate worse than death, probably.

He pulled himself up. The ceiling bounced down on him, flattening him against the floor.

He counted under his breath and scampered forward. Steam washed over him.

He slipped again, and thrust out his hands.

He could feel himself losing control. There were too many things to operate. Never mind the spleen, just keeping heart and lungs going was taking too much effort . . .

"*Topiary!*"

"What the heck do you mean?"

"Topiary! Get it? Yo!"

"Oook!"

Windle looked up through foggy eyes.

Ah. Obviously he was losing control of his brain, too.

A trolley came sideways out of the steam with shadowy figures clinging onto its sides. One hairy arm and one arm that was barely an arm any more reached down, picked him up bodily and dumped him into the basket. Four tiny wheels skidded on the floor, the trolley bounced off the wall, and then it righted itself and rattled away.

Windle was only vaguely aware of voices.

"Off you go, Dean. I know you've been looking forward to it." That was the Archchancellor.

"Yo!"

"You'll kill it totally? I don't think we want it ending up at the Fresh Start Club. I don't think it's a joiner." That was Reg Shoe.

"Oook!" That was the Librarian.

"Don't you worry, Windle. The Dean is going to do something military, apparently," said Ridcully.

"Yo! Hut!"

"Oh, good grief."

Windle saw the Dean's hand float past with something glittering in it.

"What are you going to use?" said Ridcully, as the trolley rocketed through the steam. "The Seismic Reorganiser, the Attractive Point or the Incendiary Surprise?"

"Yo," said the Dean, with satisfaction.

"What, all three at once?"

"Yo!"

"That's going a bit far, isn't it? And incidentally, if you say 'yo' one more time, Dean, I will personally have you thrown out of the University, pursued to the rim of the world by the finest demons that thaumaturgy can conjure up, torn into extremely small pieces, minced, turned into a mixture reminiscent of steak tartare, and turned out into a dog bowl."

"Y– " The Dean caught Ridcully's eye. "Yes. Yes? Oh, go on, Archchancellor. What's the good of having mastery over cosmic balance and knowing the secrets of fate if you can't blow something up? Please? I've got them all ready. You know how it upsets the inventory if you don't use them after you've got them ready – "

The trolley whirred up a trembling slope and cornered on two wheels.

"Oh, all right," said Ridcully. "If it means that much to you."

"Y– sorry."

The Dean started to mutter urgently under his breath, and then screamed.

"I've gone blind!"

"Your bonsai bandage has slipped over your eyes, Dean."

Windle groaned.

"How are you feeling, brother Poons?" Reg Shoe's ravaged features occluded Windle's view.

"Oh, you know," said Windle. "Could be better, could be worse."

The trolley ricocheted off a wall and jerked away in another direction.

"How are those spells coming along, Dean?" said Ridcully, through gritted teeth. "I'm having real difficulties controlling this thing."

The Dean muttered a few more words, and then waved his hands dramatically. Octarine flame spurted from his fingertips and earthed itself somewhere in the mists.

"Yee-haw!" he crowed.

"Dean?"

"Yes, Archchancellor?"

"The comment I made recently about the Y-word . . ."

"Yes? Yes?"

"You can definitely include Yee-haw, too."

The Dean hung his head.

"Oh. Yes, Archchancellor."

"And why hasn't everythin' gone boom?"

"I put a slight delay on it, Archchancellor. I thought perhaps we ought to get out before things happened."

"Good thinking, that man."

"Soon have you out, Windle," said Reg Shoe. "We don't leave our people in there. Isn't this – "

And then the floor erupted ahead of them.

And then, behind them.

The thing that arose from the shattered tiles was either formless or many forms at once. It writhed angrily, snapping its tubing at them.

The trolley skewed to a halt.

"Got any more magic, Dean?"

"Er . . . no, Archchancellor."

"And the spells you just said will go off . . . ?"

"Any second now, Archchancellor."

"So . . . whatever's going to happen . . . is going to happen to us?"

"*Yes*, Archchancellor."

Ridcully patted Windle on the head.

"Sorry about this," he said.

Windle turned awkwardly to look down the passageway.

There was something behind the Queen. It looked like a perfectly ordinary bedroom door, advancing in a series of small steps, as though someone was carefully pushing it along in front of them.

"What is it?" said Reg.

Windle raised himself as far as he could.

"Schleppel!"

"Oh, come *on*," said Reg.

"It's Schleppel!" shouted Windle. "*Schleppel!* It's us! Can you help us out?"

The door paused. Then it was flung aside.

Schleppel unfolded himself to his full height.

"Hallo, Mr Poons. Hallo, Reg," he said.

They stared at the hairy shape that nearly filled the passageway.

"Er, Schleppel . . . er . . . could you clear the way for us?" Windle quavered.

"*No* problem, Mr Poons. Anything for a friend."

A hand the size of a wheelbarrow glided through the steam and tore into the blockage, ripping it out with incredible ease.

"Hey, look at me!" said Schleppel. "You're right. A bogeyman needs a door like a fish needs a bicycle! Say it now and say it loud, I'm – "

"And now could you get out of the way, please?"

"Sure. Sure. Wow!" Schleppel took another swipe at the Queen. The trolley shot forward.

"And you'd better come with us!" Windle shouted, as Schleppel disappeared in the mists.

"No he shouldn't," said the Archchancellor, as they sped along. "Believe me. What *was* it?"

"He's a bogeyman," said Windle.

"I thought you only get them in closets and things?" shouted Ridcully.

"He's come out of the closet," said Reg Shoe proudly. "And he's found himself."

"Just so long as *we* can lose him."

"We can't just leave him – "

"We can! We can!" snapped Ridcully.

There was a sound behind them like an eruption of swamp gas. Green light streamed past.

"The spells are starting to go off!" shouted the Dean. "Move it!"

The trolley whirred out of the entrance and soared up into the cool of the night, wheels screaming.

221

"Yo!" bellowed Ridcully, as the crowd scattered ahead of them.

"Does that mean *I* can say yo too?" said the Dean.

"All right. Just once. Everyone can say it just once."

"Yo!"

"Yo!" echoed Reg Shoe.

"Oook!"

"Yo!" said Windle Poons.

"Yo!" said Schleppel.

(Somewhere in the darkness, where the crowd was thinnest, the gaunt shape of Mr Ixolite, the world's last surviving banshee, sidled up to the shaking building and bashfully shoved a note under the door.

It said: OOOOeeeOOOeeeOOOeee.)

The trolley ploughed to a very definitive stop. No one turned around. Reg said, slowly: "You're behind us, right?"

"That's right, Mr Shoe," said Schleppel happily.

"Should we worry when he's in front of us?" said Ridcully, "Or is it worse because we know he's behind us?"

"Hah! No more closets and cellars for *this* bogey," said Schleppel.

"That's a shame, because we've got some really *big* cellars at the University," said Windle Poons quickly.

Schleppel was silent for a while. Then he said, in an exploratory tone of voice, "How big?"

"Huge."

"Yeah? With rats?"

"Rats aren't the half of it. There's escaped demons and all sorts down there. Infested, they are."

"What are you doing?" hissed Ridcully. "That's *our* cellars you're talking about!"

"You'd prefer him under your bed, would you?" murmured Windle. "Or walking around behind you?"

Ridcully nodded briskly.

"Wow, yes, those rats are getting really out of hand down there," he said loudly. "Some of them – oh, about two feet long, wouldn't you say, Dean?"

"Three feet," said the Dean. "At least."

"Fat as butter, too," said Windle.

Schleppel gave this some thought. "Well, all right," he said reluctantly. "Maybe I'll just wander in and have a look at them."

The big store exploded and imploded at the same time, something it is almost impossible to achieve without a huge special effects budget or three spells all working against one another. There was the impression of a vast cloud expanding but at the same time moving away so rapidly that the overall effect was of a shrinking point. Walls buckled and were sucked in. Soil ripped up from the ravaged fields and spiralled into the vortex. There was a violent burst of non-music, which died almost instantly.

And then nothing, except a muddy field.

And, floating down from the early morning sky like snow, thousands of white flakes. They slid silently through the air and landed lightly on the crowd.

"It's not seeding, is it?" said Reg Shoe.

Windle grabbed one of the flakes. It was a crude rectangle, uneven and blotchy. It was just about possible, with a certain amount of imagination, to make out the words:

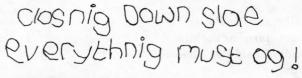

"No," said Windle. "Probably not."

He lay back and smiled. It was never too late to have a good life.

And when no one was looking, the last surviving trolley on the Discworld rattled off sadly into the oblivion of the night, lost and alone.*

"Pog-a-grodle-fig!"

Miss Flitworth sat in her kitchen.

* It is generally thought, on those worlds where the mall lifeform has seeded, that people take the wire baskets away and leave them in strange and isolated places, so that squads of young men have to be employed to gather them together and wheel them back. This is exactly the opposite of the truth. In reality the men are hunters, stalking their rattling prey across the landscape, trapping them, breaking their spirit, taming them and herding them to a life of slavery. Possibly.

Outside, she could hear the despondent clanking as Ned Simnel and his apprentice picked up the tangled remains of the Combination Harvester. A handful of other people were theoretically helping, but were really taking the opportunity to have a good look around. She'd made a tray of tea, and left them to it.

Now she sat with her chin in her hands, staring at nothing.

There was a knock at the open door. Spigot poked his red face into the room.

"Please, Miss Flitworth – "

"Hmm?"

"Please, Miss Flitworth, there's a skeleton of a horse walking around in the barn! It's eating hay!"

"How?"

"And it's all falling through!"

"Really? We'll keep it, then. At least it'll be cheap to feed."

Spigot hung around for a while, twisting his hat in his hands.

"You all right, Miss Flitworth?"

"You all right, Mr Poons?"

Windle stared at nothing.

"Windle?" said Reg Shoe.

"Hmm?"

"The Archchancellor just asked if you wanted a drink."

"He'd like a glass of distilled water," said Mrs Cake.

"What, just water?" said Ridcully.

"That's what he wants," said Mrs Cake.

"I'd like a glass of distilled water, please," said Windle.

Mrs Cake looked smug. At least, as much of her as was visible looked smug, which was that part between the Hat and her handbag, which was a sort of counterpart of the hat and so big that when she sat clasping it on her lap she had to reach up to hold the handles. When she'd heard that her daughter had been invited to the University she'd come too. Mrs Cake always assumed that an invitation to Ludmilla was an invitation to Ludmilla's mother as well. Mothers like her exist everywhere, and apparently nothing can be done about them.

The Fresh Starters were being entertained by the wizards, and trying to look as though they were enjoying it. It was one of those problematical occasions with long silences, sporadic coughs, and people saying isolated things like, "Well, isn't this nice."

"You looked a bit lost there, Windle, for a moment," said Ridcully.

"I'm just a bit tired, Archchancellor."

"I thought you zombies never slept."

"I'm still tired," said Windle.

"You're sure you wouldn't like us to have another go with the burial and everything? We could do it properly this time."

"Thank you all the same, but no. I'm just not cut out for the undead life, I think." Windle looked at Reg Shoe. "Sorry about that. I don't know how you manage it." He grinned apologetically.

"You've got every right to be alive or dead, just as you choose," said Reg severely.

"One-Man-Bucket says people are dying properly again," said Mrs Cake. "So you could probably get an appointment."

Windle looked around.

"She's taken your dog for a walk," said Mrs Cake.

"Where's Ludmilla?" he said.

Windle smiled awkwardly. Mrs Cake's premonitions could be very wearing.

"It'd be nice to know that Lupine was being looked after if I . . . went," he said. "I wonder, could you take him in?"

"Well . . ." said Mrs Cake uncertainly.

"But he's – " Reg Shoe began, and then saw Windle's expression.

"I must admit it'd be a relief to have a dog around the place," said Mrs Cake. "I'm always worrying about Ludmilla. There's a lot of strange people around."

"But your dau– " Reg began again.

"Shut up, Reg," said Doreen.

"That's all settled, then," said Windle. "And have you got any trousers?"

"What?"

"Any trousers in the house?"

"Well, I suppose I've got some that belonged to the late Mr Cake, but why – "

"Sorry," said Windle. "My mind was wandering. Don't know what I'm saying, half the time."

"Ah," said Reg, brightly, "I *see*. What you're saying is that when he – "

Doreen nudged him viciously.

"Oh," said Reg. "Sorry. Don't mind me. I'd forget my own head if it wasn't sewn on."

Windle leaned back, and shut his eyes. He could hear the occasional scrap of conversation. He could hear Arthur Winkings asking the Archchancellor who did his decorating, and where the University got its vegetables. He heard the Bursar moaning about the cost of exterminating all the cursewords, which had somehow survived the recent changes and had taken up residence in the darkness of the roof. He could even, if he strained his perfect hearing, hear the whoops of Schleppel in the distant cellars.

They didn't need him. At last. The world didn't need Windle Poons.

He got up quietly and lurched to the door.

"I'm just going out," he said. "I may be some time."

Ridcully gave him a half-hearted nod, and concentrated on what Arthur had to say about how the Great Hall could be entirely transformed with some pine-effect wallpaper.

Windle shut the door behind him and leaned against the thick, cool wall.

Oh, yes. There was one other thing.

"Are you there, One-Man-Bucket?" he said softly.

how did you know?

"You're generally around."

heh heh, you've caused some real trouble there! you know what's going to happen next full moon?

"Yes, I do. And I think, somehow, that they do too."

but he'll become a wolfman.

"Yes. And she'll become a wolfwoman."

all right, but what kind of relationship can people have one week in four?

"Maybe at least as good a chance of happiness as most people get. Life isn't perfect, One-Man-Bucket."

you're telling me?

"Now, can I ask you a personal question?" said Windle. "I mean I've just *got* to know . . ."

huh.

"After all, you've got the astral plane to yourself again."

oh, all right.

"Why are you called One – "

is that all? I thought you could work that one out, a clever man like you. in my tribe we're traditionally named after the first thing the mother sees when she looks out of the teepee after the birth. it's short for One-Man-Pouring-a-Bucket-of-Water-over-Two-Dogs.

"That's pretty unfortunate," said Windle.

it's not too bad, said One-Man-Bucket. *it was my twin brother you had to feel sorry for. she looked out ten seconds before me to give him* his *name.*

Windle Poons thought about it.

"Don't tell me, let me guess," he said. "Two-Dogs-Fighting?"

Two-Dogs-Fighting? Two-Dogs Fighting? said One-Man-Bucket. *wow, he'd have given his right arm to be called Two-Dogs-*Fighting.

It was later that the story of Windle Poons really came to an end, if "story" means all that he did and caused and set in motion. In the Ramtop village where they dance the real Morris dance, for example, they believe that no one is finally dead until the ripples they cause in the world die away – until the clock he wound up winds down, until the wine she made has finished its ferment, until the crop they planted is harvested. The span of someone's life, they say, is only the core of their actual existence.

As he walked through the foggy city to an appointment he had been awaiting ever since he was born, Windle felt that he could predict that final end.

It would be in a few weeks' time, when the moon was full again. A sort of codicil or addendum to the life of Windle Poons – born in the year of the Significant Triangle in the Century of the Three Lice (he'd always preferred the old calendar with its ancient names to all this new-fangled numbering they did today) and died in the year of the Notional Serpent in the Century of the Fruitbat, more or less.

227

There'd be two figures running across the high moorland under the moon. Not entirely wolves, not entirely human. With any luck, they'd have best of both worlds. Not just feeling . . . but knowing. Always best to have both worlds.

Death sat in his chair in his dark study, his hands steepled in front of his face.

Occasionally he'd swivel the chair backwards and forwards.

Albert brought him in a cup of tea and exited with diplomatic soundlessness.

There was one lifetimer left on Death's desk. He stared at it.

Swivel, swivel. Swivel, swivel.

In the hall outside, the great clock ticked on, killing time.

Death drummed his skeletal fingers on the desk's scarred woodwork. In front of him, stacked up with impromptu bookmarks in their pages, were the lives of some of the Discworld's great lovers.* Their fairly repetitive experiences hadn't been any help at all.

He got up and stalked to a window and stared out at his dark domain, his hands clenching and unclenching behind his back.

Then he snatched up the lifetimer and strode out of the room.

Binky was waiting in the warm fug of the stables. Death saddled him quickly and led him out into the courtyard, and then rode up into the night, towards the distant glittering jewel of the Discworld.

He touched down silently in the farmyard, at sunset.

He drifted through a wall.

He reached the foot of the stairs.

He raised the hourglass and watched the draining of Time.

And then he paused. There was something he had to know. Bill Door had been curious about things, and he could remember everything about being Bill Door. He could look at emotions laid out like trapped butterflies, pinned on cork, under glass.

Bill Door was dead, or at least had ceased his brief existence. But – what was it? – someone's actual life was only the core of their real existence?

---

* The most enthusiastic of these was the small but persistent and incredibly successful Casanunder the Dwarf, a name mentioned with respect and awe wherever stepladder owners are gathered together.

Bill Door had gone, but he had left echoes. The memory of Bill Door was owed something.

Death had always wondered why people put flowers on graves. It made no sense to him. The dead had gone beyond the scent of roses, after all. But now . . . it wasn't that he felt he understood, but at least he felt that there was something there capable of understanding.

In the curtained blackness of Miss Flitworth's parlour a darker shape moved through the darkness, heading towards the three chests on the dresser.

Death opened one of the smaller ones. It was full of gold coins. They had an untouched look about them. He tried the other small chest. It was also full of gold.

He'd expected something more from Miss Flitworth, although probably not even Bill Door would have known what.

He tried the large chest.

There was a layer of tissue paper. Under the paper, some white silky thing, some sort of a veil, now yellowed and brittle with age. He gave it an uncomprehending stare and laid it aside. There were some white shoes. Quite impractical for farm wear, he felt. No wonder they'd been packed away.

There was more paper; a bundle of letters tied together. He put them on top of the veil. There was never anything to be gained from observing what humans said to one another – language was just there to hide their thoughts.

And then there was, right at the bottom, a smaller box. He pulled it out and turned it over and over in his hands. Then he unclicked the little latch and lifted the lid.

Clockwork whirred.

The tune wasn't particularly good. Death had heard all the music that had ever been written, and almost all of it had been better than this tune. It had a plinkety plonkety quality, a tinny little one-two-three rhythm.

In the musical box, over the busily spinning gears, two wooden dancers jerked around in a parody of a waltz.

Death watched them until the clockwork ran down. Then he read the inscription.

It had been a present.

Beside him, the lifetimer poured its grains into the bottom bulb. He ignored it.

When the clockwork ran down, he wound it up again. Two figures, spinning through time. And when the music stopped, all you needed was to turn the key.

When it ran down again, he sat in the silence and the dark, and reached a decision.

There were only seconds left. Seconds had meant a lot to Bill Door, because he'd had a limited supply. They meant nothing at all to Death, who'd never had any.

He left the sleeping house, mounted up, and rode away.

The journey took an instant that would have taken mere light three hundred million years, but Death travels inside that space where Time has no meaning. Light thinks it travels faster than anything but it is wrong. No matter how fast light travels it finds the darkness has always got there first, and is waiting for it.

There was company on the ride – galaxies, stars, ribbons of shining matter, streaming and eventually spiralling towards the distant goal.

Death on his pale horse moved down the darkness like a bubble on a river.

And every river flows somewhere.

And then, below, a plain. Distance was as meaningless here as time, but there was a sense of hugeness. The plain could have been a mile away, or a million miles; it was marked by long valleys or rills which flowed away to either side as he got closer.

And landed.

He dismounted, and stood in the silence. Then he went down on one knee.

Change the perspective. The furrowed landscape falls away into immense distances, curves at the edges, becomes a fingertip.

Azrael raised his finger to a face that filled the sky, lit by the faint glow of dying galaxies.

There are a billion Deaths, but they are all aspects of the one Death: Azrael, the Great Attractor, the Death of Universes, the beginning and end of time.

Most of the universe is made up of dark matter, and only Azrael knows who it is.

Eyes so big that a supernova would be a mere suggestion of a gleam on the iris turned slowly and focused on the tiny figure on the immense whorled plains of his fingertips. Beside Azrael the big Clock hung in the centre of the entire web of the dimensions, and ticked onward. Stars glittered in Azrael's eyes.

The Death of the Discworld stood up.

LORD, I ASK FOR –

Three of the servants of oblivion slid into existence alongside him.

One said, Do not listen. He stands accused of meddling.

One said, And morticide.

One said, And pride. And living with intent to survive.

One said, And siding with chaos against good order.

Azrael raised an eyebrow.

The servants drifted away from Death, expectantly.

LORD, WE KNOW THERE IS NO GOOD ORDER EXCEPT THAT WHICH WE CREATE . . .

Azrael's expression did not change.

THERE IS NO HOPE BUT US. THERE IS NO MERCY BUT US. THERE IS NO JUSTICE. THERE IS JUST US.

The dark, sad face filled the sky.

ALL THINGS THAT ARE, ARE OURS. BUT WE MUST CARE. FOR IF WE DO NOT CARE, WE DO NOT EXIST. IF WE DO NOT EXIST, THEN THERE IS NOTHING BUT BLIND OBLIVION.

AND EVEN OBLIVION MUST END SOME DAY. LORD, WILL YOU GRANT ME JUST A LITTLE TIME? FOR THE PROPER BALANCE OF THINGS. TO RETURN WHAT WAS GIVEN. FOR THE SAKE OF PRISONERS AND THE FLIGHT OF BIRDS.

Death took a step backwards.

It was impossible to read expression in Azrael's features.

Death glanced sideways at the servants.

LORD, WHAT CAN THE HARVEST HOPE FOR, IF NOT FOR THE CARE OF THE REAPER MAN?

He waited.

LORD? said Death.

In the time it took to answer, several galaxies unfolded, whirled around Azrael like paper streamers, impacted, and were gone.

Then Azrael said:

YES.

And another finger reached out across the darkness towards the Clock.

There were faint screams of rage from the servants, and then screams of realisation, and then three brief, blue flames.

All other clocks, even the handless clock of Death, were reflections of the Clock. Exactly reflections of the Clock; they told the universe what the time was, but the Clock told Time what time is. It was the mainspring from which all time poured.

And the design of the Clock was this: that the biggest hand only went around once.

The second hand whirred along a circular path that even light would take days to travel, forever chased by the minutes, hours, days, months, years, centuries and ages. But the Universe hand went around once.

At least, until someone wound up the clockwork.

And Death returned home with a handful of Time.

A shop bell jangled.

Druto Pole, florist, looked over a spray of *floribunda Mrs Shover*. Someone was standing among the vases of flowers. They looked slightly indistinct; in fact, even afterwards, Druto was never sure who had been in his shop and how his words had actually sounded.

He oiled forward, rubbing his hands.

"How may I hel– "

FLOWERS.

Druto hesitated only for a moment.

"And the, er, destination for these – "

A LADY.

"And do you have any pref– "

LILIES.

"Ah? Are you sure that lilies are – ?"

I LIKE LILIES.

"Um . . . it's just that lilies are a little bit sombre – "

I LIKE SOMB–

The figure hesitated.

WHAT DO YOU RECOMMEND?

Druto slipped smoothly into gear. "Roses are always very well received," he said. "Or orchids. Many gentlemen these days tell me that ladies find a single specimen orchid more acceptable than a bunch of roses – "

GIVE ME LOTS.

"Would that be orchids or roses?"

BOTH.

Druto's fingers twined sinuously, like eels in grease.

"And I wonder if I could interest you in these marvellous sprays of *Nervousa Gloriosa* – "

LOTS OF THEM.

"And if Sir's budget would stretch, may I suggest a single specimen of the extremely rare – "

YES.

"And possibly – "

YES. EVERYTHING. WITH A RIBBON.

When the shop bell had jangled the purchaser out, Druto looked at the coins in his hand. Many of them were corroded, all of them were strange, and one or two were golden.

"Um," he said. "That will do nicely . . ."

He became aware of a soft pattering sound.

Around him, all over the shop, petals were falling like rain.

AND THESE?

"That's our De Luxe assortment," said the lady in the chocolate shop. It was such a high-class establishment that it sold, not sweets, but confectionery – often in the form of individual gold-wrapped swirly things that made even larger holes in a bank balance than they did in a tooth.

The tall dark customer picked up a box that was about two feet square. On a lid like a satin cushion it had a picture of a couple of hopelessly cross-eyed kittens looking out of a boot.

WHAT FOR IS THIS BOX PADDED? IS IT TO BE SAT ON? CAN IT BE THAT IT IS CAT-FLAVOURED? he added, his tone taking on a definite menace, or rather more menace than it had already.

"Um, no. That's our Supreme Assortment."

The customer tossed it aside.

NO.

The shopkeeper looked both ways and then pulled open a drawer under the counter, at the same time lowering her voice to a conspiratorial whisper. "Of course," she said, "for that *very special* occasion . . ."

It was quite a small box. It was also entirely black, except for the name of the contents in small white letters; cats, even in pink ribbons, wouldn't be allowed within a mile of a box like this. To deliver a box of chocolates like this, dark strangers drop from chairlifts and abseil down buildings.

The dark stranger peered at the lettering.

"DARK ENCHANTMENTS", he said. I *LIKE* IT.

"For those intimate moments," said the lady.

The customer appeared to consider the relevance of this.

YES. THAT SEEMS APPROPRIATE.

The shopkeeper beamed.

"Shall I wrap them up, then?"

YES. WITH A RIBBON.

"And will there be anything else, sir?"

The customer seemed to panic.

ELSE? SHOULD THERE BE ANYTHING ELSE? IS THERE SOMETHING ELSE? WHAT IS IT THAT SHOULD BE DONE?

"I'm sorry, sir?"

A PRESENT FOR A LADY.

The shopkeeper was left a little adrift by this sudden turning of the tide of conversation. She swam towards a reliable cliché.

"Well, they do say, don't they, that diamonds are a girl's best friend?" she said brightly.

DIAMONDS? OH. DIAMONDS. IS THAT SO?

They glittered like bits of starlight on a black velvet sky.

"This one," said the merchant, "is a particularly excellent stone, don't you think? Note the fire, the exceptional – "

HOW FRIENDLY IS IT?

The merchant hesitated. He knew about carats, about adamantine lustre, about "water" and "make" and "fire", but he'd never before been called upon to judge gems in terms of general affability.

"Quite well-disposed?" he hazarded.

NO.

The merchant's fingers seized on another splinter of frozen light.

"Now *this*," he said, confidence flowing back into his voice, "is from the famous Shortshanks mine. May I draw your attention to the exquisite – "

He felt the penetrating stare drill through the back of his head.

"But not, I must admit, noted for its friendliness," he said lamely.

The dark customer looked disapprovingly around the shop. In the gloom, behind troll-proof bars, gems glowed like the eyes of dragons in the back of a cave.

ARE ANY OF THESE FRIENDLY? he said.

"Sir, I think I can say, without fear of contradiction, that we have never based our purchasing policy on the amiability of the stones in question," said the merchant. He was uncomfortably aware that things were wrong, and that somewhere in the back of his mind he knew what was wrong with them, and that somehow his mind was not letting him make that final link. And it was getting on his nerves.

WHERE IS THE BIGGEST DIAMOND IN THE WORLD?

"The biggest? That's easy. It's the Tear of Offler, it's in the innermost sanctuary of the Lost Jewelled Temple of Doom of Offler the Crocodile God in darkest Howandaland, and it weighs eight hundred and fifty carats. And, sir, to forestall your next question, I personally would go to bed with it."

One of the nice things about being a priest in the Lost Jewelled Temple of Doom of Offler the Crocodile God was that you got to go home early most afternoons. This was because it was lost. Most worshippers never found their way there. They were the lucky ones.

Traditionally, only two people ever went into the innermost sanctuary. They were the High Priest and the other priest who wasn't High. They had been there for years, and took turns at being the high one. It was an undemanding job, given that most prospective worshippers were impaled, squashed, poisoned or sliced by booby-traps even before making it as far as the little box and the jolly drawing of a thermometer* outside the vestry.

They were playing Cripple Mr Onion on the high altar, beneath the very shadow of the jewel-encrusted statue of Offler Himself, when they heard the distant creak of the main door.

The High Priest didn't look up.

---

* "Lost Jewelled Temple Roof Repair Fund! Only 6,000 gold pieces to go!! Please Give Generously!! Thankyou!!!"

"Heyup," he said. "Another one for the big rolling ball, then."

There was a thump and a rumbling, grinding sound. And then a very final bang.

"Now," said the High Priest. "What was the stake?"

"Two pebbles," said the low priest.

"Right." The High Priest peered at his cards. "Okay, I'll see your two peb– "

There was the faint sound of footsteps.

"Chap with a whip got as far as the big sharp spikes last week," said the low priest.

There was a sound like the flushing of a very old dry lavatory. The footsteps stopped.

The High Priest smiled to himself.

"Right," he said. "See your two pebbles and raise you two pebbles."

The low priest threw down his cards.

"Double Onion," he said.

The High Priest looked down suspiciously.

The low priest consulted a scrap of paper.

"That's three hundred thousand, nine hundred and sixty-four pebbles you owe me," he said.

There was the sound of footsteps.

The priests exchanged glances.

"Haven't had one for poisoned-dart alley for quite some time," said the High Priest.

"Five says he makes it," said the low priest.

"You're on."

There was a faint clatter of metal points on stone.

"It's a shame to take your pebbles."

There were footsteps again.

"All right, but there's still the – " a creak, a splash " – the crocodile tank."

There were footsteps.

"No one's *ever* got past the dreaded guardian of the portals – "

The priests looked into one another's horrified faces.

"Hey," said the one who was not High. "You don't think it could be – "

"Here? Oh, come *on*. We're in the middle of a godsdamn *jungle*." The High Priest tried to smile. "There's no way it could be – "

The footsteps got nearer.

The priests clutched at one another in terror.

"*Mrs Cake!*"

The doors exploded inwards. A dark wind drove into the room, blowing out the candles and scattering the cards like polka-dot snow.

The priests heard the chink of a very large diamond being lifted out of its socket.

THANK YOU.

After a while, when nothing else seemed to be happening, the priest who wasn't High managed to find a tinder box and, after several false starts, got a candle alight.

The two priests looked up through the dancing shadows at the statue, where a hole now gaped that should have contained a very large diamond.

After a while, the High Priest sighed and said, "Well, look at it like this: apart from us, who's going to know?"

"Yeah. Never thought of it like that. Hey, can I be High Priest tomorrow?"

"It's not your turn until Thursday."

"Oh, come on."

The High Priest shrugged, and removed his High Priesting hat.

"It's very depressing, this kind of thing," he said, glancing up at the ravaged statue. "Some people just don't know how to behave in a house of religion."

Death sped across the world, landing once again in the farmyard. The sun was on the horizon when he knocked on the kitchen door.

Miss Flitworth opened it, wiping her hands on her apron. She grimaced short-sightedly at the visitor, and then took a step back.

"Bill Door? You gave me quite a start – "

I HAVE BROUGHT YOU SOME FLOWERS.

She stared at the dry, dead stems.

ALSO SOME CHOCOLATE ASSORTMENT, THE SORT LADIES LIKE.

She stared at the black box.

ALSO HERE IS A DIAMOND TO BE FRIENDS WITH YOU.

It caught the last rays of the setting sun.

Miss Flitworth finally found her voice.

"Bill Door, what are you thinking of?"

I HAVE COME TO TAKE YOU AWAY FROM ALL THIS.

238

"You have? Where to?"

Death hadn't thought this far.

WHERE WOULD YOU LIKE?

"I ain't proposing to go anywhere tonight except to the dance," said Miss Flitworth firmly.

Death hadn't planned for this, either.

WHAT IS THIS DANCE?

"Harvest dance. You know? It's tradition. When the harvest is in. It's a sort of celebration, and like a thanksgiving."

THANKSGIVING TO WHO?

"Dunno. No one in particular, I reckon. Just general thankfulness, I suppose."

I HAD PLANNED TO SHOW YOU MARVELS. FINE CITIES. ANYTHING YOU WANTED.

"Anything?"

YES.

"Then we're going to the dance, Bill Door. I always go every year. They rely on me. You know how it is."

YES, MISS FLITWORTH.

He reached out and took her hand.

"What, you mean now?" she said, "I'm not ready – "

LOOK.

She looked down at what she was suddenly wearing.

"That's not my dress. It's got all glitter on it."

Death sighed. The great lovers of history had never encountered Miss Flitworth. Casanunder would have handed in his stepladder.

THEY'RE DIAMONDS. A KING'S RANSOM IN DIAMONDS.

"Which king?"

ANY KING.

"Coo."

Binky walked easily along the road to the town. After the length of infinity, a mere dusty road was a bit of a relief.

Sitting sidesaddle behind Death, Miss Flitworth explored the rustling contents of the box of Dark Enchantments.

"Here," she said, "someone's had all the rum truffles." There was another crackle of paper. "*And* from the bottom layer, too. I hate that, people starting the bottom layer before the top one's been properly finished. And I can tell you've been doing it because there's a little map in the lid and by rights there should be rum truffles. Bill Door?"

I'M SORRY, MISS FLITWORTH.

"This big diamond's a bit heavy. Nice, though," she added, grudgingly. "Where'd you get it?"

FROM PEOPLE WHO THOUGHT IT WAS THE TEAR OF A GOD.

"And is it?"

NO. GODS NEVER WEEP. IT IS COMMON CARBON THAT HAS BEEN SUBJECT TO GREAT HEAT AND PRESSURE, THAT IS ALL.

"Inside every lump of coal there's a diamond waiting to get out, right?"

YES, MISS FLITWORTH.

There was no sound for a while, except the clip-clop of Binky's hoofs. Then Miss Flitworth said, archly:

"I do know what's going on, you know. I saw how much sand there was. And so you thought 'She's not a bad old stick, I'll show her a good time for a few hours, and then when she's not expecting it, it'll be time for the old cut-de-grass', am I right?"

Death said nothing.

"I am right, aren't I?"

I CAN'T HIDE ANYTHING FROM YOU, MISS FLITWORTH.

"Huh. I suppose I should be flattered. Yes? I expect you've got a lot of calls on your time."

MORE THAN YOU COULD POSSIBLY IMAGINE, MISS FLITWORTH.

"In the circumstances, then, you might as well go back to calling me Renata again."

There was a bonfire in the meadow beyond the archery field. Death could see figures moving in front of it. An occasional tortured squeak suggested that someone was tuning up a fiddle.

"I always come along to the harvest dance," said Miss Flitworth, conversationally. "Not to dance, of course. I generally look after the food and so on."

WHY?

"Well, someone's got to look after the food."

I MEANT WHY DON'T YOU DANCE?

"'Cos I'm old, that's why."

YOU ARE AS OLD AS YOU THINK YOU ARE.

"Huh! Yeah? Really? That's the kind of *stupid* thing people always say.

240

They always say, My word, you're looking well. They say, There's life in the old dog yet. Many a good tune played on an old fiddle. That kind of stuff. It's all stupid. As if being old was some kind of thing you should be glad about! As if being philosophical about it will earn you *marks*! My head knows how to think young, but my knees aren't that good at it. Or my back. Or my teeth. Try telling my knees they're as old as they think they are and see what good it does you. Or them."

IT MAY BE WORTH A TRY.

More figures moved in front of the firelight. Death could see striped poles strung with bunting.

"The lads usually bring a couple of barn doors down here and nail 'em together for a proper floor," observed Miss Flitworth. "Then everyone can join in."

FOLK DANCING? said Death, wearily.

"No. We have *some* pride, you know."

SORRY.

"Hey, it's Bill Door, isn't it?" said a figure looming out of the dusk. "It's good old Bill!"

"Hey, Bill!"

Death looked at a circle of guileless faces.

HALLO, MY FRIENDS.

"We heard you'd gone away," said Duke Bottomley. He glanced at Miss Flitworth, as Death helped her down from the horse. His voice faltered a bit as he tried to analyse the situation.

"You're looking very . . . sparkly . . . tonight, Miss Flitworth," he finished, gallantly.

The air smelled of warm, damp grass. An amateur orchestra was still setting up under an awning.

There were trestle tables covered with the kind of food that's normally associated with the word "repast" – pork pies like varnished military fortifications, vats of demonical pickled onions, jacket potatoes wallowing in a cholesterol ocean of melted butter. Some of the local elders had already established themselves on the benches provided, and were chewing stoically if toothlessly through the food with the air of people determined to sit there all night, if necessary.

"Nice to see the old people enjoying themselves," said Miss Flitworth.

Death looked at the eaters. Most of them were younger than Miss Flitworth.

241

There was a giggle from somewhere in the scented darkness beyond the firelight.

"And the young people," Miss Flitworth added, evenly. "We used to have a saying about this time of year. Let's see . . . something like 'Corn be ripe, nuts be brown, petticoats up . . .' something." She sighed. "Don't time fly, eh?"

YES.

"You know, Bill Door, maybe you were right about the power of positive thinking. I feel a lot better tonight."

YES?

Miss Flitworth looked speculatively at the dance floor. "I used to be a great dancer when I was a gel. I could dance anyone off their feet. I could dance down the moon. I could dance the sun up."

She reached up and removed the bands that held her hair in its tight bun, and shook it out in a waterfall of white.

"I take it you *do* dance, Mr Bill Door?"

FAMED FOR IT, MISS FLITWORTH.

Under the band's awning, the lead fiddler nodded to his fellow musicians, stuck his fiddle under his chin, and pounded on the boards with his foot –

"Hwun! Htwo! Hwun htwo three four . . ."

Picture a landscape, with the orange light of a crescent moon drifting across it. And, down below, a circle of firelight in the night.

There were the old favourites – the square dances, the reels, the whirling, intricate measures which, if the dancers had carried lights, would have traced out topological complexities beyond the reach of ordinary physics, and the sort of dances that lead perfectly sane people to shout out things like "Do-si-do!" and "Och-aye!" without feeling massively ashamed for quite a long time.

When the casualties were cleared away the survivors went on to polka, mazurka, fox-trot, turkey-trot and trot a variety of other birds and beasts, and then to those dances where people form an arch and other people dance down it, which are incidentally generally based on folk memories of executions, and other dances where people form a circle, which are generally based on folk memories of plagues.

Through it all two figures whirled as though there was no tomorrow.

The lead fiddler was dimly aware that, when he paused for breath, a spinning figure tap-danced a storm out of the mêlée and a voice by his ear said:

YOU WILL CONTINUE, I PROMISE YOU.

When he flagged a second time a diamond as big as his fist landed on the boards in front of him. A smaller figure sashayed out of the dancers and said:

"If you boys don't go on playing, William Spigot, I will personally make sure your life becomes absolutely foul."

And it returned to the press of bodies.

The fiddler looked down at the diamond. It could have ransomed any five kings the world would care to name. He kicked it hurriedly behind him.

"More power to your elbow, eh?" said the drummer, grinning.

"Shut up and play!"

He was aware that tunes were turning up at the ends of his fingers that his brain had never known. The drummer and the piper felt it too. Music was pouring in from somewhere. They weren't playing it. It was playing them.

IT IS TIME FOR A NEW DANCE TO BEGIN.

"Duurrrump-da-dum-dum," hummed the fiddler, the sweat running off his chin as he was caught up in a different tune.

The dancers milled around uncertainly, unsure about the steps. But one pair moved purposefully through them at a predatory crouch, arms clasped ahead of them like the bowsprit of a killer galleon. At the end of the floor they turned in a flurry of limbs that appeared to defy normal anatomy and began the angular advance back through the crowd.

"What's this one called?"

TANGO.

"Can you get put in prison for it?"

I DON'T BELIEVE SO.

"Amazing."

The music changed.

"I know this one! It's the Quirmish bullfight dance! Oh-lay!"

"WITH MILK"?

A high-speed fusillade of hollow snapping noises suddenly kept time with the music.

"Who's playing the maracas?"

Death grinned.

MARACAS? I DON'T NEED . . . MARACAS.

And then it was now.

The moon was a ghost of itself on one horizon. On the other there was already the distant glow of the advancing day.

They left the dance floor.

Whatever had been propelling the band through the hours of the night drained slowly away. They looked at one another. Spigot the fiddler glanced down at the jewel. It was still there.

The drummer tried to massage some life back into his wrists.

Spigot stared helplessly at the exhausted dancers.

"Well, then . . ." he said, and raised the fiddle one more time.

Miss Flitworth and her companion listened from the mists that were threading around the field in the dawn light.

Death recognised the slow, insistent beat. It made him think of wooden figures, whirling through Time until the spring unwound.

I DON'T KNOW THAT ONE.

"It's the last waltz."

I SUSPECT THERE'S NO SUCH THING.

"You know," said Miss Flitworth, "I've been wondering all evening how it's going to happen. How you're going to do it. I mean, people have to die of *something*, don't they? I thought maybe it was going to be of exhaustion, but I've never felt better. I've had the time of my life and I'm not even out of breath. In fact it's been a real tonic, Bill Door. And I – "

She stopped.

"I'm *not* breathing, am I." It wasn't a question. She held a hand in front of her face and huffed on it.

NO.

"I *see*. I've never enjoyed myself so much in all my life . . . ha! So . . . when – ?"

YOU KNOW WHEN YOU SAID THAT SEEING ME GAVE YOU QUITE A START?

"Yes?"

IT GAVE YOU QUITE A STOP.

Miss Flitworth didn't appear to hear him. She kept turning her hand backwards and forwards, as if she'd never seen it before.

"I see you made a few changes, Bill Door," she said.

NO. IT IS LIFE THAT MAKES MANY CHANGES.

"I mean that I appear to be younger."

THAT'S WHAT I MEANT ALSO.

He snapped his fingers. Binky stopped his grazing by the hedge and trotted over.

"You know," said Miss Flitworth, "I've often thought . . . I often thought that everyone has their, you know, *natural* age. You see children of ten who act as though they're thirty-five. Some people are born middle-aged, even. It'd be nice to think I've been . . ." she looked down at herself, "oh, let's say eighteen . . . all my life. Inside."

Death said nothing. He helped her up onto the horse.

"When I see what life does to people, you know, you don't seem so bad," she said nervously.

Death made a clicking noise with his teeth. Binky walked forward.

"You've never met Life, have you?"

I CAN SAY IN ALL HONESTY THAT I HAVE NOT.

"Probably some great white crackling thing. Like an electric storm in trousers," said Miss Flitworth.

I THINK NOT.

Binky rose up into the morning sky.

"Anyway . . . death to all tyrants," said Miss Flitworth.

YES.

"Where are we going?"

Binky was galloping, but the landscape did not move.

"That's a pretty good horse you've got there," said Miss Flitworth, her voice shaking.

YES.

"But what is he *doing*?"

GETTING UP SPEED.

"But we're not going *any*where – "

They vanished.

They reappeared.

The landscape was snow and green ice on broken mountains. These weren't old mountains, worn down by time and weather and full of gentle ski slopes, but young, sulky, adolescent mountains. They held secret ravines and merciless crevices. One yodel out of place would attract, not the jolly echo of a lonely goatherd, but fifty tons of express-delivery snow.

The horse landed on a snowbank that should not, by rights, have been able to support it.

Death dismounted and helped Miss Flitworth down.

They walked over the snow to a frozen muddy track that hugged the mountain side.

"Why are we here?" said the spirit of Miss Flitworth.

I DO NOT SPECULATE ON COSMIC MATTERS.

"I mean here on this mountain. Here on this geography," said Miss Flitworth patiently.

THIS IS NOT GEOGRAPHY.

"What is it, then?"

HISTORY.

They rounded a bend in the track. There was a pony there, eating a bush, with a pack on its back. The track ended in a wall of suspiciously clean snow.

Death removed a lifetimer from the recesses of his robe.

NOW, he said, and stepped into the snow.

She watched it for a moment, wondering if she could have done that too. Solidity was an awfully hard habit to give up.

And then she didn't have to.

Someone came out.

Death adjusted Binky's bridle, and mounted up. He paused for a moment to watch the two figures by the avalanche. They had faded almost to invisibility, their voices no more than textured air.

"All he said was 'WHEREVER YOU GO, YOU GO TOGETHER'. I said where? He said he didn't know. What's happened?"

"Rufus – you're going to find this very hard to believe, my love – "

"And who was that masked man?"

They both looked around.

There was no one there.

In the village in the Ramtops where they understand what the Morris dance is all about, they dance it just once, at dawn, on the

246

first day of spring. They don't dance it after that, all through the summer. After all, what would be the point? What use would it be?

But on a certain day when the nights are drawing in, the dancers leave work early and take, from attics and cupboards, the *other* costume, the black one, and the *other* bells. And they go by separate ways to a valley among the leafless trees. They don't speak. There is no music. It's very hard to imagine what kind there could be.

The bells don't ring. They're made of octiron, a magic metal. But they're not, precisely, silent bells. Silence is merely the absence of noise. They make the opposite of noise, a sort of heavily textured silence.

And in the cold afternoon, as the light drains from the sky, among the frosty leaves and in the damp air, they dance the *other* Morris. Because of the balance of things.

You've got to dance both, they say. Otherwise you can't dance either.

Windle Poons wandered across the Brass Bridge. It was the time in Ankh-Morpork's day when the night people were going to bed and the day people were waking up. For once, there weren't many of either around.

Windle had felt moved to be here, at this place, on this night, now. It wasn't exactly the feeling he'd had when he knew he was going to die. It was more the feeling that a cogwheel gets inside a clock – things turn, the spring unwinds, and this is where you've got to be . . .

He stopped, and leaned over. The dark water, or at least very runny mud, sucked at the stone supports. There was an old legend . . . what was it, now? If you threw a coin into the Ankh from the Brass Bridge you'd be sure to return? Or was it if you just threw *up* into the Ankh? Probably the former. Most of the citizens, if they dropped a coin into the river, would be sure to come back if only to look for the coin.

A figure loomed out of the mist. He tensed.

"Morning, Mr Poons."

Windle let himself relax.

"Oh. Sergeant Colon? I thought you were someone else."

"Just me, your lordship," said the watchman cheerfully. "Turning up like a bad copper."

"I see the bridge has got through another night without being stolen, sergeant. Well done."

"You can't be too careful, I always say."

"I'm sure we citizens can sleep safely in one another's beds knowing that no one can make off with a five-thousand-ton bridge overnight," said Windle.

Unlike Modo the dwarf, Sergeant Colon did know the meaning of the word "irony". He thought it meant "sort of like iron". He gave Windle a respectful grin.

"You have to think quick to keep ahead of today's international criminal, Mr Poons," he said.

"Good man. Er. You haven't, er, seen anyone else around, have you?"

"Dead quiet tonight," said the sergeant. He remembered himself and added, "No offence meant."

"Oh."

"I'll be moving along, then," said the sergeant.

"Fine. Fine."

"Are you all right, Mr Poons?"

"Fine. Fine."

"Not going to throw yourself in the river again?"

"No."

"Sure?"

"Yes."

"Oh. Well. Good night, then." He hesitated. "Forget my own head next," he said. "Chap over there asked me to give this to you." He held out a grubby envelope.

Windle peered into the mists.

"What chap?"

"That ch— oh, he's gone. Tall chap. Bit odd-looking."

Windle unfolded the scrap of paper, on which was written: OOoooEeeeOooEeeeOOOeee.

"Ah," he said.

"Bad news?" said the sergeant.

"That depends," said Windle, "on your point of view."

248

"Oh. Right. Fine. Well . . . good night, then."

"Goodbye."

Sergeant Colon hesitated for a moment, and then shrugged and strolled on.

As he wandered away, the shadow behind him moved and grinned.

WINDLE POONS?

Windle didn't look around.

"Yes?"

Out of the corner of his eye Windle saw a pair of bony arms rest themselves on the parapet. There was the faint sound of a figure trying to make itself comfortable, and then a restful silence.

"Ah," said Windle. "I suppose you'll want to be getting along?"

NO RUSH.

"I thought you were always so punctual."

IN THE CIRCUMSTANCES, A FEW MINUTES MORE WILL NOT MAKE A LOT OF DIFFERENCE.

Windle nodded. They stood side by side in silence, while around them was the muted roar of the city.

"You know," said Windle, "it's a wonderful afterlife. Where were you?"

I WAS BUSY.

Windle wasn't really listening. "I've met people I never even knew existed. I've done all sorts of things. I've really got to know who Windle Poons *is*."

WHO IS HE, THEN?

"Windle Poons."

I CAN SEE WHERE THAT MUST HAVE COME AS A SHOCK.

"Well, yes."

ALL THESE YEARS AND YOU NEVER SUSPECTED.

Windle Poons did know exactly what irony meant, and he could spot sarcasm too.

"It's all very well for you," he mumbled.

PERHAPS.

Windle looked down at the river again.

"It's been great," he said. "After all this time. Being needed is important."

YES. BUT WHY?

249

Windle looked surprised.

"I don't know. How should I know? Because we're all in this together, I suppose. Because we don't leave our people in there. Because you're a long time dead. Because anything is better than being alone. Because humans are human."

AND SIXPENCE IS SIXPENCE. BUT CORN IS NOT JUST CORN.

"It isn't?"

No.

Windle leaned back. The stone of the bridge was still warm from the day's heat.

To his surprise, Death leaned back as well.

BECAUSE YOU'RE ALL YOU'VE GOT, said Death.

"What? Oh. Yes. That as well. It's a great big cold universe out there."

YOU'D BE AMAZED.

"One lifetime just isn't enough."

OH, I DON'T KNOW.

"Hmm?"

WINDLE POONS?

"Yes?"

THAT *WAS* YOUR LIFE.

And, with great relief, and general optimism, and a feeling that on the whole everything could have been much worse, Windle Poons died.

Somewhere in the night, Reg Shoe looked both ways, took a furtive paintbrush and small pot of paint from inside his jacket, and painted on a handy wall: Inside Every Living Person is a Dead Person Waiting to Get Out . . .

And then it was all over. The end.

Death stood at the window of his dark study, looking out onto his garden. Nothing moved in that still domain. Dark lilies bloomed by the trout pool, where little plaster skeleton gnomes fished. There were distant mountains.

It was his own world. It appeared on no map.

But now, somehow, it lacked something.

Death selected a scythe from the rack in the huge hall. He strode past the huge clock without hands and went outside. He stalked through the black orchard, where Albert was busy about the beehives, and on until he climbed a small mound on the edge of the garden. Beyond, to the mountains, was unformed land – it would bear weight, it had an existence of sorts, but there had never been any reason to define it further.

Until now, anyway.

Albert came up behind him, a few dark bees still buzzing around his head.

"What are you doing, master?" he said.

REMEMBERING.

"Ah?"

I REMEMBER WHEN ALL THIS WAS STARS.

What was it? Oh, yes . . .

He snapped his fingers. Fields appeared, following the gentle curves of the land.

"Golden," said Albert. "That's nice. I've always thought we could do with a bit more colour around here."

Death shook his head. It wasn't quite right yet. Then he realised what it was. The lifetimers, the great room filled with the roar of disappearing lives, was efficient and necessary; you needed something like that for good order. But . . .

He snapped his fingers again and a breeze sprang up. The cornfields moved, billow after billow unfolding across the slopes.

ALBERT?

"Yes, master?"

HAVE YOU NOT GOT SOMETHING TO DO? SOME LITTLE JOB?

"I don't think so," said Albert.

AWAY FROM HERE, IS WHAT I MEAN.

"Ah. What you mean is, you want to be alone," said Albert.

I AM ALWAYS ALONE. BUT JUST NOW I WANT TO BE ALONE BY MYSELF.

"Right. I'll just go and, uh, do some little jobs back at the house, then," said Albert.

YOU DO THAT.

Death stood alone, watching the wheat dance in the wind. Of

251

course, it was only a metaphor. People were more than corn. They whirled through tiny crowded lives, driven literally by clock work, filling their days from edge to edge with the sheer effort of living. And all lives were exactly the same length. Even the very long and very short ones. From the point of view of eternity, anyway.

Somewhere, the tiny voice of Bill Door said: from the point of view of the owner, longer ones are best.

SQUEAK.

Death looked down.

A small figure was standing by his feet.

He reached down and picked it up, held it up to an investigative eye socket.

I KNEW I'D MISSED SOMEONE.

The Death of Rats nodded.

SQUEAK?

Death shook his head.

NO, I CAN'T LET YOU REMAIN, he said. IT'S NOT AS THOUGH I'M RUNNING A FRANCHISE OR SOMETHING.

SQUEAK?

ARE YOU THE ONLY ONE LEFT?

The Death of Rats opened a tiny skeletal hand. The tiny Death of Fleas stood up, looking embarrassed but hopeful.

NO. THIS SHALL *NOT* BE. I AM IMPLACABLE. I AM DEATH . . . ALONE.

He looked at the Death of Rats.

He remembered Azrael in his tower of loneliness.

ALONE . . .

The Death of Rats looked back at him.

SQUEAK?

Picture a tall, dark figure, surrounded by cornfields . . .

NO, YOU CAN'T RIDE A CAT. WHO EVER HEARD OF THE DEATH OF RATS RIDING A CAT? THE DEATH OF RATS WOULD RIDE SOME KIND OF DOG.

Picture more fields, a great horizon-spanning network of fields, rolling in gentle waves . . .

DON'T ASK *ME* I DON'T KNOW. SOME KIND OF TERRIER, MAYBE.

252

. . . fields of corn, alive, whispering in the breeze . . .

RIGHT, AND THE DEATH OF FLEAS CAN RIDE IT TOO. THAT WAY YOU KILL TWO BIRDS WITH ONE STONE.

. . . awaiting the clockwork of the seasons.

METAPHORICALLY.

And at the end of all stories Azrael, who knew the secret, thought:

I REMEMBER WHEN ALL THIS WILL BE AGAIN.